ABOUT THE AUTHOR

Helmut Glenk was born in an Australian internment camp to parents of German origin who had been deported from Sarona, Palestine. This background has inspired much of his research as well as his writing. He is also the author of the authoritative historical non-fiction book *From Desert Sands to Golden Oranges,* focused on the Sarona settlement.

SARONA

By

Helmut Glenk

 www.trafford.com

North America & international
toll-free: 1 888 232 4444 (USA & Canada)
phone: 250 383 6864 ♦ fax: 812 355 4082

Also by Helmut Glenk

FROM DESERT SANDS TO GOLDEN ORANGES

SHATTERED DREAMS AT KILIMANJARO

CONTENTS

BACKGROUND

An historical novel set in Palestine during the turbulent period of the late 1930s and the early 1940s.

Despite the events engulfing Palestine and the world at large, love, that most powerful of human emotions, grew between two young people, a young German man and a Jewish girl, and endured the difficult circumstances to survive for a lifetime.

In the 1870s, when the Holy Land was a remote impoverished province of the Turkish Ottoman Empire, small groups of pious Germans, known as Templers, migrated there to establish farming communities in the hope of building a spiritual Temple of God. One of their early settlements, founded in the desolate Sharon Plain, just north of the port of Jaffa, was named Sarona. It was the first European agricultural settlement in the Holy Land and its progress and success was closely observed by some early Jewish pioneers in the Holy Land.

In the 1880s groups of Jews started to migrate to the Holy Land in significant numbers. Most had fled persecution in Russia and Eastern Europe and they also established settlements and agricultural enterprises. It was the beginning of the Zionist movement which aimed to establish a Jewish homeland.

After the defeat of Germany and Turkey in the First World War, Palestine became a British Mandate territory. For more than sixty years the German and Jewish settlers lived in their separate towns and settlements but because their businesses and work were often closely interlinked, a mutual respect developed between them. However, the two groups did not mix socially.

This peaceful co-existence was shattered in the 1930s as hostilities between the British, Jews and Arabs emerged and grew steadily. As the hostilities escalated the Germans were viewed with suspicion by all parties particularly when the National Socialists came to power in Germany and adopted anti-Semitic policies and a war in Europe became ever more apparent.

At the outbreak of the Second World War, all Germans in Palestine were interned as Enemy Aliens and eventually deported.

In 1947, the United Nations voted in favour of partitioning Palestine into Arab and Jewish sectors. When the British withdrew in 1948, the State of Israel was proclaimed and Sarona became the centre of government for the infant nation and was renamed Hakirya.

It took another sixty years for many of the wounds of that period to heal and for Sarona to blossom once more.

PART ONE

SECRET LOVE

CHAPTER 1 – 1935/36

Erich had turned eighteen and bought a second-hand motor cycle from a good family friend. The BSA was a large machine with a rear pillion seat which would be handy if he wanted to take a passenger. For years he had watched enviously as many other young men of his small German farming settlement had bought motor cycles; he had yearned to join them in their rides when he became old enough and had saved money for this purpose since commencing work. At last his boyhood dream could be fulfilled. He knew that his parents had been a little apprehensive about his purchase but he was determined to have the mobility and freedom to travel independently beyond the boundaries of the settlement, and further than he could go on his bicycle.

Erich had grown up in the tightly knit German Templer community of Sarona which was established in 1871 on a small rise in the Sharon Plain just a few kilometres north of Jaffa near the junction of the Audsche (Yarkon) River and the Wadi Musrara. It was the first such European venture in the Holy Land, which at that time was a neglected province of the Turkish Ottoman Empire and Erich's grandfather had been one of the original settlers. The Templers were pious Christians who, although not missionaries, believed that they should demonstrate Christian ideals and values by example in their family and community living. The culture of the Templer settlements was characterized by a strong work ethic, frugality, unwavering religious belief, mutual help, and staunch German patriotism. Non-Templers were regarded with suspicion and there was almost no social interaction with non-German groups although the Templers did share their agricultural experience and technical knowledge with the early Zionist settlers. As Sarona grew and prospered, the settlers sold their produce – potatoes, vegetables, fruit, milk, olives, oil, and wine – to Jewish and Arab merchants in nearby Tel Aviv and Jaffa. The Jewish market for the settlement's dairy produce was so important, that the settlement made provision for a Jewish religious supervisor to certify that the milk, butter and cheese were *kosher*, ritually fit for consumption by religious Jews.

Erich was born in 1917, when despite the difficulties imposed by the Great War, the settlement was well-established and independent, having almost faltered in its early years when many settlers succumbed to dysentery and malaria. By that time, Erich's father, Wilhelm, had established an orange grove, using an irrigation system that drew water from deep wells by means of motorized pumps – the deep wells were a revolutionary innovation in Palestine. Sophie, Erich's mother, was also a Templer who had migrated from Germany as a child; her family was part of the founding group of Wilhelma, another German settlement, near Lydda, east of Jaffa.

By the time Erich and his older sister, Helga, reached their teens, the ravages of the Great War had been repaired and the rising generation was questioning some of the constraints of the traditional Templer way of life. The growing prosperity of the settlements, combined with the considerable freedom of movement afforded by the advent of motor cars and motor cycles, led to a grudging acceptance by the elders that the adolescents would often leave the settlement to shop and dine out in restaurants in nearby Tel Aviv, or simply seek entertainment in the city; some of the young even frequented the horse races. Dancing, playing cards, drinking alcohol and smoking by the young notwithstanding, the Templer community continued to adhere to its ideals of religious faith, honesty, good citizenship and mutual help.

Erich had obtained permission from the British police to drive his motor bike to the Serail in Jaffa, four kilometers away, to undergo his licence test and have the bike registered in his name. He had been warned to drive slowly on his way to Jaffa and although he had to fight the urge to turn the accelerator and get there faster, it did not take him long to reach his destination.

The Serail was a busy British administrative headquarters, established after the Great War when Britain became the Mandatory authority for Palestine. Erich's appointment was with the British Police Licensing Sergeant, a frequent visitor to Sarona who knew most of the residents. Nevertheless, Erich made sure to arrive early to allow the Sergeant to properly observe the formalities. He asked Erich some elementary questions on the road rules, tested his eyesight and then followed him on a police motorcycle through the busy, narrow, winding streets of Jaffa to test his practical skills. Erich passed easily as he had been practising for the past two years and after paying the considerable fee of one pound Sterling, he received his licence.

Erich left the Serail feeling elated and decided to celebrate his newly acquired freedom. He took the Jaffa-Tel Aviv road north, though the German Walhalla settlement before turning left towards the Rothschild Boulevard, the wide tree-lined street through the middle of Tel Aviv. There were numerous small Jewish coffee shops in the Lev Tel Aviv area but he had heard that Gold's, where German was spoken, served delicious homemade German and Austrian style cakes, and decided to try it for himself.

He found the small shop, entered and seated himself at the small corner table from where he could watch the passing traffic. He had not yet gathered his thoughts when a sweet soft voice asked him for his order. He glanced up and found himself looking into two glowing dark brown eyes set in a stunningly beautiful face, framed by honey blonde tresses. Erich was smitten – the dark eyebrows, the perfectly shaped nose, the mouth with two full rosy lips separated by glistening white teeth, the soft, innocent voice, the sweet smile, and the open expression - the beauty left him speechless!

"What would you like to order?" she asked again.

His heart was throbbing! His mouth was dry and with his lips stuck to his gums he found himself unable to speak! He sat gazing into those dark unblinking eyes until he gathered his thoughts, swallowed and stammered, "Just a cup of coffee and some apple strudel with cream, please." As she turned and walked away from him to the rear of the shop he noticed her figure – a narrow waist, tight buttocks and slender ankles protruding beneath her flowing floral skirt.

Only a few minutes later she returned smiling, carrying his order on a small tray. As she leaned forward to place the cup and plate on the table, Erich could not help but notice the firm but not overlarge breasts beneath her blouse. Sensing his gaze, she blushed and quickly turned away. He ate slowly and sipped his coffee all the while following her with his eyes as she moved about the shop serving other customers. She knew she was being watched and would glance and smile shyly at him whenever the opportunity arose. Completely captivated by her smiles, Erich finished his coffee and strudel, paid his bill and quietly left the shop.

As he rode home, Erich knew he would have to return and speak with this absolutely gorgeous girl. His thoughts were incoherent: he had never felt like this about any girl he had seen or met; this one was obviously Jewish, which would be a problem as in Sarona a minority had embraced the anti-Jewish views of the National Socialist government in Germany even though Germans and Jews had lived together harmoniously in Palestine for decades. Going out with someone outside the community was always a problem but dating a Jewess would be really frowned upon; and what were her views about dating a German? Erich's father, although not antisemitic, was otherwise a strong supporter of the German government, which he hoped would make Germany a strong and respected nation once more; Erich was also a proud and patriotic German. This girl was just so beautiful, her smiles seemed to be genuinely affectionate, surely she was not just teasing him.

As he rode the short distance back to Sarona, Erich decided that regardless of the consequences and what was happening in the wider world he would see her again and speak with her; he would summon his courage and ask her name and see if she would speak with him. Along the sandy stretches of *Meer Strasse* that led directly into Sarona he opened the throttle of the bike and left a cloud of dust in his wake. He slowed just before reaching the outskirts of the settlement because many of the residents complained constantly that the young men stirred up the dust and damaged the narrow unsealed roads of the settlement with their motorbikes. Erich did not want to be reprimanded for fast driving on his first day as a licenced rider. When he reached his home, Erich rode into the backyard, pushed his bike into the shed and took care to close the front gate before entering the large kitchen. His mother, who was preparing the evening meal, looked up and said: "I didn't know that getting a licence would take so long. You look so happy you obviously got it."

"Yes, I did, Mother. It has been a great day. I passed the test without any problems whatsoever."

*   *   *   *   *

In the days that followed, Erich couldn't get the beautiful waitress out of his mind. Her image flashed constantly before his eyes and his resolve to see her again grew stronger. The knowledge that he would be teased and ridiculed and that the ensuing gossip would only embarrass his family quelled his temptation to mention her to his friends and he reminded himself that he didn't even know her name or if she even cared for him.

Erich was fortunate that he had to wait only one week for an excuse to revisit Gold's; a dental appointment in Tel Aviv. Normally he hated going to the dentist but on this occasion the prospect of pain and discomfort was completely eclipsed by the opportunity the appointment afforded to go to Golds to meet the most beautiful girl he had ever seen.

The visit to the dentist brought none of the anticipated discomfort or pain; Erich took this as a good omen for his plans. It was mid-afternoon when he entered the café to see the girl of his heart serving another customer. She looked up as the door opened, met his eyes with hers and turned away blushing. It seemed to Erich that no sooner had he sat down that she came to take his order. She was as radiant as he had remembered her – those dark striking eyes looked straight at him as he ordered. His heart throbbed as he took a breath to ask her name but she had already turned away, leaving him wondering if he had missed his opportunity.

When he had finished his coffee she came to take his plate and cup he whispered urgently, "What is your name?"

"Ruth," she replied with an upward glance, her dark eyes sparkling as a blush spread across her face.

"When do you finish work? My name is Erich and I really would like to speak with you. Could I meet you somewhere?"

"I finish at four o'clock and I could meet you two blocks from here at the corner of Montefiore and Nahmani Streets."

"I'll see you there!" he replied as they looked into each others eyes again. "How much do I owe you for the coffee and cake?"

"Seventy mils," she replied. He reached into his pocket and paid as he all but skipped from the shop.

Although Ruth had agreed to meet Erich, after he left the shop she became apprehensive about meeting a stranger known to her only by his first name and obviously a German. What if someone saw her in his company? Had she agreed too hastily to meet him? She had been caught off guard when he had asked her - maybe she should not go. What would Erich do if she did not meet him? Probably come back to the shop which might be even more embarrassing. She was all too familiar with the concerns of her Jewish community and the tensions that were growing between the Germans and Jews. She was sure her family would not condone such a meeting – they would be dismayed to think that she was going to meet him at all. But her attraction to the handsome young German was strong. He seemed so sincere and genuine, even a little shy, when he spoke to her - surely he would not take advantage of her. She had been attracted to him the first time he had come to the shop and had longed for his return. Clearly, he must have had similar feelings toward her otherwise he would not have returned and asked her to meet him.

With a full hour to elapse before they would see each other again Erich decided to ride his motor bike to the *Südstrand* (South Beach), a popular beach with the Sarona settlers just south of the headland at Jaffa. He passed the large German Wagner factory and through the other German settlement in Jaffa, with its old wooden houses that had been bought in 1869 by the Templers from an American religious sect that had failed to thrive. He blew his horn constantly as he dodged pedestrians, donkeys and animal drawn carts in the narrow bustling, winding lanes and alleyways of old Jaffa. When he at last reached the beach it was deserted; the wind was blowing stiffly off the Mediterranean Sea and white capped waves could be seen as far as the eyes could see. Erich took the firm sandy road along the top of the sand-dunes, opened the throttle of his bike and zoomed along. His exhilaration made him even more impatient for their meeting but the minutes seemed to tick by at an agonizingly slow pace. Where should he take Ruth to talk undisturbed? Would she be willing to come with him? What if she did not turn up? She will be there he reassured himself.

At five minutes to four Erich was waiting at the appointed cross roads. As a European he blended with the bustling pedestrian traffic in this Jewish precinct. Four o'clock came, ten past four, quarter past four; anxiously he looked by turns at his watch and in the direction from which he expected Ruth to come, but there was still no sign of her – had she misled him? Was he at the right spot?

Just after Erich had left Gold's, an elderly Viennese Jewish couple arrived; they were regular customers and well-known to Mrs Gold whose baking was popular amongst the many European Jews who had migrated to Palestine. Her shop provided a little old world charm that reminded them of their former home. It was this couple's habit to come in to enjoy a good cup of coffee and some cake after they had been shopping in Tel Aviv; they were never in a hurry, and usually lingered to chat over a second cup of coffee. So it was on this occasion – the very day Ruth wanted to leave punctually. At four o'clock, the old people showed no intention of leaving. Anxiously, Ruth looked at the clock. Mrs Gold had noticed the smiles and body language between Ruth and Erich earlier and sensed Ruth's anxiety now, but decided that Ruth should stay a little after closing time to understand that customer service is due to every customer, even when it is inconvenient for the shopkeeper. When the couple left, a little after four, she called to Ruth, "I don't think we will have anymore customers today. As it is already after four, you can leave and I will clean up the table."

"Thanks, Mrs. Gold. I have to meet someone."

"I know, I know. You had better hurry!" Mrs. Gold said with a huge grin as Ruth rushed from the shop.

Erich was in a quandary - should he continue to wait at the corner or go to the shop to look for Ruth? – when she suddenly appeared running towards him along the crowded footpath, her skirt flowing out behind her. "I'm so sorry I'm late," she blurted breathlessly. "I was hoping you would still be here."

"It's all right, though I must admit I was getting a little concerned - I was fairly sure you would come after our few words in the shop - but I'm thrilled you are here."

"Unfortunately I couldn't leave on time as we had some late customers and they had to be served. Mrs Gold makes sure that every customer is served properly and she sets a very high standard of service. As soon as they left I told Mrs Gold I had to meet someone, she just smiled and said I could go quickly. I'm sure she knew exactly what I was up to - she doesn't miss a thing but she is also a softie."

"Don't worry, Ruth - everything is fine now that you're here, but this footpath is not a good place to talk. I have my motorbike nearby and we could go for a short ride and find a quieter spot where we can speak more easily with one another. That's of course, if you are willing to come with me."

"Where do you plan to go?" she asked hesitantly, "I have to be home by about five thirty otherwise my parents will be worried."

"I thought maybe just a kilometre or two to the north beach. There along the foreshore I'm sure we will find a quieter spot."

"OK. I'll come but please don't drive fast - I have never been on a motor bike before."

"You will be fine, just sit still and hold onto me. I promise I won't drive fast. We are not going far and you will be home when you need to be."

On reaching the beach front of Tel Aviv they stopped and surveyed the area; very few people were strolling along the beach in the cool wind. They walked a short distance to a bench seat overlooking the sea near the Strand Hotel where they sat quietly for a few moments holding hands and looking into each others eyes.

"Ruth we are total strangers to one another; I know nothing about you. Where do you live?" Erich opened somewhat tentatively.

"Well, Erich, you already know I am Jewish. My family name is Stein, and my family is not strictly orthodox. I like reading and music, especially dance music. I have an older brother who wants to become a policeman. I was born here in Tel Aviv in 1918, just after the Australian cavalry came to Jaffa. We used to live in Ness Ziona but about ten years ago, when the Montefiore land was subdivided and sold, we moved to the outskirts of the new settlement where my parents established a small mixed farming business with friends. They sell fruit, vegetables, eggs, and a few chickens."

"I know where Montefiore is. It is not far from my home in Sarona."

"Really! Then we are practically neighbours. Sarona is an easy walk from Montefiore – just across the Wadi Massara."

"So how come you work in Tel Aviv, Ruth?"

"When I left school, the Golds, who are life-long friends of my parents, offered me a job in their coffee shop."

"Do you help with the baking?"

"No, they do all their own baking. I just serve the customers and help generally in the shop."

"I must say the piece of strudel I had was absolutely delicious - and the waitress was extremely charming." Erich teased, causing Ruth to blush.

"All the cakes are good. We have many long-standing customers who have become good friends of the Golds. Some people come from far away for their cakes. But now, Erich, tell me what you do."

"Well I am eighteen and grew up in Sarona, the German settlement – but you already know that. My family name is Bergerle. My grandparents were amongst the original settlers and we still live in the old family home. During the war, my mother, older sister and I were interned by the British in 1918 with the other German families from our settlement and taken to Helouan in Egypt – my father was captured earlier as a prisoner of war and sent to a camp in Egypt. I was two years old before I saw my father for the first time. After the war our whole family was deported from Egypt to Germany where we lived in an old castle in Bad Mergentheim. Of course, I cannot remember much about that."

"Why did you come back to Palestine after that?" she asked.

"Sarona is our home. All the German deportees wanted to come back but the British wouldn't let us until 1920. We certainly didn't want to live in Germany - my parents had never lived in Germany, they grew up in Palestine which was their home and livelihood."

"But, weren't all your things taken when you left? My parents told me that the Germans lost everything."

"Yes, everything that could be taken was stolen – all the household goods, tools and livestock were stolen and our property was damaged. But my family still owned their land, and their house and sheds were still standing. My father often said how neglected and overgrown everything was in the gardens and orange groves. Nothing had been irrigated and many trees had died.

"I went to school in Sarona for eight years before going on to *Ecole des Freres* in Jaffa, the local French Catholic school. When I was sixteen I left school and started working with my father in managing our orange grove and small vegetable garden. Nearly all our oranges are exported to Europe as the famous Jaffa Oranges."

"Why did your parents send you to a Catholic French school when you are German? I always thought the people of Sarona were of the Templer faith. Do you speak French?"

"You're right we are all Templers in Sarona. I think my parents sent me there because the education for us Germans here is fairly limited and they wanted me to have a few more years of schooling rather than just finishing after eight years at the Sarona School. I can speak a little French but when I first went there I couldn't speak any at all. The brothers there were very strict and also taught us English and Arabic although most of us could already speak Arabic but not write it. I was never keen to study further in Germany or go to the Templer High school in Jerusalem, or to learn a trade. I just wanted to help and work in our orange grove. We own another small piece of land which my father developed and we now grow vegetables there. Although it is hard work I am happy with what I am doing. Now, you tell me something about your family."

"Well, like you, I am a third generation Palestinian – both my parents were born here to families that had fled the anti-Jewish persecutions in Russia. My father's parents settled in Rishon le-Zion in 1883, the same year that settlers from Sarona came to help dig a well to save the Jewish settlement. My mother's parents settled in Ness Ziona in 1884 and when my parents married they remained in Ness Ziona before moving us to Montefiore."

Ruth looked at Erich's wrist watch. "I think I'd better get home - it is already close to my normal getting home time. My parents will worry if I am not home on time, especially with all the recent troubles with the Arabs."

"I will give you a lift back."

"Please, don't drive right to our home as it will not be good for me if I'm seen being brought home by a German. Anti-German feelings are starting to run high amongst some of our people - my brother amongst them."

"OK, I will drop you off some distance from your home. But Ruth, I really want to meet with you again. Our time today was just so brief. When can we see each other again?"

"I don't know when or where. I want to see you again too," she said with a fond smile as she squeezed his hand. "It could be a little awkward. But I have an idea - are you going to the races at Sarafant on Sunday? We are all going as my uncle has two horses racing there."

"Yes, I also intend to go. One of our friends in Sarona has a stallion racing in the sprint and we all think it is going to win. The horse is being ridden by one of his Arab workers. But I really don't think it will be possible for us to meet there. We will just have to wait and see what opportunity arises. Why don't we try to meet again next Tuesday evening after you finish work, at the same place and same time?"

"I'll look forward to that, but I am hoping for something on Sunday," she said with a cheeky smile on her face and a twinkle in her eyes.

Erich rode carefully through Tel Aviv with Ruth holding onto him. He was keenly aware of her soft arms wrapped firmly around him. Ruth felt such longing as she rested her head against Erich's broad back. "What a fine young man he is," she thought, "I can't wait to see him again."

Erich set her down about half a kilometre from her house and they promised each other that they would meet again. Ruth quickly brushed her windswept hair before walking the rest of the way home and Erich quickly drove the last few kilometres back to Sarona whistling the song *Es ist der schönste Tag im meinem Leben*, with the lyrics going through his mind "It's the best day of my life, I've fallen in love the first time...". He just couldn't get the beautiful Ruth out of his mind.

* * * * *

Before any other activity on a Sunday, the Sarona settlers all gathered at the community hall for the church service, summoned by the bell that tolled for fully ten minutes. On this occasion the Elder leading the service spoke about the perils of gambling and the associated evils. Gambling was not condoned by Templer philosophy and especially not by the older generation of settlers who had endured the hardships and suffering in the early days of the settlement. But the world was changing: people were better off; new social activities had emerged during the 1920s; and gradually the old barriers were crumbling as more liberal views came to the fore, although these were only begrudgingly finding acceptance by the older members of the community.

However, of greater concern to the community elders, and with far-reaching consequences to the community, was the political philosophy of the Third Reich, and the Elder also addressed that. He spoke with conviction of the need to have a strong inner belief in the love of God and to uphold of the Christian Templer faith. The new political doctrine was creating difficulties for people as it set German patriotism above their religious faith. In particular, Nazi doctrine was causing tensions in families whose young people were being encouraged to join groups such as the Hitler Youth and the League for German Girls instead of participating in the community's traditional youth activities.

After the conclusion of service Erich was approached by someone who worked at the German Consulate in Jaffa/Walhalla. "Ah, Erich! Good morning! I was hoping to see you today."

"Good day to you, Mr. Mueller. Why did you want to see me?"

"Erich, late yesterday morning we received our dispatch bag from the Government in Berlin and there is an envelope addressed to you with an instruction that you must collect it in person. I was wondering if you could pick it up tomorrow."

"Yes, Mr Mueller. I will call by and collect it. I suspect I know what it contains. I will see you tomorrow."

"What do you have planned for today?" Mr Mueller enquired.

"Some friends and I are going to the races at Sarafant. Mr Wald's beautiful black stallion is racing, it is being ridden by young Abdul and we are all going to watch him win."

"Yes, I have heard that quite a few Saronians are going to Sarafant today. Good luck, but don't put all your money on him if you are going to bet. Just a little word of advice - in racing there never is a sure winner - remember there are some good Arab horses racing as well."

*　　*　　*　　*　　*

It was a beautiful cloudless day at Sarafend, to the east of Tel Aviv and Sarona. Race days always generated excitement and an expectant atmosphere although race meetings were irregular and only held during the cooler part of the year. The racecourse, which was essentially a long straight course on the sandy plain near Ramleh, had been developed by the British after the war. Horse racing was a traditional British upper-class social activity that became popular with the other nationalities in Palestine, particularly the Arabs. Race meetings also provided a pleasant distraction from the civilian unrest that had grown to grip Palestine since the Arab riots of 1929.

On race day numerous temporary shelters were erected for shade. A large marquee was also set up with tables, chairs and table cloths for food and drink to be served to the officials, their wives and guests. The British ladies who regarded race days as major social events, dressed for the occasion in fashionable dresses and hats. Horses from British military and police forces, and from Arab, Jewish and sometimes German owners were entered for the races. The amateur jockeys were local men of small stature who were able to ride a horse. Competition amongst the horse owners, as well as the nationalities was fierce, and trophies were awarded to the winners. Numerous Arab and Jewish bookmakers attended to take bets from the crowd in attendance. People arrived by all manner of transport - car, horse-drawn vehicles, bicycles, motorbikes - some even riding horses and donkeys, and settled themselves in the shade of the shelters where chairs and small tables had been placed. There were no grandstands or other fixed seating and most spectators brought their own food and drink, although there were some Arab vendors. The race meeting had a distinctly relaxed picnic atmosphere.

Erich came with his best friend, Alfred, riding as pillion passenger. A large group of Sarona boys had ridden together on their motor bikes, many had brought their girlfriends with them. They met with others from Sarona and with Germans from the other nearby settlements. It was fun to catch up with friends and relatives. During all the preliminary talk and revelry Erich was able to leave the group unnoticed and wander around the race course to look for Ruth. The different nationalities did not usually mingle with the other groups, but Erich could not see Ruth in the Jewish crowd. When the first race, a brush hurdle race much loved by the British who had a long tradition of fox hunting, began, Erich had still not returned to his group.

As the start of the second race approached, a large crowd of Jewish spectators gathered at the running rail spectator area near the winning post. Many of them had backed a Jewish-owned horse. Erich at last spotted Ruth wearing a bright blue and white sundress that complemented her olive skin and beautiful body. "If only I could catch her attention," Erich thought to himself. The second race began but Erich didn't shift his gaze from Ruth. A loud cheer went up from the group as the horses galloped past the winning post. It was obvious that their favoured horse had won because people were jumping, laughing and slapping each other on the back. The race over, Ruth looked around and caught sight of him watching her. She smiled happily and gave him a wink, he raised his hand in greeting, but both knew they could not be seen together. Erich turned to return to his own group, content just to have seen Ruth so happy.

"You look as if you are in a daze." Alfred's comment brought Erich back to reality. "I was looking for you. Do you want to come and place a bet? I have just been given a tip by an Arab merchant who knows my father; he told me about a good horse in the next race. I saw you eyeing those Jewish fillies; you know they are not for you but there are several German ones in our settlement with eyes on you - you would have no trouble getting one of them to the winning post," Alfred teased.

"You never know your luck. Anything is possible!" Erich responded.

The fifth race was the feature of the program. When the horses with their jockeys slowly made their way to the starting line, six furlongs away, the excitement and anticipation amongst the Saronians intensified. Would their stallion win? Far away in the distance the horses and coloured jackets of the jockeys could hardly be distinguished with the naked eye as the horses moved into their starting position. The race started, but looking down the straight it was impossible to see which horse was leading; only the figures of horses against a background of a cloud of dust could be seen. At the two-furlong sign, the Sarona stallion was clearly in the lead but Abdul, the jockey, was riding him hard. Could he hold on? Had he run too fast too early? When their favourite was only one hundred metres from the finish line, the German crowd was jumping and cheering him on as other horses challenged him for the lead. Abdul, in the black, white and red colours of the Sarona Sports Club, held his mount in the lead and the Sarona stallion was the first across the finishing line. There were many happy smiles amongst the relieved Saronians as they collected their winnings. They all clapped and cheered enthusiastically when the silver cup was presented to the owners, Mr and Mrs Wald.

After that race many Saronians left for home but Erich and some of his young friends stayed on. They had had a good win and were keen to increase their winnings – they had been told that a gelding, brought all the way from Transjordan by an Arab merchant, was a good chance in one of the later races. Erich also hoped to catch another glimpse of Ruth before the day ended. He was not disappointed and signalled to her that he had a win; she acknowledged his gesture with a big smile and threw him a kiss. The boys put their winnings on the gelding and after its win they had even more reason to celebrate. In high spirits they rode back to Sarona and went straight to Kuebler's Bar to join the celebrations already underway. It had been a great day at the Sarafant races.

*　　*　　*　　*　　*

As he had told Mr Mueller he would, on Monday morning, Erich rode the short distance from Sarona to Walhalla, the small Templer settlement on the outskirts of Jaffa where the German Consulate was located. The building, constructed in the early 1930s in the modern Bauhaus style, was prominent amongst its humbler, traditional neighbours. The Templer Bank was located in the same building. A large German flag fluttered above the road from the flag pole which protruded diagonally from the first floor balcony. Situated as it was on the outskirts of Jaffa, Walhalla was an ideal administrative centre, close to both the port and the railway station. In addition, it was also the home of the Wagner Foundry and

Engineering Works, which employed many Sarona residents as well as Jews and Arabs. It was the largest factory of its kind and supplied and installed the pipes and pumps for irrigation and water supply in the burgeoning Palestine economy. Walhalla had been started by the Jaffa Templer community in the late nineteenth century when the Jaffa settlement could no longer accommodate the growing population.

*   *   *   *   *

Erich was known to most of the consulate staff, many of whom were from the German communities of Jaffa and Sarona, so when he asked to see Mr Mueller, he was shown to his office without delay.

"Good morning, Mr Mueller. I have come as you asked me." he said as he entered.

"Ah, Erich! Good morning," Mr Mueller responded as he rose to shake Erich's hand. "Please take a seat and give me a moment to get your envelope."

He handed Erich a large sealed envelope. Erich knew what it contained and smiled as he opened it. He was quite right - it contained his call-up papers for military service with the Wehrmacht. After the call-up the previous year of all the young German males born in Palestine in 1914 and 1915, he knew to expect to be in the next group.

"I sense that it has not come as a surprise," Mueller smiled. "But before you go, I need you to sign a form acknowledging that you have received the papers. You understand that you will not be alone, because all your friends of the same age will be joining you. It is part of your duty to the Führer and Germany, for the building of the new German Reich."

"I have to say that I am quite looking forward to it, it will be a wonderful experience. I will see Germany for the first time, and have an opportunity to see at first hand the great changes taking place there."

As he left the building, a thought crossed his mind; as he was so close to Ruth's workplace, should he call into Gold's to let her know? No, he decided, it would be better to wait the extra day for their appointment, when he could talk privately and at length with her.

On his arrival home he found his parents and sister, Helga, eating lunch.

"You were right father, I have received my call-up papers," he greeted them cheerily, waving the envelope.

"Well, my son, you must do military service so that if it becomes necessary to serve our German nation, you will be prepared. As you know, I did the same during the Great War and I can tell you that it will be a marvellous experience. I am so proud that you are going, especially now when pride has been restored in our German language and culture, our people are working again and our defence forces have been re-established. When I read the *Völkischer Beobachter* in our library it fills me with pride at what has already been achieved in such a short time and the far-reaching plans for the future. Soon Germany will be strong once more and that shameful and humiliating Versailles Treaty will no longer burden us. Young people like you and Helga will have a bright future in the new German Reich. It is good to be a German and even Germans like us, living abroad, are receiving the benefits."

Suddenly Wilhelm caught sight of Sophie's face and realised that his wife was not overjoyed at the prospect of her son serving in the army, even the new army of the rising new Reich.

"When do you have to go?" he asked lamely.

"Early in the New Year a German ship is expected here to collect us and I must be ready. The documents are quite specific as to what I can take with me. You know, I will be away for at least two years, but I'm looking forward to my first opportunity to visit Germany – of course, I can remember nothing of Bad Mergentheim. And I will be arriving in the middle of winter and will see snow for the first time. But Father, how will you cope here while I am away? You can't single-handedly manage the vegetables and the oranges."

"I will employ a few more Arab workers as necessary. Hassan is developing into a good reliable worker and I'll give him some more responsibilities. Your call-up was not unexpected – Uncle Kurt asked me if I would employ Klaus, who has just finished his schooling, to replace you during your absence. We will manage; after all, it is the least sacrifice we can make for our new Germany. You know, I think doing military service and seeing Germany blossom again will be the making of you; you'll enjoy the experience and it will broaden your outlook."

* * * * *

The next day, Erich did not need to find an excuse to be out as he had to return his papers, signed, to the Consulate. He then went on to Tel Aviv, arriving a little early for his rendezvous with Ruth. She arrived smiling radiantly only a minute or two after four; he was struck anew by her charm and beauty as they embraced.

"Can we go to the same place as last time?" Erich suggested, "I have brought some lemonade for us to drink as we talk."

"That is fine with me. Nobody will know either of us is in that part of town during the winter months. I told my parents that I might be a little late today; I told them that there would be a small group having a birthday celebration at Gold's. I just hope my mother doesn't mention anything to Mrs Gold about it when they next speak," she said, tightly squeezing his rough hands.

Once again they chose a bench after a short walk along the foreshore.

"Ruth, I must tell you something very important."

"Let me guess. You have been caught out - someone saw us together."
She laughed mischievously. "How did you answer that? Or maybe you
have a German girlfriend you want to tell me about!"

"No, nothing like that. It is a more serious matter," he said as Ruth
looked straight into his eyes. "Yesterday, I received my call up papers
for military service in Germany."

"Oh no!" she gasped, adding quickly, "But why do you have to go? You
don't live there. You were not even born there! Did you volunteer?"

"No, Ruth, I did not volunteer. Compulsory military service has been
introduced again in Germany for all young men of eighteen years. And
even though I was born in Palestine, I am a German citizen – my family,
like all the German families in Sarona, have always retained our German
nationality. We are patriotic Germans and therefore we never took out
Palestinian citizenship. So now, I have no choice but to go. The first group
of young men went about eighteen months ago, now it is the turn of my
age group. Military service is obligatory for all able-bodied young German
males, even those, like me, who live in foreign countries."

"When will you be going?" she asked anxiously.

"Most likely in about six week's time. There are five of us from Sarona
but the group will include some from the other settlements. We have to
wait until a ship arrives to take us to Germany early next year."

"Can you not put it off until later? We've only just met and already we
are being pulled apart. I will miss you so much," she said sadly.

"Oh, I will miss you, too. I have never felt so deeply for anyone as for
you, Ruth. I simply love you and I have loved you ever since I first saw
you. But I cannot postpone my call up; I have no valid reason and all
sorts of questions would be asked. I would probably even be branded
a coward or traitor within our own community. My father would be

especially devastated; he is a strong supporter of the new Germany and has already told to me what an honour it is to serve the Führer and our Fatherland. I'll be quite honest with you, Ruth, I really don't mind going and doing my duty. I know that may sound a little selfish to you, but there is no reason why our love and affection for one another should not remain strong even if we can't see each other. The separation will be a good test for us. I sincerely hope that when I come back, we will still have one another. We are still both very young."

"But who knows what will be in two years time," Ruth was sobbing softly and large tears were rolling down her cheeks from her dark eyes. "Oh Erich, I love you!"

"I love you too" They kissed as they held each other in a tight embrace. Silently they sat – each with their own thoughts.

"Will you write to me?" she whispered quietly, after a few moments of silence.

"If I can, of course I will, but it will be awkward to write directly to you – where should I send my letters? I don't think that it will be a straightforward matter. At this stage, even if you want to write to me, I do not have an address in Germany and I am not sure how the mail works in the military - maybe the letters are checked to see where they come from. It could be embarrassing."

"I am so afraid you will stay on in Germany. Please let me know somehow if that happens."

"Oh Ruth, I have absolutely no intention of staying in Germany beyond my military duty. My home is here and my family needs me to work in our vegetable garden and orange grove. Most importantly you are here – I will be coming back to you." He held her tightly as their lips met once more. "For now, let's enjoy the time available before I leave - it is almost the end of the orange harvest and I will have some more time when it is finished. Also, our late autumn and early winter vegetables will soon be ready for sale, and as most of them are sold through a Jewish merchant in the Tel Aviv wholesale market, I will have a good excuse to go to Tel Aviv. We will try and see each other as often as we can and still keep our love as our own secret. My darling, don't even worry that this might be the end – I am sure that our love will be even stronger in two years time. Come on, dry your eyes and let's take a walk along the beach."

With their arms around each other, they strolled on the fine sand, immersed in their thoughts and quite oblivious to time or place. Preoccupied, they walked quite a distance before they realised that Ruth was already late and that Erich's family would be wondering what could have kept him at the Consulate.

"My, that took a long time," he was greeted by his mother. "We thought you'd got lost and were ready to send out a search party to look for you," she added sarcastically.

"No such drama, Mother," he answered tersely, "I met a friend and we had a cup of coffee".

"Oh? Who was that? Fritz was round here looking for you - he said that a whole group was going to Walhalla to Lorenz's Café to have a few drinks and watch a new film just arrived from Germany. Your father also wanted you to help him fix the door on the shed. I think he needed to take the whole door off the hinges."

"Never mind, it was just an Arab friend who I had not seen for a while."

"I hope you've done nothing silly. We have to be so careful these days - the Jews constantly accuse us of being pro-Arab, and even of helping them with their regular uprisings, while the British keep a close watch on us Germans because they don't like our new German government. You do remember that the *Bürgermeister* (Mayor) told us all that it is vital for us to stay strictly neutral in the conflict between the Arabs and the Jews. And our Templer Council is of the same view - that under no circumstances should we take sides. They want what is best for us, so we must pay attention."

"Mother, you know that I am fully aware of all these directions and I can assure you that I have not breached them in any way. Now, I had better go out to father to see if I can still give him a hand."

*   *   *   *   *

Early in January 1936, *Milwaukee,* a ship of the German Hamburg Line, dropped anchor just off Jaffa for a stay of four days. As was the tradition in Sarona, the captain and crew were invited to the settlement to enjoy some local hospitality; a function was organised at the Community Hall and the ship's band asked to provide music. This time the function had a two-fold purpose – the usual opportunity for the settlers to enjoy some German entertainment, and the need to farewell in style the young military conscripts. The members of Milwaukee's crew were amazed to find such a strong attachment to German culture in a settlement so far from home.

The concert was held in the early evening so that young and old from the settlement could attend. The women brought homemade cakes, pretzels and *Flahden* (small pizzas) for the meal; the Sarona Wine Co-operative supplied wine and spirits; *Gassos* (lemonade) was purchased from Orth's lemonade factory; and beer from Kuebler's Tavern. The German flag was prominently displayed above the stage and the evening began with formalities: the mayor of Sarona addressed the gathering and was followed by the German consul and the ship's captain. The formalities came to an end with the singing of the German national anthem, *Deutschland, Deutschland über Alles,* and the *Horst Wessel Lied.*

The formalities were not long and the remainder of the evening was planned to be one of enjoyment and light entertainment. The mixed choir sang several songs including the *Sarona Song,* deeply meaningful to the settlers who all joined in. The Sarona Brass Band and the ship's band played marches, popular music and traditional German folksongs to accompany a sing-along. Later in the evening when the children and many of the older citizens had left, the ship's band played dance music. This was greatly appreciated as usually the dancers had to make do with gramophone records.

Erich and his four colleagues formed the centre of attention of the evening. In addition to giving them heartfelt good wishes for safety, the adults of the settlement begged them to return to Sarona at the conclusion of their military training. Of the previous batch of trainees, a number had stayed in Germany where employment was easy to find, unlike Sarona. Some young men had returned home only to go back to Germany to seek work and there was a genuine fear in the settlement that the loss of these youngsters would threaten the settlement's long term viability and create a gender imbalance in the short term. However the problems faced by the settlement were not only internal. Tel Aviv was growing; suburbs were springing up to the north and east of Sarona, putting irresistible upward pressure on land prices, making agricultural land too expensive for the young Germans. Unless their families owned sufficient land for them to work, these children of the settlers had no opportunities.

*   *   *   *   *

As he had each Tuesday since their first meeting, Erich met Ruth after she finished work at their usual place and they rode out to the North Beach. This time however, it was a sad occasion as Erich was due to ship out early the next day. It was a cool winter's day and the strong breeze blowing straight off the Mediterranean drove white capped waves up the beach, forcing them to walk, arm in arm, on the soft dry sand away from the water's edge. They had already walked a long way and could see the Audsche estuary in the distance when Erich suggested, "Let's have a drink and something to eat in one of the places along the foreshore."

"Oh, yes. I would like to make today special; who knows when we will see each other again?" Ruth whispered, squeezing him tightly. He turned his body to face her, gazed into her dark eyes and, quite oblivious to his surroundings, kissed her passionately.

They chose a quiet little café with a beautiful view over the sea. The few clouds in the sky were illuminated in shades of grey, orange and pink by the slowly sinking sun. After the waiter had taken their orders, leaving them alone at the table, Erich reached into his shirt pocket and gave Ruth an envelope. "This is something for you," he said. Ruth gently opened the flap and pulled out a card embossed with a bright blue forget-me-not flower and an attached portrait photo of Erich. On the back of the photo he had written *Dein Erich* (Your Erich). "I'll never ever forget you, Erich, and I will cherish your photo as long as I live. I'm so sorry I have no memento for you," she declared.

"No need to be sorry, my darling, I have your love and wonderful memories that will never fade. And I have the firm hope that we will still have each other when I return."

"Yes, we will," Ruth whispered.

Erich dropped Ruth off as he had always done a few hundred metres from her home. It was late for Ruth to arrive home, but she offered no greeting or explanation to her family as she went straight to her room. Her mother, Zara, sensed that something was amiss; she knocked on Ruth's door and opened it to find Ruth lying on her bed sobbing quietly.

"What's happened, Ruth?" she asked softly as she sat on the bed and gently rubbed her daughter's back.

"You wouldn't understand, *Imma*" was the choked reply.

"Mothers always understand and you know you can trust me, so why can't you tell me?"

"I don't know."

"It's something about love, isn't it?"

"How did you know that?" Ruth said as she sat up and looked wide-eyed at her mother.

"A mother's instinct. I have noticed that you often come in much later than normal on Tuesday afternoon. Can I help you? Is there something you want to share with me?"

"There is, but I don't know how to tell you. I'm afraid that you and *Abba* may become very angry with me."

"Ruth, are you in trouble?" Zara asked.

"No, but I am in love. Imma, can we please keep what I tell you between the two of us?"

"It depends what you are going to tell me, Ruth. You know that Abba and I always share any family problems."

"OK, but whatever you do, please don't tell David as he will be angry with me. You know his feelings and political views"

"Why should I tell David when it has nothing to do with him?"

"Imma, promise that only you and Abba will know what I tell you."

"Yes, I promise you that."

"Imma, I have fallen deeply in love with the most wonderful boy you could imagine and he feels the same way towards me. His name is Erich. He is kind and understanding and very handsome, but he is German

- he lives in the Sarona settlement. But he is not like the Nazis we hear so much about now - he does not despise Jews - in fact he is very caring and sensitive. He is just a wonderful person."

"But that is no reason to cry. There is more to what you are telling me."

"Yes, Imma, Erich and I met at Gold's one afternoon in November, and from the moment we saw each other we both felt a powerful bond between us - I have never felt like that before toward anyone else. It was quite strange this heady feeling of wanting one another. We have been seeing each other secretly for two months now. Imma, please don't jump to any conclusions - we have done nothing wrong. He has the same problem in his home; falling in love with a young Jewish girl would not be tolerated in his community or his home. His father is a strong supporter of the new German nation and the Führer.

"A few weeks ago, just two weeks after we met, Erich received his call up papers for military service in Germany. Four of his friends from Sarona are also going, as well as some from the other German settlements. He is leaving tomorrow morning on a German ship anchored at Jaffa. He will be gone for two years and I fear I might never see him again." she sobbed as she hugged her mother and the tears wet her cheeks.

"Oh, Ruth, my darling, one's first love is always difficult. You know, I fell in love at your age with a young man; he was the man of my dreams and hopes and I was sure there was no-one else like him in the world. But he left our small community in Ness Ziona and I never saw him again. I met several other nice young men but when I met your father I knew I had met the right partner. You know, I haven't thought of that first young man for years.

"You are young, so very young, and your life will take all sorts of twists and turns. Who knows whether Erich will be back in your life in two years time or at all? It won't be the end of the world even though it is hard for you to understand that now. I take it that Erich's parents don't know about you."

"No, they don't. He doesn't know how to tell his parents. He knows his father would be very upset but thinks his mother is more tolerant. But since the Aryan racial purity laws were announced a few months ago, the situation is particularly difficult. We can't even write to each other, but Erich promised me he will return to Palestine."

"My darling, I know it is frustrating, but there is absolutely nothing you can do at this time except await the outcome. Who knows what is before us; what tomorrow may bring let alone what will be in two years time. Young hearts are so full of life, it is possible that you or he will meet some else and fall in love with them. Maybe you will still care for and love each other when he returns. Come dry your tears, and when you are ready come out and have something to eat and drink."

"Oh Imma, I love you so. You always understand and have an answer. I know that my love for Erich will endure his absence. Please don't say anything to David – you know his view of the Germans."

"Don't worry, I won't. I am sure everything will turn out."

*   *   *   *   *

The next day dawned overcast and cool. A few intermittent rain showers fell during the morning and a strong wind blew from the west making conditions at the Jaffa port rather unpleasant with waves breaking over the rocks near the breakwater and against the sea wall next to the harbour. The British harbour master determined that the sea conditions made it unsafe for the Arab boatmen to ferry passengers and luggage out to the ship. The young men had been instructed to assemble at the port at eight o'clock to complete the formalities prior to sailing. There seemed to be a great deal of activity at the port as the passengers for Germany, some private travellers as well as the young conscripts, gathered with their family groups next to their bags and parcels in the hall of the Customs House. The group from Jerusalem had commenced their journey by train on the previous day and had stayed overnight with relatives or friends in Sarona or Wilhelma. The atmosphere in the

31

Customs House was tense; the grey light matched the apprehension of the mothers and girlfriends of the conscripts, while the young men themselves were excited to be undertaking such a grand adventure. For most of them it was not simply their first visit to Germany but their first time out of Palestine. Overall hung the knowledge that unless the wind subsided they would be forced to wait another day to embark.

By mid-morning, the formalities completed, most of the people gathered left the Customs House to wait in one of the many small Arab cafes in nearby old Jaffa town. These cafes and eating places were well known to the local Germans who frequented them whilst waiting for arrivals from Germany or when farewelling friends and relatives leaving for overseas. These cafes depended for much of their business on such captive clients.

Around two o'clock, a few patches of blue sky appeared through the grey clouds, the wind subsided and the waves abated accordingly. At three o'clock the harbour master decided that conditions were suitable for the loading of the ship to commence. The luggage and many cases of renowned Jaffa Oranges from the Sarona growers were carefully loaded onto the open ferry boats by the Arab boatmen, who, just as their forefathers had, with much shouting and gesturing, skilfully negotiated their way in all sorts of conditions, past the many other ferry boats, through the calm waters inside the breakwater, around the rocky outcrops into the Mediterranean swells to the *Milwaukee* heaving at anchor. The sea was too rough to lower any ladders and as the boats came aside the ship, they secured themselves to its hull with ropes, allowing sufficient slack to accommodate the rise and fall of the swells. With precise judgement they lifted each item of luggage and placed it aboard the ship through a side hatch whenever the waves lifted the boat level with the opening. Their skills honed by long experience, they rarely missed the opportunity afforded by each rising wave.

By late afternoon, the luggage had all been loaded and it was time for the passengers to take their leave and step into the boats. Erich turned to his parents to say farewell when his father broke the heaviness of the moment with an announcement, "Well Erich, we have a surprise for you. Your mother and I have booked a holiday in Germany later this year. We are hoping that you may be able to obtain leave from your military training so that we can meet and enjoy a few days together. It will be wonderful to see our revitalised Fatherland. We are also planning to attend the *Reichsparteitag* at Nürnberg, to hear the speeches and see the leaders of the Reich in the flesh. We will write to you with further details and when we know where you are located."

"That is a great surprise! I hope we can work it out. Just to meet you will be fantastic, but to be able to spend a few days together in Germany will be even better. I suppose though that we will have to see how things turn out. Father, good-bye for now; stay well. I hope to see you later this year but if not, then in two years' time." Erich replied, firmly shaking his father's hand.

"Well my son, enjoy your time in Germany. It is, as I have told you before, an honour to do your duty and serve the German Reich. I'm sure you will also gain a better understanding of what our nation stands for. Look after yourself, do us all proud and come home in good health. *Auf Wiedersehen*, Erich."

Erich's mother could not maintain the brave façade her husband had presented. Her tears flowed as she hugged Erich, and spoke softly, "Erich, my dear son. I'll miss you but I am happy for you to go to Germany. You go with my blessing to do your military training; it will be the making of you and a few years away from home will give you a much broader outlook on life. Take care and come home again safe and sound. We need you. Good-bye." She wiped away her tears before hugging him once more and kissing his face.

"Ah, Mother. Please don't worry. I'll be back; it is only two years. It seems that I might see you and father before then. Please, be brave and look after yourself," he said as he gave his mother a tight hug and another kiss.

Their farewells made, the young men walked through the Customs House and boarded one of the open boats moored against the stone quay. There was an air of excitement as each boat was cast off by the Arab boatmen and the boat steered out into the open water past the breakwater and into the Mediterranean. After the last boat had cast off, the families and friends made their way outside and lined up along the old stone sea wall. From this elevated vantage point they waved to their sons as the boats left the calm waters behind the breakwater and headed directly into the waves which were breaking in great sprays against the black rocks that flanked the harbour entrance.

As Erich turned his head to look back at the shore, his eyes caught the sight of a young woman standing apart from the main German group. His eyes met hers and, as if by instinct, he knew instantly that it was Ruth. She too had come to wave him goodbye. He raised his arm and waved back. From the distance he saw her raise her hands to her lips and blow a kiss which he returned. His heart was pounding and he wondered if he would ever see her again. Would she still love him when he returned?

As the figures on the seawall became smaller and more indistinct, and hull of the *Milwaukee* loomed ever larger before them. A side hatch had been opened on the leeward side where the waves were more subdued and the Arab boatmen manoeuvred their boats in turn towards the opening before fastening the boat with a rope to the ship. Now they stood to help their passengers board the *Milwaukee;* they ordered one passenger at a time to stand and come to the side of the boat, then, in the instant that the boat rose to the top of the wave they would lift him onto the small platform-like landing protruding from open hatch. For most of the young men, sea-sickness had displaced the euphoria with which they had stepped aboard the open boats, and it was with subdued feelings that they stood at the railing and watched the coastline of Palestine recede.

CHAPTER 2 – 1937/1938

On arrival in Germany, Erich and his comrades from Palestine were separated, each posted to a different training base – Erich was sent to a facility near Nagold. At first he was desperately lonely, and the rigours of boot camp, quite different to the physically hard agricultural work he knew, were punishing. After six months however, he began to enjoy the camaraderie and realised that a strong bond had developed amongst the new recruits. The contact with young men from every part of Germany as well as Germans from overseas made him see that he had been living in a very tiny corner of the world. He valued the new friendships he had forged and understood how important they were for coping with the strict discipline, meeting the challenges, and especially in sustaining their spirits during the long boring periods when they were confined to their base.

Fortunately, the rigours of training were relieved with regular periods of leave when the young men could shed their field grey training uniforms, don their dress uniforms, with jackets and peak hats, and visit the nearby towns or, if time permitted, travel to visit family and friends. At the local bars there were always plenty of charming girls with whom to dance and share a drink, but Erich longed to return to Palestine – to his family and to Ruth, the girl to whom he had given his heart and who was constantly in his thoughts.

Integrated with the military training were sessions of instruction on National Socialism including, of course, indoctrination in the superiority of the Aryan race and implacable antisemitism. Erich found some of this doctrine difficult to accept: on the one hand, as a patriotic German, he shared the national pride of the revitalised German people based as it was on tangible evidence of improved living standards as people found work again after the Great Depression, the construction of massive new Autobahns and the new flowering of German language and culture; yet, on the other hand, the denigration of anything non-Aryan, in particular, Jewish, was difficult to reconcile with his first hand experience of life in Palestine where he dealt daily with both Arabs and Jews. His family's well-being, as well as that of the whole German community back home, was closely linked to the Jews with whom they had close commercial ties. He had not experienced any of the evil the Jews were alleged to be. Furthermore he had a Jewish girlfriend who despite all that he had heard was still very, very dear to him. She was the only girl he really loved.

Erich held fast to his fond memories of Palestine, unaware that conditions there were changing. The violence between the Arabs and Jews was already a fact of life but he had no idea that it was about to enter a new phase of escalation which would engulf the German settlers despite their attempts to remain aloof from it. Beginning in the 1920s, as the flow of Jewish immigrants to Palestine began to increase, the tension and violence increased correspondingly. As anti-Jewish riots increased in frequency and ferocity during the 1920s, the *Yishuv*, the Jewish community in Palestine, realised that it could no longer rely for protection on the British police or army and established a militia for self-defence the *Haganah*, which the British regarded as an underground movement and tried to suppress through arrests and imprisonments. Nevertheless, the *Haganah* grew steadily in strength and sophistication as it secretly purchased arms and smuggled them past the British, and recruited and trained its own fighters. In very short time, it had become the "unofficial" army of the Jews in Palestine.

After the rise to power of the Nazis in Germany in 1933, and especially after the amalgamation of Germany and Austria in 1938, the influx of German and Austrian Jews to Palestine increased substantially. That they were refugees from violent antisemitism and that they were city dwellers rather than farmers did not allay the Arab fear that the Zionist goal of establishing an independent Jewish state was imminent and might mean the loss of land and even, possibly, the expulsion of non-Jews. Consequently, groups of young Arabs formed and directly involved themselves in ongoing anti-Zionist actions. Within the *Haganah,* some of the more militant members rejected the constraints of self-defence, and arguing that they needed to be able to mount attacks, broke away and formed *Irgun Beth,* which undertook reprisals for any Arab attacks on Jews. Action and counter action caused an unending escalation of hostility and violence between the two peoples.

Shortly after Erich's departure, the Arab opposition became more organised. The stimulus was the death of a prominent Arab leader in late 1935 and its first co-ordinated action was the calling in early 1936 of a national Arab strike which lasted for six months and was accompanied by fierce outright violence against the Jews. Several Jewish farming areas and orchards were destroyed and some of the outlying Jewish communities had to be evacuated to safer areas. The *Irgun* responded by bombing Arab markets.

The British were forced to use the military to quell the violent protests in Jaffa and to restore order. In an attempt to prevent further trouble, the authorities imposed curfews and issued identification passes; they cordoned off large areas and searched them, and they established checkpoints for scrutinising identification passes. Nevertheless, Arabs and Jews continued to snipe at one another while the British police and military struggled to maintain order thereby becoming targets for the warring paramilitary groups.

A Royal Commission, known as the Peel Commission, inquired into the causes of the riots and means to prevent similar uprisings and restore law and order. When the Commission recommended that Palestine be partitioned into a small Jewish State and an Arab State attached to Jordan, it triggered another major and violent Arab uprising. This time, the British were compelled to use overwhelming force to quell the uprising; for additional manpower they commissioned some thousands of Jewish auxiliary police for security and intelligence work, which entailed close collaboration with the *Yishuv* in recruiting, training and arming Jewish settlers.

During the period of the Great Arab Revolt, from 1936 to 1939, it became clear that there would be no reconciliation between the Arab and Jewish populations. In an attempt to placate Arab unrest, the British placed severe limits on further Jewish immigration to Palestine. As Nazism consolidated its hold on Germany and Germany threatened and annexed neighbouring countries, many European Jews unsuccessfully sought permits to enter Palestine as refugees; the *Yishuv* strenuously opposed the British restrictions on Jewish immigration, but to no avail. Avraham Stern, split from *Irgun* with a number of followers to establish a new group, *Lohamei Herut Israel* (Freedom Fighters of Israel), better known as the *Stern Gang*. They regarded the British as the main obstacle to the establishment of a Jewish homeland.

*   *   *   *   *

Ruth's sorrow lingered in the weeks following Erich's departure but she eventually realised there was nothing she could do but wait for Erich's return. The dimming of her bright spirits had not gone unnoticed by her best friend, Eva who tried hard to probe Ruth for the reason why her demeanour had changed. Although bursting to tell Eva about Erich, Ruth simply evaded Eva's questions by saying that everything would be alright. Eva decided to arrange and host a birthday party for Ruth, who was turning nineteen, as a means of boosting her flagging spirits. The party was a great success: the singing and dancing continued well into the night; Ruth was the centre of attention and attracted many young male admirers with her good looks and shapely figure.

"You are so attractive that the boys just fall over you," Eva said somewhat enviously at the end of the party "but you never seem to show interest in any of them."

"Oh Eva, I like a few of them but I really don't want to start a serious relationship with anyone in particular," Ruth replied.

"Why not? Itamar has been trying really hard for quite some time to win your attention."

"Yes, I know he has. I think he is very nice and even handsome but somehow, I just don't want to become too close to him. You know the way people in our community gossip."

"At nineteen you aren't too young for a serious relationship and people will gossip when you are twenty and twenty-three – only then, they may be saying that you were too picky and have missed the boat."

"That's true, Eva, but while I like Itamar, I don't think I love him, if you know what I mean."

"Oh, you romantic dreamer! I guess you are still waiting for the man of your dreams."

"Yes, I am. I'm patient and prepared to wait for a while yet – even for a few years if necessary," Ruth said with an inwards smile. Eva would never guess what she really meant by these words.

*   *   *   *   *

As the governing authority, the British declared a public holiday on 12 May 1937 for the Coronation of King George VI, and suitable celebrations were planned throughout Palestine to mark this grand historic occasion. Ruth was looking forward to a free day so she was surprised when her brother David turned to her at breakfast and made clear that he expected her to join him at a rally.

"What rally?" she asked.

"At the German Consulate, to publicly demonstrate strong Jewish opposition to Germany's antisemitic policies. We need as big a crowd as possible to deliver our message with force. You should be with us - especially as you don't have to work today," David insisted.

"Do you think there will be clashes?" Ruth asked.

"I know the organizers want a peaceful demonstration - it is not directed against the Arabs or the British, so we don't expect clashes or any sort of violence. Of course, there are no guarantees – you know how some people allow themselves to be swept along by their emotions."

"What about the local Germans, David? They are certainly not doing us any harm."

"That's true, and they are not the target of the rally. It is the political leadership in Germany that is creating the hatred, although unfortunately, I have to say, some local Germans openly embrace the policies of their government in Germany. You can come with me - some friends will be coming here so that we can go together – we plan to leave at eleven o'clock."

"Well then, if it is aimed only at the government of Germany, I'll join you and your friends."

As planned, the small group set off on foot for Tel Aviv where they met other groups with whom they continued, on foot, to Jaffa. As if to emphasise the remoteness of the Coronation and defy British control, most buildings in Tel Aviv were flying the blue and white flag and every demonstrator carried a small flag.

A large crowd was assembled outside the German Consulate where the German flag, with the hated swastika at its centre, hung above the street from the flagpole that sloped out from the balcony. Voices could be heard shouting slogans to which the crowd responded with ever-louder calls. Suddenly, a young Jewish man appeared holding a very long pole with a burning rag at its end. He was hoisted on the shoulders of several others. When with a stretch, he was able to set alight the German flag, the crowd roared its approval. The celebration was short-lived however, as the police arrived with military backing to disperse the crowd. Despite the abrupt and confused ending to their rally, the demonstrators left satisfied. "I am sure we have made our point," David commented to Ruth as they walked back to Montefiore.

* * * * *

In mid 1937, more than fifteen months since Erich had left Palestine, Erich's unit was selected to participate at the *Reichsparteitag,* the annual Nazi Party rally and congress, in Nürnberg. The 1937 rally was the ninth congress and its theme was the "Rally of Labour" with a special emphasis on the reduction of unemployment since Hitler's rise to power. It was also be a display of military might and more than 30,000 members of the RAD (*Reichsarbeitsdienst,* the Nazi State Labour Service) marched.

The commanding officer of the barrack was overjoyed at the honour and suspended the regular physically gruelling training to allow day-long marching drills to ensure that his men would do honour to Germany as well as to their unit and themselves. The drilling was mind-numbing in its repetitiveness but no less physically demanding than the training it had displaced, but the men were as keen as their CO to shine.

On the first day of the rally they assembled on the road leading into Nürnberg to commence their march through the town. Erich was over-awed and thrilled by the cheering of the dense crowds lining the streets, the brass bands, the banners and flags as they marched through the town. Like his comrades, he concentrated hard to keep in step and in line. But the spectacle that greeted them as they entered the stark concrete forum on Zeppelin Field was beyond their imagining - towering above the podium was an immense shield of an eagle holding a swastika medallion. Oversized flags and huge banners of swastikas formed the backdrop around the arena. After completing their march past, Erich and his unit had to stand as the daytime rally continued to unfold. The many thousands of people assembled were stimulated by the loud patriotic music and driven almost into hysteria by the rousing speeches of the Nazi leaders, punctuated by the rhythmic shouts of *"Sieg Heil"* and the accompanying Nazi salutes. Units from all sections of the Wehrmacht were paraded, armoured and tank columns formed part of the military review as *Luftwaffe* squadrons flew overhead in tight formation.

The show of military strength left Erich quite awe-struck. "How strong our nation has become again! How lucky am I to be part of this wonderful enterprise!" he thought. Yet inside him, a conflict gnawed – he was proud to be a German and proud of Germany's great achievements, but while the undimmed image of Ruth was the prism through which he viewed the entire world, he could not embrace the anti-Jewish hatred that was central to National Socialism.

When the daytime rally finished, the men were pleased to be dismissed; they remained in a state of exhilaration but hunger, thirst and bodily fatigue could not be denied. When darkness fell, another spectacular display opened in the arena as one hundred and fifty-two searchlights pierced the night sky to create a "Cathedral of Light" into which hundreds of torch bearers marched to conclude the day on a mystical note that conjured the national myths of blood and *Volk*.

*   *   *   *   *

When two years had passed since Erich's departure, Ruth began to count the days. She had not expected to hear from him while he was away and she was not yet concerned. "After all, it's only February. I will just have to wait a little longer," she consoled herself. "I miss him, so I hope that means that he misses me and still cares for me."

But when February passed into March and then into April with no word, Ruth took to walking past Bergerle's vegetable fields to look for Erich. Forlornly she would scan the fields but saw no sign of him. She was tempted on several occasions to ask his father – she presumed it was his father at work with the Arabs in the field - but could not bring herself to risk betraying their secret.

Fortunately, she remembered that one of Gold's regular customers worked at the Customs House at the Jaffa port. He was a friendly man who always spoke with her whenever he came in for his coffee and cake. She decided to take a chance; on his next visit, she asked him, "Mr Jakobsohn, has a Mr Erich Bergerle returned to Palestine in the last few months? I knew him before he went to Europe; he was a regular customer, but we haven't seen him for a long time."

"I do not know offhand, Ruth, but I will check the passenger manifests to see if he has come back and I will let you know."

A few days later, Ruth experienced a strange mixture of relief and anxiety when Mr Jakobsohn told her that no-one by that name had disembarked at Jaffa.

* * * * *

The Stein family was eating lunch and David was venting his feelings of frustration at the prevailing situation. "I cannot understand why the British won't allow more of our people to enter Palestine – thousands have fled from Germany to France and England, and many more want to come here, but the British won't lift their stupid immigration quotas because they are anxious to appease the Arabs. Look at what happened at the Evian Conference recently – no-one wanted to take Jewish refugees fleeing Germany. Yet here we are, willing to receive them and provide for them, but the British won't allow us. Perhaps we should encourage the British to exchange the local Germans for Jewish refugees – maybe the Germans who are so proud of the new Germany should be sent there to live."

"Oh, David," Ruth responded, "that would be so unfair – most of the local Germans were born here and don't want to leave."

"Unfair? Do you think that what is happening to our people in Germany – born and raised as German – is fair? Who cares about fairness? We have to do what best serves our long-term interests!"

"David, it is because of what is happening to our people in Germany that I think it would be unjust to force the local Germans out."

At this David became quite agitated; he turned on Ruth. "Why do you always stick up for the local Germans? Every time I say something about them you seem to feel a need to support them, to defend them."

"No, David. I am neither supporting nor defending them. But I do feel that your hostility to them is unreasonable and as I have said before, they have done us no harm here in Palestine. In fact, they even helped our pioneers get established."

"Ruth! Here in Palestine, our immediate concern is the local Arab population, but in Europe our people are facing a far greater threat and there are far more Jews there than here. Just read the papers and you'll see."

"I do know what is happening over there," Ruth responded, her voice rising in anger, "but I will not agree that we should take it out on the Germans living here."

"Why not? It may be the only way we can do something. Perhaps we should even consider kidnapping a few Germans and holding them hostage."

"Stop that now, David!" their father, Avraham, intervened. "I will not tolerate stupid, provocative talk. We need to focus our attention and efforts on ensuring our own safety without provoking other groups or the authorities. We cannot help our brethren in Europe if we are insecure here."

"I'm sorry, Abba; you are quite right. It just annoys me that Ruth constantly sticks up for the Germans. It seems that no matter what happens, she always comes to their defence."

"That's not true!" Ruth retorted forcefully. "You are trying to associate the Templers with the Nazi government. But the Templers live in their settlement right next to us in Montefiore and we have never had trouble with them. Nevertheless, you imply that they are all bad. In the main, they are good, decent people who have lived here for several generations – just like us."

"Enough, both of you! Shouting will resolve nothing. As your father, I want to remind you that we are living in testing times and we are likely to be tested much further – I want us to hold together as a family. David, all of us share your passion for a Jewish homeland, but you cannot allow yourself to adopt extremist views. If we can believe the newspapers, we may soon have our own state – it seems that the British are now seriously considering partitioning Palestine into Jewish and Arab regions – we should be encouraged by these reports."

*   *   *   *   *

On a hot day in July 1938, Wilhelm entered the kitchen deep in thought. "You look upset," Sophie said anxiously, as Wilhelm sat himself down at the kitchen table.

"What has happened?"

"I have just been speaking with Jonathan, our *Bürgermeister*. He was at a meeting between representatives of our settlements and Sir John Woodhead, the head of the British commission examining the proposal to partition Palestine."

"Yes, I read about the Commission some time ago in the Palestine Post."

"Well, Sir John has asked our representatives for their views on partition. If it goes ahead, it will have disastrous implications for us! Can you image if some of our settlements were under Arab control and others under Jewish rule? You can just imagine what would happen then: it would mean the end of our way of life; our German customs; our culture; and maybe even our language."

"But Wilhelm, nothing will happen quickly! These matters take a long time to sort out," Sophie said.

"Do they? We only know that it is being seriously considered, otherwise the British wouldn't be asking our leaders for their opinion. They see partitioning Palestine as a solution to the problem they created here after the war. I just hope it doesn't happen. What future will Helga and Erich have here if it does?"

CHAPTER 3 – 1939

Erich did not return to Palestine until February 1939; his absence had coincided exactly with the Great Arab Revolt, so he returned to a land that had changed significantly. As the violence between the Arabs and the Jews had escalated, so too did the violence between the British and the Jews and the British and the Arabs, both the Jews and Arabs believing that the British favoured their opponents. The Germans were caught in the middle of all this unrest and uncertainty. Keen to remain aloof from the de facto war between the Arabs and Jews, the German community leaders continued to urge the settlers to be strictly neutral in all their dealings with both parties. The Germans had lived in harmony with both the Arabs and Jews for decades and despite the social delineations, many strong personal ties had developed. But in a war, both sides suspect neutral parties of bias, and this was the fate of the Templers.

The anti-Semitic policies and actions of the German government fostered suspicion of the German settlers amongst the Jews, especially as Jews fled Nazi Germany in increasing numbers and sought refuge in Palestine. Sporadic boycotts of German produce did some minor harm to the economic well-being of the German farmers and business people but generally the commercial interaction between Jews and Germans in Palestine continued to grow. The Sarona community continued to provide rent-free lodging in their settlement for a religious Jew who supervised the dairy to certify its milk and dairy products as kosher for sale in Tel Aviv. They also continued to seek the pharmaceutical, specialist medical and dental services provided by Jews in Tel Aviv, just as they continued to shop in Jewish shops in Tel Aviv and trade with Jewish merchants.

However, the Germans also continued their good relations with the Arabs who provided much of the labour for the German enterprises as well as being purchasers of German goods and produce.

Unfortunately though, the political influence of the National Socialist German Labour Party had also increased amongst the German settlers as more of them became active party members, as cells of the German Labour Front were established in workplaces, and as the youth were encouraged to join either the Hitler Youth or the League of German Girls. An intense debate arose within the Sarona community between those who wished to maintain the community's core religious values and worship of God and those who had adopted the new political doctrine and admired the Führer to the point of reverence.

It was to this atmosphere that Erich returned. He'd had no contact with Ruth during his three year absence: neither could send the other any letters for fear of causing embarrassment; and neither could know the feelings of the other. On his return to Palestine, Erich's first thoughts were of Ruth; did she still work at Golds? Did she feel betrayed by his extended absence? Did she still love him? Of one thing he was certain - he yearned to see her again, his absence had not diminished his love for her. The only possible avenue of contact was through Golds, but he was reluctant to go there not knowing what to expect. He opted instead to write a letter, seal it in a personally addressed envelope and slip it under the door of the closed coffee shop one evening.

The next morning, when Ruth arrived for work Mrs Gold greeted her with a broad smile. "I have a little surprise for you," she said handing the envelope to Ruth.

"Oh, my God!" Ruth gasped as she looked at the envelope addressed to her and with *Persönlich* printed in large letters across the top. She instantly knew who it was from but just stared at the envelope, hesitant to open it, not knowing its contents.

"Ruth, darling, just go to the back room where you can be alone when you open it. I have a hunch that it brings good news," Mrs Gold urged in a warm tone.

"But Mrs Gold, Erich has been gone for nearly three years now and I heard nothing from him in all that time. I am so afraid that he does not want me anymore." Ruth called as she hurried to the storeroom, her voice tremulous with fear and hope.

With anxious hands she tore open the envelope; her heart pounded loudly as she unfolded Erich's letter. As if frightened to read too closely, she first skimmed the hand written words before taking a deep breath and reading it slowly.

"My dearest Ruth

It has been nearly three years since I last embraced you when we said good-bye. I hold dear a clear image of you standing on the sea-wall at Jaffa, windswept as you waved to me – a memory I will never forget. Much has happened during these three years, but my love for you has not diminished and you were in my thoughts every day. I don't know how you feel towards me now, but I know that I still love you. Now that I am back I hope we can meet again and catch up on what has happened. Can we meet at our old meeting place on the corner of Montefiore and Nahmani Streets tomorrow after you finish work?

I don't know if you still work for Mrs Gold but I have written to you in the hope that even if you no longer work there, she will pass this letter on to you. If that is the case, I will wait at our usual spot for the next two weeks as well.

I'm so happy to be back again and do really hope you will meet me.

With all my love

Erich"

She read it again, more slowly still, the sound of her heart pounding loudly in her ears. Oh what joy!

With an irrepressible smile, Ruth returned to the shop.

"Oh, Mrs Gold, you were right again. It is wonderful news and I am so happy, I could burst. Erich is back! He still loves me and wants to meet me after work tomorrow just like he used to before he went away. I'm so looking forward to seeing him again; I just hope that the bond between us is as strong as it was."

"You see, Ruth, I told you it would all work out. I sensed from the first time he came here that he was absolutely smitten with you. I could also say the same about you because you told me as much. I am happy for you Ruth but I'm also just a little worried about how your relationship will proceed - the world has changed so much in the last three years and you know as well as I do just how much the tensions have increased between we Jews and the Germans. In this tiny country, where once we lived together co-operatively, there is now three-way fighting between Jews, Arabs and the English, and all three are suspicious of the Germans; it seems to me that the situation is only going to get worse as time goes on."

"Yes, I know. We recently received a letter from our relatives in Germany and they wrote about the *Kristallnacht* in November last year and the terrifying hostility and violence the Jews face daily now in Germany. Our relatives are frantically trying to get out of Germany and come here to Palestine; my parents are willing to take them in but it is difficult for them to get out of Germany and even more difficult to get an entry permit for Palestine."

"Yes, I know what people are going through, nevertheless I bear no ill feeling towards Erich – he and his family are not responsible for our changed circumstances or for the situation in Germany. In fact, Ruth, if you want to use the shop for your meetings, he is welcome to come here after we close. Here it is quiet and private, you can make yourselves a cup of coffee and have any of the cake left at the end of the day. Believe me,

I am worried for you. You know that we now have our own extremists who harbour such a deep hatred towards any Germans that if they were to learn of your relationship, they may harm you and Erich, perhaps not physically but by innuendo and gossip. You know you can trust me."

"Oh, how can I thank you! You have always been so understanding and now so supportive and wise." Ruth exclaimed, hugging Mrs Gold. "Right now, I can only think about seeing him again. I cannot think about the difficulties until I am sure that everything is well between us."

* * * * *

The next day, Erich was waiting at the meeting place well before four o'clock – he was determined not to be late on this occasion. He was certainly eager but also rather apprehensive: would Ruth come to meet him? Would he wait in vain? How would she behave toward him after all this time? What would she say to him? Nervously, at intervals of thirty seconds, he looked down at his watch to check the time and then lifted his gaze to scan the bustling footpath for any glimpse of his beloved Ruth. His agony was cut short when, right on four o'clock, he caught sight of her as she ran towards him waving, a magnificent smile illuminating her face. She looked more beautiful than ever – gone were the last remnants of her childhood looks. Her dark eyes sparkled and her long honey-blond hair flowed as he remembered but her shapely figure had blossomed into beautiful young womanhood. He recognised the same strange inner feeling he had experienced when he first met her almost four years earlier.

With a pounding heart he moved towards her; without a word they embraced in the middle of the footpath, oblivious of their surroundings, as only lovers can do. Erich held Ruth tightly to him and lifted her off the ground as their lips met in a passionate kiss. Each realised in that magic moment that their love for one another had not diminished during their long separation but seemed to have strengthened.

"Ruth, I have missed you so much, I just love you!" he whispered between tender kisses.

"Oh Erich, I have missed you, too. I was so worried when you didn't return at the end of two years," she sobbed, as her tears of joy ran soaked into Erich's jacket.

"Let's go somewhere quiet where we can talk we have so much to catch up. My bike is just around the corner."

Erich drove through Jaffa to the first beach south of the Jaffa headland; it was quieter than the northern beaches which had become lively precincts due to Tel Aviv's rapid expansion of the past three years. At the quiet south beach there was also far less likelihood that they might be recognised. He parked his bike at the top of the high sand dunes that overlooked the long southward sweep of beach. It was the first time he had visited the beach since his return and as if by instinct, his eyes searched for the distinctive natural features that were so prominent in his happy memories of childhood summer holidays at the beach. "Adam's Rock" still protruded from the water, dark and defiant against the waves; the water around it was deep and only the strong swimmers could reach it. He remembered the first time he had tried to clamber onto it. It was tricky as it could only be done from the seaward side using the swell to lift one high enough to gain a foothold. But how exhilarating it had been to climb to the top for the first time and wave to his family on the beach! The *"Insele"* was a low rock formation just above the waterline - like a little island - and a welcome resting point on the long swim to "Adam's Rock". A short distance away was "Columbus' Egg", a round rock formation that stood high and solitary from the sparkling blue Mediterranean. *Südstrand* was still a favourite holiday place for many of the Germans and families, who would come from as far as Jerusalem, for an annual seaside holiday and informal reunions with other German families. Of course, the beach was deserted in winter and the contrast to summer, when it was bustling with swimmers and holiday makers, was stark.

Erich and Ruth took off their shoes and followed the narrow but well worn sandy track to the beach. The warm rays of the late afternoon sun cast long shadows as they strolled in silent communion, arms about each other, towards the southern end of the beach, stopping from time to time to embrace.

At the southern end of the beach the dunes rose much higher; the gravestones in the old Greek cemetery reflected the golden light of the setting sun. Erich and Ruth decided to take one of the overgrown tracks to the cemetery to sit on the warm stones and talk, but as they neared the top of the ridge they found a small secluded clearing in the vegetation, just a few steps off the track itself through a narrow opening. They sat down on the dry cool sand - they had stumbled upon the clearing accidentally but they immediately adopted it as their private place, where they could meet and talk away from any bustling crowds or prying eyes.

"Oh, Erich. How glad I am that you have returned to me! This last year has been so difficult – I had expected you to return after two years, but there was absolutely no sign of you! I knew from friends of my parents, who still go to Sarona for coffee and cake at Günthners, that the men who left with you had all returned, but I couldn't make specific enquiries about you. Several times I walked past your family's orange grove and saw your father working with the Arab workers - you have no idea how tempted I was to ask him about you, but I just couldn't work up the courage as I knew your parents didn't know anything about me. In the end I thought you may have married and stayed on to live in Germany – it was better than thinking that something serious had happened to you during training."

"I'm so sorry that you worried about me. I was also concerned because I didn't know what you were doing or what your feelings were towards me. So much could have happened, especially to someone as young and beautiful as you. When I wrote the letter to you and left it at Golds', I didn't even know if you were still working there, let alone how you would respond. I was in an agony of doubt: did you still love me? Had you started a new relationship with some else? Would you come to meet me? So I was just overjoyed when I saw you coming towards me with that wonderful smile on your face. I knew straight away that there was still a real bond between us. Oh, Ruth, I just love you," he said, hugging Ruth tightly. "I had wanted to return home to Sarona after completing my military service but my father wrote to me about the changing situation in Palestine. He was most concerned at how the political situation in Germany was affecting the Germans living here and making our lives more difficult.

"In our family's case most of our oranges are sold to Germany and we get paid in *Reichsmark*. It used to be our main source of income, but in recent years the *Reichsmark* has become worthless outside of Germany. Here in Palestine we can no longer buy anything in *Reichsmark* and so we often have to resort to bartering for goods with traders in Germany. Last year, my uncle bought a new car in Germany and rather than paying for it with money from here he was able to negotiate the purchase in exchange for a shipment of oranges. The same situation applies with other goods such as machines or tools. It is much easier if you have relatives in Germany to whom you can transfer *Reichsmark* and they in turn can buy things for you and send them to Palestine, but my family has no relatives left in Germany. Fortunately, as well as growing oranges, my family has been doing very well with the sale of vegetables and some other fruit we produce and sell here in Palestine through Jewish merchants at the Tel Aviv markets. There is a growing market here for all our products especially with the continuing influx of your people from Europe and the rapid expansion of Tel Aviv.

"So my parents thought that it would be a good idea for me to attend an agricultural college in Germany after completing my military training. With my newly-acquired knowledge, we will be able to recognise opportunities to diversify our farming to take advantage of local conditions and reduce our reliance on the export of oranges. The agricultural course was very interesting and I learnt a great deal – of course, the climate in Germany is dramatically different to what we have here. But I'm sure you don't want all this technical detail – it was the study that kept me away for an extra year, but I had no way of telling you."

"If only I had known," Ruth whispered as she squeezed his hand, "I would have been more certain of myself. Several young men have been keen to take me out. One was particularly persistent to begin a serious relationship with me and I went out with him on a few occasions - he is a kind and caring man and my parents liked him - but I could not forget you or my deep feelings towards you. It was a very trying time but fortunately, my parents didn't press me at all - I told my mother about you on the night before you left and she has always said that things would work themselves out somehow.

"My brother has now qualified as a policeman and is posted in Tel Aviv - he has realised his ambition. Since you left, the British have appointed many young Jewish men as auxiliary policemen. There has been so much unrest since 1936. We fear for my brother at times with all the violence but he is more determined than ever to help bring about the establishment of a homeland for our people – he is actually quite fanatical and it is difficult to speak rationally with him about Germans, Arabs or the British as he thinks they are all against us.

"As you mentioned, more and more Jewish families are fleeing Germany and trying to settle here but the British have placed stringent limits on the numbers that can enter Palestine. The desperate ones enter Palestine illegally by any means they can and our communities, which shelter and protect these illegals, are constantly harassed by the British trying to find them; anyone without an official identification card is arrested. The Arabs resent these new arrivals and see Jewish migration as a threat to them so there are constant skirmishes with the Arabs. It has become quite dangerous for Jews to go into places where there is an Arab majority. Most of us stay indoors at home, especially at night because so many people have been killed and injured. Last year, when there was another Arab uprising in Jaffa, we didn't venture out at all. It took the British and Jewish police and the army several days to restore order but the unrest and violence still continues despite the many arrests on both sides. Sadly the whole situation is going from bad to worse with more and more bloodshed - there is no end in sight.

"Meanwhile, I am still working at Golds - they are so good to me, Mrs Gold especially. She is just so big-hearted and understanding. I can speak with her about any issues and she always listens carefully before sharing her thoughts. I just love her! She even said that whenever we want to talk in private, we can use her shop after closing time and help ourselves to coffee and any cake that is left. She really means well for both of us."

*   *   *   *   *

In the following weeks, the days that Ruth and Erich appointed for their meetings were fine and they preferred the freedom of their hideaway on the sand dunes rather than to be confined indoors for their times together. But one rainy day in March, Erich unexpectedly found himself in Tel Aviv; he telephoned Ruth at the cake shop to see if he could meet her after work. She was delighted and asked Mrs Gold for permission for Erich to come to the shop after closing time.

"Of course he can come! I made that offer to you weeks ago but because you've never taken it up, I just assumed that Erich didn't want to come here. There is some strudel left, which I will put aside for him as you told me how much he likes it. The cream is in the refrigerator. You might as well use it up and we can beat some fresh tomorrow – it comes from the Sarona dairy anyway. You know where the coffee is - just make yourselves at home. I will leave you in peace!" Mrs Gold said warmly.

"Thank you so much, Mrs Gold. Your kindness and understanding are overwhelming in these times," Ruth replied.

It was five o'clock when Erich knocked on the door. The shop was in darkness as Ruth had drawn the blinds on the shop-front windows. She showed him to the back room, which as a workroom and staff area, was sparsely furnished with just a single small table and two chairs. It was certainly no romantic setting lined as it was with a refrigerator, a small oven, a workbench and shelves to store baking trays and implements, crockery and ingredients. After their initial embrace they stood admiring each other before Ruth invited Erich to sit at the table "I'll make you a coffee and I have a surprise for you."

"I would love a coffee. I've been on the move all afternoon and haven't had a drink since lunchtime."

"In that case, I will make a pot of coffee."

Ruth poured the coffee into two cups, took the strudel from the refrigerator and topped it with a very large dollop of cream.

"There you are," she said as she presented it, "service with love and a smile."

"Oh my - I will not say no to that! Did you especially keep this for me?"

"No, actually, it was Mrs Gold. I told her how much you liked her strudel."

"How kind of her. Please pass on my thanks."

After his first mouthful he added, "It is absolutely delicious."

After a pause, Ruth placed a folder on the table and shyly said, "Erich I have something here for you. It is a photo of me. I had it taken by a professional photographer especially."

Erich opened the folder, picked up the photo and gazed at it intently. "Oh, Ruth! You know that I will treasure it - it is the only photograph I have of you, but it is extraordinary how faithfully the photographer captured you in a happy and relaxed pose. Thank you, my darling." He rose to hug Ruth and kiss her again and added, "Maybe we should get him to take a photo us together."

"I am glad you like it. I was happy with my expression as well. I would dearly love to have a photo of us together, but it could be a bit risky in the current circumstances. I think it might be better if we waited a bit longer before we did that."

And so they chatted together, enjoying each other's company until it was time to clean up, wash the dishes and go to their homes.

*   *   *   *   *

During springtime Erich and Ruth met regularly in Tel Aviv, a great deal of their time was spent pondering their future as the spectre of war grew larger and more threatening in Europe.

One late afternoon Erich was aghast when he saw Ruth coming towards obviously upset; gone was the radiant smile, the dark eyes were sad and the normally carefree face was clouded.

"What has happened?" Erich asked anxiously as he hugged Ruth.

"Oh Erich, my *Safta*, my dear grandmother, passed away two days ago; we had her funeral yesterday," Ruth spoke quietly between sobs as her tears darkened Erich's jumper. "She was so special to me; she cared for me when I was small and my parents were both working hard to make ends meet. She was kind and wise - my brother always teased me and said I was her pet.

"I regret now that I did not tell her about you; I am sure she would have been very understanding and supportive as she never expressed any negative feelings for the Germans here in Palestine. In fact quite the opposite; I can recall that she mentioned with admiration on a number of times the achievements of the Germans and the assistance they gave the Jews when both were struggling to build settlements and new communities in Turkish-ruled Palestine. She was so proud what she and her family achieved in those early years.

"At the funeral service the Rabbi mentioned that Safta was one of the last original pioneering women of Nahalat Reuben and that she was present in 1891 when Jewish settlers gathered there and waved a blue and white flag with *Ness Ziona* (Flag/banner of Zion) written on it. You know Erich, that flag was later adopted by the Zionist Congress and the settlement became known as Ness Ziona."

"Ruth, my dear, I am so sorry to hear such sad news." Erich said comfortingly as he gently rubbed Ruth's back. "Had she been ill? I guess I assumed that you had no grandparents because you never mentioned them and also I suppose because I have none. She must have been a good age."

"She was eighty-eight and had been in relatively good health for her age. Last week she said she didn't feel well, but still got up everyday; we were therefore not all that concerned. When she died in her sleep it was a great shock to us all. Oh how I miss her! I didn't even have an opportunity to say good-bye." Ruth sobbed.

"It's very sad and I feel for you and your family, but Ruth at least you were able to grow up with her and enjoy her love and attention. So it is in life. Time will heal your sorrow and you will always have those happy memories and good times to reflect on. We should also never forget the hardships and tribulations our forefathers went through to achieve what we have today. Can we sit down somewhere quiet and have a cup of coffee together?"

"You know that I would love to, Erich, but during this week of mourning, I feel that I must be with my parents. Please try to understand, my love. I'll look forward to seeing you next week."

*   *   *   *   *

Despite the troubles that surrounded them, both Erich and Ruth felt so happy and invincible after their meetings that one moonless Spring night, after dropping Ruth near her home Erich decided to take a shortcut to Sarona along the Nablus Road and then turning onto a track through the orange groves to his home. The track was both sandy and narrow, with tall prickly pear plants growing along both sides. Although the plants were cut back regularly to keep the track open, care was needed not to brush against the tough thorns. Erich had driven some hundred metres along the track and slowed in the dry loose sand, his motor revving, when without warning two hooded figures jumped out in front of him. In his headlights he could clearly see one of them pointing a pistol in his direction.

"*Kif!* Stop! *Halt!*" they shouted at him. By this time, several other hooded men had emerged from the prickly pear bushes behind him; he was trapped, unable to turn back or accelerate forward.

"We have caught you, Jew! Now we will teach you a lesson for trying to find our hiding place and reporting us to your secret police," the armed Arab chortled.

"But I am a German, I'm not Jewish." Erich replied firmly.

"You are lying. You have no German flag on your motorbike. All the Germans mark their vehicles so that we can easily identify them and therefore not harm them."

"Look! I live in Sarona, the German settlement less than a kilometre from here, I left my emblem at home. Come with me and I will show it to you."

"Do you think we are stupid? You would only lead us into a trap."

"Show us your wallet, licence and identification card. What do they say?"

"I don't have them with me. My papers are all at home also. Just believe me I am German. I'm on my way home."

"Yeah? So why are you coming from Montefiore if you are a German? That's a Jewish village."

"I just went for a joy ride on my motorbike and on my way home I decided to take this track back to Sarona. It is a shortcut."

Cold drops of perspiration were forming on Erich's forehead and face. Of course he knew that there was no love lost between the Arab fighters and Jewish militants - there had been numerous skirmishes with gunfire around Sarona and in the orange groves and vineyards. One of the shoot-outs had been so close to the settlement that bullets had whistled between the buildings and settlers threw themselves to the ground to avoid being hit. After that incident, the British authorities stationed an Arab policeman in the Sarona village for additional security.

In order to protect themselves from being shot at by the Arabs the Germans had adopted the practice of placing small German flag emblems on their cars and motor bikes. This open display of the swastika emblem incensed the Jews against the Germans. Out of respect for Ruth, Erich did not display his emblem when they were together, and hence he did not have it with him. In practical terms too, both their lives could have been made most uncomfortable if they were spotted together on a motorbike with the German flag.

"We don't believe you - look at your face shiny with sweat – you're nothing but a frightened Jew! You deliberately came out without identification so that you could lie your way out if you are caught - well it won't work," he grinned maliciously, his white teeth bared.

"Please! You must believe me! I am German - I have lived in Sarona all my life. My family, relatives and friends all live there. If you let me go there I can prove my identity."

"Enough of this lying and silly talk. We are going to teach you a lesson for spying on us - you will never try it again. Turn off the lights and come with us," the Arab said menacingly. Erich knew he had no choice but to do as he was ordered. The leader gestured to the others who closed around Erich. One of them pushed a pistol barrel firmly into Erich's back and he heard the pistol click as it was primed.

"Don't do anything silly like trying to escape," the leader said curtly, frisking Erich, "any false move and we will shoot. You will not get away. Do as you are told."

The group walked Erich a short distance up the track to an opening in the hedge through which they pushed him into an orange grove.

"Now tell us just what you were up to, coming here after dark. Were you looking for us?"

"I have told you, I am on my way home to Sarona. I live there with my family. I am a German and have absolutely nothing to do with the Jewish militants. You know that we Germans have not taken sides in all the unrest, and you also know that many of us are quite sympathetic towards you. We provide work for many Arabs – both men and women. In my family we employ Yasmine to help my mother in the home with housework and the washing, and my father has two full-time Arab workers, Saeed and Hassan, to help us in the orange grove and vegetable garden. They are very loyal and good workers who have been working for us for more than ten years. During the orange harvest we take on casual Arab workers. You must believe me!"

"What rubbish! You are a Jew sent to spy on us and then report our location to the authorities so they can arrest us. You are unarmed because it makes your claim to be German believable if you were captured. Who sent you here, the Haganah or the Irgun?"

"No-one sent me. I am German. I have nothing to do with either of them."

"Well, if you won't answer our questions truthfully, that's it. Do you want to be blind-folded or face your fate with open eyes?" the Arab asked mockingly.

Erich heard the click of another pistol as it was primed.

"You are making a big mistake. You are killing an innocent person. I was not spying on you. I was on my way home. Just let me go." Erich pleaded

"Shut-up! You can only go if you can prove that you are German. So far you haven't been able to do that."

Ominously they forced him to stand in front of a high prickly pear bush.

"Stop, please stop I can prove I am a German." Erich desperately called out.

"What lies are you going to tell us now? What frightens you more - pain or death?"

"I want to show you something."

"What have you got to show? You told us you left all your papers at home. This is just a trick."

"No trick – I promise."

Erich undid his belt and let his trousers fall to his ankles, exposing his genitals.

"You see? I have not been circumcised. I am not Jewish!"

A bright torch was shone on his penis and loud laughter followed.

"He is a German after all." one of them commented.

"Cover yourself - we've seen enough. You can go but take care to tell no-one that we are here. If you betray us, we know your motor bike and where to find you, we will deal with you." the leader told a very relieved Erich.

* * * * *

When summer arrived, the activity on the beach increased to such an extent that Erich and Ruth had to find new meeting places, far from the crowds amongst which there were likely to be acquaintances of one of them. On a hot July night, Erich met Ruth after she finished work and took her to a small restaurant on the beach front just north of the Audsche estuary, well north of the north and south beaches of Jaffa where their friends were most likely to be.

It was already evening as they set off for home but Erich still had to stop at the orange grove, just on the outskirts of Sarona, to turn off the pump motor as the trees would have received sufficient water. Normally this work was done by Abdullah, the overseer of the Bergerle's orchard - most of the orange growers employed an overseer to protect their crops against theft during the harvest and to manage the irrigation of the trees – but Abdullah was ill and Erich had taken up his irrigation duties during the hot summer to ensure a good crop in autumn and early winter.

A glorious full moon was rising in the east and the sounds from Sarona were clearly audible in the balmy summer evening – the dance music from Günthner's café, the rumble and crash of skittles from the bowling alley at Kuebler's bar accompanied by the occasional shout of *"Kranz"* and *"Platte"* as both old and young pursued their pastimes. On the eastern side of the pump house stood a garden bench on which Erich and Ruth sat with their arms around each other to watch the moon rise and enjoy each other's company for a little longer.

"You know Ruth, this land has belonged to my family for over sixty years. It was my grandfather who first ploughed the ground here. Originally he planted a vineyard but as it became evident that a much better return could be made from oranges he decided to plant this orange grove. Many other early Sarona vineyards have been ripped out for orange groves. We still have a couple of *dunams* with grapes and my father still belongs to the Sarona-Wilhelma Winegrowers Co-operative, which owns the large wine cellar. Most of the grapes for the wines now come from our sister settlement of Wilhelma. One day, I hope to own this beautiful orchard to carry on our family tradition." Then wistfully, he added, "It would be wonderful if we could do that together."

Ruth nestled closer. "Oh, Erich, I can't see that happening right now. Everyone is saying that war is coming in Europe and the troubles here in Palestine are getting worse. Maybe we will have to go elsewhere to be together."

"Yes, I've thought that too, but where could we go? Cyprus? Turkey? Or further – South Africa, the United States or Australia? But I can't leave my home and my parents, it would break their hearts, and if I left with you, I could probably never return to my community, which I admire and respect. I'm caught in the middle in this crazy world - with an undying love for you but no less a love for my family."

"I know Erich; I feel the same way and just wish that there could be a solution for us that would allow us to live together. Being forced to meet in secret and having to avoid being seen together is driving me insane. We should be allowed to live our lives like any other young couple in love without shame and prejudice. We've done nothing wrong and nor have our families, but all our problems come from someone else over whom we have no control. It doesn't seem to matter what we think or do, we can change nothing."

They fell silent, pondering their future. The moon had risen and cast eerie shadows across the orchard. The dance music floating from Sarona had become even more clearly audible in the still night air when Erich asked Ruth if she would like to dance. Her heart leapt – she had so longed to dance with Erich, she didn't hesitate,

"Yes of course, I'd love to!"

As they rose to their feet and enfolded their arms about each another, Ruth rested her head against Erich's powerful shoulder. They melted into each other as they shuffled in the fine dry sand to *Zwei Herzen im Dreiviertel Takt* (Two hearts in three quarter time). When the record finished they remained holding each other and stole a sweet kiss.

As the next record started, Erich squeezed Ruth even closer to him. Their eyes were closed as the lyrics of the song *Du, Du liegst mir im Herzen, Du, Du liegst mir im Sinn* (You, you lie my heart, you, you lie in my thoughts) echoed in their own hearts. As they danced, Erich quietly sang along with feeling. Ruth was mesmerised as she absorbed the words "And, and when I love you, then, then love me too".

Totally oblivious to the world, the dancing couple was unaware of the silent approach of a figure through the shadows of the orchard. A voice shattered their tranquillity,

"I am glad that you are OK, Erich!"

It was Assif, the nightwatchman employed by the Sarona community to safeguard their properties and provide some security during the hours of darkness. The settlers had always prided themselves on their honesty, but during the 1930s their concerns grew about the protection for themselves and their properties from outside marauders. Assif was from Syria - the community deliberately chose a non-local Arab for this task – having lived in Sarona for five years, he was trusted by the German community that employed him and spoke German in their Swabian dialect.

"What are you doing here?" Erich asked after he had regained his composure.

"I was doing my patrol when I saw a light shining near the pump house. As I got closer I could see that it was moonlight reflecting from the mirror of your motorbike. I was worried that you had been ambushed or hurt because you are not normally at the orchard at this time of night so I crept through the orchard. I'm sorry I gave you and your friend such a fright; I understand and promise I won't tell anyone about you being here," his white teeth flashed as he grinned and turned away.

"I know I can trust you Assif." Erich replied, feeling abashed at so soon having forgotten his own encounter with Arab militants in the orchard. He silently resolved that he would never again allow Ruth's intoxicating presence to blind him to the ever-present dangers.

When Assif was out of earshot, Ruth's anxiety surfaced, "Erich, can you really trust him. What if he tells others in your community?"

The spell of the evening was broken, and Ruth's practicality emerged, "I really need to get home. My parents will be wondering about my safety even though I told them I would be home late. My father especially gets very worried."

"I am sure we can trust Assif. He has probably caught many other young couples as they tried to find a quiet spot for themselves somewhere. It is not easy for people of our age to get away from prying eyes; rumours start and spread very quickly. Assif knows our people only too well to start spreading stories – he would soon lose his job if he did. But yes, you're quite right. It's high time we both got home otherwise I will be asked a few tricky questions as well."

*   *   *   *   *

After that abrupt end to what had promised to be an idyllic evening, Ruth and Erich resumed their frustratingly restrained and time-constricted regular weekly meetings – the beach was busy in the summer months and they couldn't use "their" hideaway as they had been able in winter. One afternoon, late in August 1939, Ruth was surprised to receive a telephone call at Golds' from Erich saying that it was extremely important that they meet that evening – they had met the previous evening and spoken, yet again, of their future.

"What is so urgent?" Ruth asked anxiously, as she embraced Erich at their usual meeting spot. "Only yesterday we spoke about our future together. What has happened? You sounded so serious when you called me. Not like you at all!"

"Ruth, we can't speak here on the footpath in the middle of Tel Aviv. Let's go to our little hideaway at the South Beach."

When they reached the beach they were surprised to see only a few people, all at the northerly end of the beach, and they made their way southward along the firm sand near the water's edge. The sun was low in the sky but the sand in the clearing was still warm and, as if to emphasise the peace and tranquillity of the tiny haven, the sweet scent of sand lilies was all-pervasive. This place was their "home" away from the hostility and hatreds of the world and the prying eyes that were the handmaidens of those hatreds. As if to catch a glimpse of the storm clouds that were rapidly darkening the skies of Europe, the couple looked westward in silence - both knew that their destiny and lives would be shaped by the tumultuous events that would take place in Europe and both felt the sinister foreboding.

In silence, they turned to one another and embraced affectionately before sitting to speak. Erich broke the silence after a few minutes. "Ruth, my darling, I have a secret which I need to share with you, but you must promise me that you will tell no-one else," he said looking directly into Ruth's dark eyes.

"I promise," she whispered with an involuntary shudder as if knowing that she was about to hear bad news.

"This morning I received a formal directive from the German consul in Jaffa to report immediately for active military service in Germany. It seems that war is imminent. Tomorrow morning, with the other young Germans who have completed their military training, I have to embark on a ship lying at anchor off Jaffa. I am sworn to secrecy so you must not tell anyone about this order but I had to tell you - I just couldn't leave you without saying good-bye. If the authorities find out that I have broken my oath I could be treated as a traitor and the consequences would be severe."

"I promise I won't tell a soul. You know you can trust me. There are already so many secrets between us," she sobbed quietly as she absorbed the unwelcome news. Tears wet her cheeks as she squeezed tightly against Erich.

A few minutes passed without a single word before Erich reached into his pocket for a small package which he gave to Ruth. "I have a small keepsake for you. It comes with all my love, from the very depths of my soul."

Ruth's hands trembled as she removed the ribbon and paper of the neatly wrapped box. She gasped when she saw the golden bracelet that glowed in the rays of the setting sun. As she lifted it for a closer look, she saw the engraving inside, *"Liebste Ruth, Mit aller Liebe, Erich. August 1939"* (Dearest Ruth, with all my love, Erich. August 1939) Tears again welled in hers eyes as she clung to Erich whose embrace tightened correspondingly and they allowed their powerful emotions to take their course.

"Ruth, I must return home – it is my last night with my family too, and I told them I wouldn't be gone for long – that I was just had to see a friend in Jaffa. How I wish it had not come to saying good-bye again after such a short time reunited with you.

"Erich, my darling, when will I see you again?" she whispered.

"Who knows how long the war will be? Hopefully, it will be short and I will be able to return to you quickly. Whatever happens, I will always love you dearly. Let us hope that some day, soon, we can hold each other in our arms again."

"My dearest Erich, I promise I will love you to my dying day. I just pray that nothing will happen to you and that some day you will return to me," she sobbed.

"Be strong, Ruth, and I am sure one day we will meet again."

Slowly they walked back to Erich's motor cycle wondering if they would ever return to their secret place on the South beach.

*   *   *   *   *

The time available was so short that Erich had not shared with Ruth the other matter weighing heavily on his heart, his concerns for the welfare of his own parents. They well remembered the harsh treatment they had received from the British during the Great War – their deportation first to Egypt and then to Germany before being allowed to return to their properties which had been looted and vandalised during their long absence. As German nationals in a British Mandate country it was likely that they would again be treated harshly if Germany and Britain became enemies once more. Their situation in Palestine was further complicated because the British were also caught in the middle of the hostilities between the Arabs and the Jews, and although the German community tried to remain neutral, many Jews were openly hostile to them because of events in Germany itself. Those hostile Jews would be happy to see the Germans interned and deported; others saw an opportunity to acquire the German properties. As Tel Aviv had grown rapidly, it had encircled Sarona, forcing up the land values and diminishing the agricultural returns. Over the last few years, Erich's parents had rebuffed several approaches by Jewish interests prepared to pay good prices in Swiss francs or US dollars for their land. Quite apart from their sentimental attachment to the land which they had held for more than sixty years, they understood that the directive from the German consulate that no German land should be sold to non-German interests was an attempt to safeguard the future of the German settlements in Palestine.

Much would depend on the outcome of the imminent war.

* * * * *

Next day, as the sun's first blush coloured the clear summer sky, the young men from the southern German settlements assembled in the Customs House at Jaffa to be ferried to the Romanian ship *Transylvania* lying at anchor half a kilometre from shore. This time, there were no relatives or friends present – they had been requested to make their farewells at home and keep the port clear to allow a speedy embarkation, attracting as little attention as possible and thereby preventing suspicions from being aroused. Most of the young men were in high spirits and eager to meet the challenges that lay ahead; a few were more sombre and subdued in the face of the looming uncertainties. The German consul had cleared all the administrative matters ahead and the embarkation went smoothly. A small flotilla of Arab boats quickly ferried their passengers past the rocky outcrops to the *Transylvania* which would carry them to Greece.

The sea was calm and flat as they made their way out, unlike the day of Erich's departure in 1936, but the mood of the crowd grew noticeably heavier as the boats cleared the rocks and the ship's great bulk overshadowed them. Something prompted Erich to look back at the port - he saw a lonely female figure standing and waving frantically. Instantly he recognised Ruth standing at the same spot, high on the seawall from where she had waved when he left in 1936. He blew a kiss and waved wildly. This time though, she looked so lonely and forlorn on the deserted sea front in the half light of early morning. A thought flashed through his mind – will this be the last time we see each other?

PART TWO

WAR YEARS

CHAPTER 4 – 1939/1940

The sudden secret departure of so many young men had caught the Sarona community by surprise. The German consulate staff had succeeded in their mission; the high level of secrecy had been maintained right through to the departure of the recruits, which had proceeded without incident, disruption or protest. Only the immediate families of the young men knew what was going on, but afterwards it became obvious to all the Saronian settlers that war was imminent.

Some families in Sarona made frantic arrangements with the consulate to leave for Germany as soon as possible; their future in Palestine was unclear and they feared internment and possible deportation as during the First World War. Others simply wanted to be reunited with family members in Germany.

Conversely, many Saronians who had travelled to Germany for the summer suddenly feared they would be left stranded in Germany when war broke out. Summer holidays in Germany had become popular among Saronians during the 1930s as the economic wellbeing of the settlers improved and the shipping between Palestine and Europe became more frequent. The emergence of a new revitalised Germany and a feeling of national pride was a further stimulus to travel to Germany to see at first hand the changes that were taking place.

On 3 September 1939, only two days after Germany invaded Poland, Great Britain and France declared war on Germany. Within a few hours of the declaration of war, and without any warning, the British police and military encircled Sarona and erected a high barbed wire perimeter fence around the settlement. There was no escape for the local Germans, including the Bergerle family; their settlement had become an internment camp. Germans living outside the perimeter fence in nearby areas were brought into the camp by the British police and military and placed in homes according to the space available. A couple from the Sudetenland, total strangers who had only been in Palestine for a short time, were billeted with Erich's parents. They had fled Germany because their political views were opposed to the Nazi regime, but despite their protests, they were German nationals and therefore enemy aliens in the eyes of the British. Wilhelm and Sophie provided the couple with a room and bedding and shared their kitchen and eating area with them, but it was an awkward time for both the involuntary hosts and their uninvited guests now thrown into close proximity. Not only were the billets total strangers, they were destitute and dependent on their host who held markedly different political views.

In return for the hospitality they received from the Bergerles, the man willingly laboured where he could for Wilhelm. But just one week after the fence was erected, all the interned men of military age were ordered to pack their personal belongings for transfer to a camp in Acre on the coast north of Haifa. The responsibility for directing the agricultural enterprises fell to the women, children and the few elderly men left in Sarona. Fortunately, the dairy herds were kept in large barns inside the settlement so the daily feeding and milking could continue, but the maintenance of the orange groves and vegetable gardens outside the camp was more difficult. With Wilhelm and the male billet gone, Sophie and Helga went each day to the entrance gate where they were permitted to give instructions to their Arab workers as to what needed to be done in the orange grove and vegetable garden outside the camp. No-one was allowed to leave the camp which was closely guarded by British police and auxiliary Jewish policemen, among them Ruth's brother.

* * * * *

Only a few days after leaving Jaffa, the *Transylvania* docked in Athens. Erich and his comrades spent two days there before boarding a train to Germany where they were posted to their various units. Erich and several of his friends were posted to a newly formed Special Forces unit near Berlin where they were given further training to enhance their basic military training. They learned self-defence combat, camouflage and concealment skills; they were trained to make explosives from common household chemicals; they learned to build booby traps and studied detonation devices and systems. The young men were bitterly disappointed not to have been part of the hugely successful invasion of Poland, but they were told not to despair, that they would soon see real combat.

*　　*　　*　　*　　*

During the Polish campaign, the *Battalion Ebbinghaus*, a unit of Polish-speaking Germans deployed behind military lines to spearhead military thrusts, achieved notable success. In the wake of this, a new company, known as the *Batallion Brandenburger* (Brandenburger Battalion), was formed and stationed at the barracks at Brandenburg-an-der-Havel near Berlin. The concept of the these units had been developed by Captain Hippel, who had served with Colonel Lettow-Vorbeck in German East Africa during the Great War. There he had observed at first hand the importance of local knowledge and native language in conducting a guerrilla campaign and hit-and-run missions. One such group had fought for the entire duration of the war against overwhelming enemy forces without being defeated. Hippel believed that such units, comprised of men fluent in foreign languages and familiar with the customs of the enemy, could operate to great effect behind enemy lines by creating confusion and securing strategic infrastructure.

Just before the war started many *Auslandsdeutsche* (Germans from overseas), who had undergone military training, were recalled to Germany and encouraged to join the newly established Brandenburger Battalion. Erich was amongst this group and it was not long before several companies were formed and ready for deployment for special missions.

SARONA NOVEMBER 1939

In November 1939, Wilhelm was among a number of Sarona internees who were brought back from the Acre Internment Camp to Sarona to help with the daily work of feeding and milking the cows twice each day and cleaning the barns. It had become obvious, in only a short time that the work was far too much for the women and elderly. But the milk from Sarona was very much needed by the British and the residents of Tel Aviv.

"I am so pleased to be back in Sarona with my dear ones," Wilhelm said as he hugged both Sophie and Helga on entering his home again. "We may still be interned and not allowed out but we are together again and I can do some real work. Acre was so frustrating and boring; just nothing to do except sit around and talk. Sometimes we went for a walk on the beach under heavy guard. We would take the opportunity to gather shells which we then made into bracelets, brooches and necklaces - it helped us to pass the time. Look Helga I brought something back for you." He pulled a shell necklace from his pocket and held it out; Helga grabbed it with glee and put it on, tying the ends together.

"Oh, Father! Thank you so much. It is really special in these hard times," she said, giving him an enthusiastic kiss.

"Here, my dear Sophie, I haven't forgotten you," he said as he pulled his hand from his pocket a second time holding a beautifully designed shell brooch.

"It is beautiful," Sophie said as she admired the brooch. "Thank you! Did you make it yourself?"

"Yes I did. I knew as soon as I had found the large shell that I would make a brooch for you. I hope you like it.

"Don't worry, the war will soon be over and you now have a memento of our internment in Palestine. We Germans only took a few weeks to conquer Poland and I'm sure that England and France will soon see the

78

folly of having declared war. It will only take another German victory in Europe, maybe against France, to bring them to the peace table. But this time, we will not be dictated to, nor subjected to such shameful conditions as were imposed in the Treaty of Versailles. You'll see, the Führer will lead our nation to victory and we will then be released and able to get on with our lives again.

"Have you heard anything from Erich? I wonder if he was part of our victorious campaign in Poland."

"No, not a word has been heard from any of our boys. We are only allowed to write twenty-five words a month. I have written twice but had no reply. Everything has to go through the British military censor here before being sent to Germany. I do not even know his address I just sent it to the Army Department and hope it gets to him somehow." Sophie explained.

"One of the things I am really looking forward to is one of your good cooked meals, Sophie. The food at Acre was just disgusting – tough chewy goat's meat and rice with a few overcooked vegetables. We were so grateful when the camp guards allowed our families here in Sarona to send us some food - baked goods and fresh fruit and vegetables. Everyone at Acre enjoyed the supplies that were sent from here. We must continue to send food as it will help maintain the morale of those that are still there. The internees from the other settlements were jealous that some of the Sarona internees were allowed to return home.

"Speaking of fresh food what has happened to our oranges this harvest, and our vegetable gardens? Has anyone been out of the camp to see them? What has happened to all the produce? We had just planted a whole field of cabbages and the potatoes should have been harvested." Wilhelm asked.

"No one has been allowed out through the gate. We are lucky to have Saeed. He has been very good – both loyal and reliable. I meet him at the front gate of the camp every morning and give him instructions.

This year, almost the entire orange crop went to waste because we couldn't export them, and there were no pickers or packers available even if we could have found local buyers. Saeed told me that some of the crop was stolen, but most of the fruit just fell off the trees and rotted. He brought us some - we still have a few – and he said he would bring me some more when we need them.

"Saeed and some others Arab workers dug the potatoes and brought bags of them to the camp for us all to share. They did the same with the other vegetables and with fruit from other growers, too - that was some of the food we packed and sent to you in Acre. We were able to negotiate for the British to provide a truck to transport the goods to you.

"Luckily it has rained a few times recently so that watering has not been an issue. I am sure much of our produce is being stolen - just taken and sold by outsiders who pocket the money. They know only too well that we are locked up with no-one to guard our properties outside the camp. We did all the hard work growing the crops and they are now reaping the profits - but what can we do about it? You know all our assets and bank accounts have been frozen and placed under the control of the Public Custodian. We are supposed to let him know of any income we get and he has to approve any money we want to withdraw from our bank account. Fortunately, Saeed was able to sell a few of our potatoes and vegetables for cash and he gave me some money.

"Only a few days ago we received a letter from Hans and Hilda. Their holiday in Germany has left them stranded. They were due to return ten days after the war started but now they cannot leave Germany and are living with Hilda's parents. They have asked if you could look after their vineyard and orange grove. They obviously are not aware of our internment and of you having been interned separately at Acre. I spoke with our community leaders but again there is really nothing to be done. I've also spoken with Saeed but he said that it is pointless to harvest the grapes because they cannot be used - there is nobody in the Sarona winery to make wine, and the grapes cannot be sold."

Wilhelm snorted with anger, "Haven't our leaders spoken to the British about this? Surely something can be done – it is our livelihood! It is madness to let all these crops go to waste."

"Yes, they have, but the British response is that we are at war, these are war-time conditions and we unfortunate Germans are now their enemy. They have given clear instructions that no-one is permitted to leave the camp. According to international law, they are responsible for our health and well-being in the camp, but not for our farms and orchards outside the camp. Wilhelm, it is not just farmers and planters like us that are affected - none of the German tradesmen can work, and the Wagner factory is closed. We are probably a bit more fortunate than others because we have a loyal employee who can do a few things for us," Sophie replied.

"Tomorrow I will speak with our leaders here to see if we can change this impossible situation. For generations we have put all our energies into these properties and at least our honest work should be treated with some respect," Wilhelm said. His buoyant homecoming mood had quickly given way to frustration.

"Wilhelm, don't get angry; it will not do you any good. If you antagonise the British they may even send you back to Acre. Our leaders have spoken with the camp commandant several times but nothing has changed."

Although no-one could leave, British government officials and police regularly came into the Sarona camp to check on the wellbeing of the internees or to conduct random searches of homes. The British also set up necessary infrastructure in the camp – an administration office for all business with the Public Custodian, a Camp Commandant's office, a basic medical facility, and a canteen for the supply of all basic necessities. The school was converted to a police barracks and some British officials moved into some of the large, recently-constructed houses. Although the internees were not allowed to leave the camp, doctors and a dentist were allowed regular access to attend to the health needs of the internees, as was the Jewish pharmacist, whose shop was situated in the settlement. Veterinarians were also able to enter the camp to tend to sick livestock. These visiting professionals were all from Tel Aviv but were all well known to the internees, having attended them for many years.

MONTEFIORE DECEMBER 1939

Early in December, Ruth consulted the family's doctor, who confirmed what she had suspected for several weeks - that she was pregnant. She mulled the matter over for several days wondering how to break the news to her parents. While still pondering her situation, she walked around the high perimeter fence of the Sarona camp.

"If only Erich was here to share the happy news with me," she thought. "I miss him so much! I wonder where he is and I worry about his safety. How can I let him know? He would know what to do for sure. If only he could hold me in his arms we could discuss our situation and I could then face the future with confidence."

She had decided on one thing – the child was as much Erich's as hers and she would let it live – she would not abort her pregnancy. Who knows, she thought, after the war, when Erich returns, we will sort things out, maybe even get married. At that thought her eyes filled with tears and she continued her walk, deep in thought. She was careful to avoid walking near the entrance gate for fear of being sighted by her brother - she could not bear the thought of confronting him right now. It was enough that she knew what a scene he would make when he learned what state she was in and the identity of her child's father.

It was a cold wintry December evening just before Christmas when Ruth told her parents that she was pregnant.

"Oh, my God! Ruth, what have you done?" her stunned mother asked, "Who is the father of the child? Why didn't you tell us earlier?"

"You know, Imma, how I told you about Erich, the young German from Sarona. Well we loved each other dearly but could only see each other secretly because of the tensions between us and the Germans. How we longed to share our feelings and love with our families and welcome each other into our communities - but of course, that was impossible with all the prejudice and hatred that developed. Erich is now in Germany in the army - I don't know where he is or how to contact him. Just before he left we were intimate several times. The doctor told me that the baby is due in late May."

"I cannot believe my own daughter would fall pregnant without marriage – let alone to a German," shock gave way to anger in Avraham's voice. "I am completely stunned. Ruth, do you really want to have this baby? Have you given any thought to having it aborted?"

"I will not have an abortion! Never!" Ruth shouted at her father, "How can you even think it?"

"Ruth, I am worried about you and the wellbeing of your child - our future grandchild. What will the future hold for the child in our small community here in Montefiore? Our future here in Palestine is uncertain. The struggle in Europe casts a deep shadow of doubt over our future here. Nothing can be predicted and we are fighting for our very survival. What if the British pulled out now? There would be total chaos - they aren't sympathetic to our cause but they at least provide some law and order. Even if we lived in the best of times, how would you cope with all the challenges of raising a child without a father?"

Ruth's anger had not abated. She retorted, "I have made up my mind and will not abort my baby! It was conceived in love and when it is born I will love and care for it with all my strength. I still love Erich - he is a wonderful, wonderful loving man. He may be German but that doesn't make him evil. He is a kind, caring and sincere person and I will always love and admire him. I am proud to bear his child. As for the uncertainties that surround us, you are just trying to frighten me.

The British won't leave and the future will have to take care of itself. We cannot know what will happen."

"If he was so caring, Ruth, he would not have got you pregnant. Anyway, I am not trying to frighten you, but I am trying to be realistic."

"Abba, can't you understand we were and still are very much in love."

"Ruth, don't you see that you will bring shame on us as a family? I cannot understand how my daughter could get herself into a situation like this. I need time to think about this before I say anything that I may regret later." He rose, turned his back and angrily slammed the door as he stormed out of the room.

Ruth was feeling dismal - tears ran down her cheeks as she stood stooped, her hands resting on the kitchen table. Her mother moved close to her and put her arms around her.

"Sit down, Ruth. Father is upset and shocked. He has always been so very proud of his beautiful daughter and is seriously worried about you and your welfare. Truly, he only wants what is best for you. I hope that you know that we both love you very much as our daughter and that won't change. I am sure when your baby is born we will accept our grandchild with love. I promise to help and support you as much as I can. And just as in the past, you can come to me at any time for anything. You know that I will stand by you.

"Now we have to tell your brother before he finds out from someone else or notices your swollen tummy. Let me break the news to him as he will certainly be very angry when he hears about your pregnancy and even more so when he learns who the father is - you know his opinion of Germans, and who can blame him given their persecution of our people in Europe? You know how passionate he is for the establishment of a Jewish homeland here in Palestine and of course, the German settlers here are opposed to that, too. But I have to say that he too is my child, and I support the ideals he stands for, so I think it is best that I speak with him when you are not here."

"Oh, thank you, Imma," Ruth sobbed, "I know it must be hard for you to come to grips with all this, but I meant what I said - I will not have an abortion. The baby will be my link to Erich the only man I have loved outside my family. Imma, he is a good person, he doesn't share the Nazi attitudes towards us. If only the times were different."

"I am sure that you are telling the truth, darling but we cannot change our circumstances or the feelings of other people. These are extremely difficult times for all of us and you will face hostility. You need to prepare yourself for that yet you must not allow yourself to become bitter against your own people – you will have to learn that very few people can rise to the occasion at the outset, although almost all will accept you eventually.

"But now, what about you? As you see, I noticed nothing to make me suspect anything – and you seem to be well. Is all well with you?" Zara asked.

"Yes, Imma. A few weeks ago I felt a little squeamish on a couple of days but that has all passed now and I'm feeling fine. As you know, I haven't missed any work – which reminds me that I still have to tell Mrs Gold. Naturally, I had to tell you and Abba before anyone else. I'm sure Mrs Gold will understand - she has been so kind to me - she knows about Erich and put a positive slant on our relationship. She has been just wonderful."

"I'm glad that you have Mrs Gold's support – you see, you already have one ally outside the family. Now, you really should have a rest – this has been quite a difficult session for all of us. Abba and I need a little time for ourselves to gather our thoughts about your unexpected news. Thank you for trusting us and taking us into your confidence first, I'm sure it wasn't easy for you."

BRANDENBURG FEBRUARY 1940

After four months of strenuous training, in February 1940 Erich and some of his fellow recruits were ready to be placed into specialised companies within the Brandenburger battalion – they were fewer in number than at the outset of the training because some of the recruits had simply been unable to withstand the rigours of the training and had already been assigned to other units of the German army. Because they were trained for action behind enemy lines, both to cause havoc for the enemy and, more challengingly, to protect infrastructure vital to the German army, they were required to reach peak physical fitness, swim fully clothed for long distances, be expert at first aid, self-defence and hand-to-hand combat, be proficient marksmen with small arms, and fully understand demolition techniques and the defusing of explosive charges. They had also been required to demonstrate their ability to work together in small units, survive in the field and use camouflage. Morale was high amongst the successful graduates who were given a weekend off-base before assignment.

When Erich reported back from his leave he was called to the commandant's office.

"Heil Hitler," Erich saluted and stood to attention as the officer returned the salute.

"Erich, I expect you are now looking forward to some real action," Captain Kimmel began.

"Yes sir! Having completed training I'm confident and ready to serve and apply our skills in an operational role. I am hopeful that I will be with some of my friends from Palestine," Erich responded smartly.

"During training we observed all of you closely, but you Erich, have some very special attributes that we want to utilise. We noted your ability to mix easily and confidently with people of other nationalities. That is something we value very highly in the Brandenburgers."

"Thank you sir," Erich replied unsure of where this was leading.

"I do not know what your next assignment is but I have been given orders by the High Command that you are to report for duty in Vienna. Your orders are in this envelope," he said handing an envelope stamped "Secret". "Erich, wherever you may go and wherever you serve I wish you all the best. The Brandenburgers are a fine group of men dedicated to the Führer, to Germany and to victory. Heil Hitler!"

Erich was both excited and disappointed as he bade farewell to his close friends, many of whom he had known all his life: disappointed because he had hoped to serve with them in the looming battle against France and England; but excited to reach Vienna and learn just what role he would play and where he would be stationed. He allowed himself to think that it might be somewhere in the Middle East - close to home and maybe even afford the opportunity to see Ruth. Now that would be something!

The rail journey from Berlin to Vienna carried him south through a winter wonderland. The entire German countryside was under a clean white blanket from which the bare tree trunks and branches protruded in dramatic contrast. Gradually the scenery became more undulating and then mountainous and the small towns and villages in the valleys, with their church spires and domes and red-roofed houses with smoke rising from the chimneys, were exquisitely picturesque. In southern Germany he noticed the many terraced vineyards, the bare vines stark against the snow, waiting for the return of spring. How different to his father's vineyard on level ground - he would hate to have to pick grapes here and carry them up and down the steep slopes. Often he observed children playing in the snow, some with sledges on the slopes and some practising skiing. The wooded spruce areas with the snow resting on the branches of the trees made everything look so peaceful and lush to his eyes, accustomed to the dryness and harshness of Palestine. Everything appeared so serene that it didn't seem possible that Germany was at war.

When Erich reported for duty in Vienna, he was surprised to find another nine Brandenburgers, some of whom he had seen at the barracks in Berlin. They were from Germany, Austria, Hungary, Romania, Italy and Russia - all German citizens but fluent in at least one other language plus English.

They assembled in a briefing room where they were addressed by two senior officers.

"My fellow Brandenburgers," Colonel Bircke began, "you have all been chosen for a vital mission that will be of immediate and far reaching benefit for the Great German Reich in this war that has been forced on us and which we must now win. As you know the Brandenburger Battalion is under the command of the German Abwehr (military intelligence) and in addition to combat duties we have other roles to fulfil to protect the Reich from its enemies.

"Your mission, gentlemen, will be the protection of the oil supply from Romania to Germany which is vital for the entire war effort, especially with the imminent war in the west. Without oil and fuel our whole military might, including our new motorised armour units, the *Luftwaffe* and *Kriegsmarine*, cannot operate. Our industry and our people are also completely dependent on oil and fuel for their daily activities, which in turn underpin our war effort. At present the Reich buys millions of litres of oil every month from Romania and it is crucial that the supply not be interrupted.

"We know that over the past year or so our enemies, particularly the English, were able to place a number of agents, trained saboteurs, into the oil refineries and pumping installations at Ploesti. Since last September, when England and France declared war on the Reich, the incidence of minor sabotage to disrupt both the supply and distribution of oil and fuel has escalated dramatically. From our people there we know that a major disruption is planned when our ground offensive against France commences. Not only will production be seriously disrupted but we also have good reason to believe that the overland railway facilities and shipping on the Danube will be targeted to prevent supplies reaching Germany.

"The political situation in Romania is not particularly friendly to us, both the King and the government are sympathetic to the English. We are trying very hard through diplomatic channels to win the Romanian government's support.

"When you go to Ploesti you will be working as foreign civilian workers at the refinery, but you will be required to carry your military identification with you at all times. Your employment has already been organised as has your accommodation. Before you depart you will have another short intense training period here to enable you to get to know each other so that you can work as a unit. During the training you will be briefed on the refinery layout and operations at Ploesti and of course you will receive some instruction in the Romanian language and key phrases used in everyday conversation. There are so many foreign workers in the region we don't anticipate any difficulties. Once there you will be linked to some contacts who will assist you.

"There is no need for me to emphasise the need for absolute secrecy about this mission. Any leaks about this mission will not only jeopardise your own lives, and the lives of our soldiers, but has the potential to harm the entire German people.

"Once the mission starts there will be absolutely no contact with your family or friends. If you wish to communicate with your family before you leave, I urge you to do so now - we have a supply of twenty-five word *Feldpost* letters. It is sufficient simply to say that you are well and send your greetings. Your letters will be scrutinised and if any are in any way inappropriate, they will not be forwarded. For those of you from overseas your letters will be sent through the Red Cross to your loved ones."

Erich wrote a brief letter to his parents and sister. He wondered, as he had so often done since he left home, how they were getting on. Autumn and the early winter in Palestine was always a busy time with the orange and grape harvests. Many other crops were also harvested before winter came. It was also the time of the annual *Dankfest* (Thanksgiving) celebrations.

The only letter he had received from Palestine was in November last year and it had been heavily censored either by the British or Wehrmacht censors. It had been written by his mother and written in the singular - it contained no mention of his father or what was happening in Sarona. He found that strange and hoped nothing untoward had happened to his father who had always been a very proud and patriotic German and quite outspoken about the Führer and the new Germany. Erich wondered whether this may have got his father into trouble with the authorities in Palestine but consoled himself by thinking that if something serious had happened to his father then somehow he would have been notified. Since then he had received nothing from his parents, not even a Christmas greeting. Perhaps there was a letter in transit that had been delayed or misdirected in the mail system.

His thoughts also turned to Ruth, wondering what she was doing and how she was coping with all the changes. If only he could write to her and let her know how much he missed her. Oh, how he longed to hold her in his arms and share a kiss. "Maybe," he thought, "victory will be ours in the next twelve months and I can return to the people I love".

MONTEFIORE MAY 1940

When Ruth's contractions began, her mother took her to the small former German hospital in Jaffa for the birth of her child. Neither woman could have known that this was the place where Erich was born in 1917, but each ever after remembered it as the birthplace of Miriam, Ruth's healthy daughter. Ruth did know that it was the practice of Erich's community to add names for the grandmothers of the child, but she decided to follow her own European Jewish custom, which never named children after a living relative. Like any new mother, Ruth was thrilled with her healthy baby but her joy was tempered by Erich's absence and the knowledge that Erich had no inkling that he had become a father, although she had no doubt that he would be proud of Miriam.

After a stay of only a few days in the hospital, Ruth returned to her parents' home where she had created a small nursery in her room.

During her pregnancy, she and her mother had knitted a number of baby garments and many friends of the family had passed on items such as blankets, linen and outgrown clothing, a pram, a cot and other items that were difficult to buy because of the war. Most people known to the family had been generous and supportive although a few did shun Ruth, especially after they learned that the father of the child was a German.

Fortunately, her father had worked through his feelings; he reassured Ruth that he loved her as he always had and although he couldn't condone what she had done, he welcomed his grandchild as a member of the family and of his household. However, Ruth's brother, David, was unable to accept the situation – he felt that his sister had brought shame on the family by having a child out of wedlock, and, as a Jewish nationalist, he was horrified that she could have even begun a relationship with a German.

If Ruth was at all apprehensive at returning home with her baby, her fears were allayed when she saw the large bunch of flowers that awaited her – the card read *"Welcome to our dear grand-daughter Miriam. We hope you enjoy many, many happy years in our family. With all our love, your Saba and Safta"*. Her mother had bought the flowers from the well-known nursery in Sarona through the agency of a Jewish doctor who regularly visited the Sarona camp. With tears glistening in her eyes, Ruth hugged her parents and whispered, "I love you so. Thank you for such a welcoming homecoming. The flowers are just gorgeous and I know that little Miriam will spend many happy days growing up here."

"We love you too, and we love our grand daughter. Now, I think you and Miriam should have a little rest," Zara said caringly, "we all need to get used to having a new member of our family."

A few days later, Mrs Gold came to visit Ruth and Miriam. "You are looking well, Ruth," she said with her characteristic warm smile as she presented Ruth with a lovely bunch of strongly scented red roses, "I am so pleased everything has gone well for you. Your little Miriam is just beautiful. I can already see she has your lovely eyes and her father's fair hair."

"Oh thanks, Mrs Gold, you do notice things, and thank you for the flowers, they are lovely. Yes, I am feeling well and pleased to be home again; Imma and Abba have made us very welcome in their house, and our neighbours and friends have all been supportive. But I really miss Erich; I think of him all the time, wondering what he is doing and where he is. I just pray and hope that he is OK. But most of all, I just wish that I could share this happy news with him."

"I can understand your feelings Ruth, but try not to worry so much about something you cannot change. As I have always told you, I'm sure that in the long run everything will turn out fine for you and Miriam."

"Tell me, how are things at the shop?" Ruth inquired. "I really miss the regulars who came in to enjoy your cakes with a cup of coffee."

"Well actually, it has become really quiet over the past few months: the English no longer come because of the growing hostility between them and us; and our own people are struggling financially, many have to provide for friends and relatives who have fled here from Europe. The whole focus of life has changed since the war started. It is such a different world we now live in."

SARONA JUNE 1940

A loud sharp knock on the front door shattered the quiet of a late afternoon in the Bergerle home. Helga opened the door to find two Palestinian police officers.

"Good day," they greeted her, and one continued, "We have come to summon you to come to the community hall with us, right away. That is, all four of you."

Helga sensed from his tone that this was not an order to be disobeyed.

"What is this all about?" asked Wilhelm as he came to the door.

"You must come with us to the community hall immediately. All internees have to assemble there."

"Why? What has happened?" Wilhelm asked, sensing that something was amiss.

"We have no time to explain. We are under orders from the Camp Commandant, so please comply."

As they had no choice, the three Bergerles and the lady billeted with them walked with the policemen to the hall where many were already assembled. When the last of the settlers had arrived, a roll call was made to ensure that everyone from the camp was in the hall.

The camp commandant then informed the gathering that they would all remain in the hall while a house-by-house search for cameras, radios and weapons, especially firearms was conducted by military personnel.

The British had good reason to suspect that there were still radios in the community, despite earlier searches and an order that made it illegal for internees to possess a radio. But as Germany had swept through the Low Lands and into France in recent times, a buoyant mood had been clearly evident amongst the internees. Each victory had been celebrated by the internees who defiantly sang the German National Anthem – *Deutschland, Deutschland über Alles* - but the news of these successes could only have been received by radio.

The internees sat glumly waiting.

"This is absolute madness," Wilhelm muttered to his wife. "They already confiscated all our registered firearms when the war started - they knew exactly who owned guns because we had to register them. But they will never find my Kruger pistol from the last war - I wrapped it and the ammunition in an oily cloth and put them in a tin which I buried and covered with a concrete slab. And I know that others did the same thing. Likewise with the cameras; only some were handed in, but others that had great sentimental and personal value were kept and hidden. And, why not? As you know, I kept the camera you gave me for our silver wedding. I was not going to part with that!"

"What have you done with it?" Sophie asked.

"It is in my sock drawer rolled inside a pair of socks."

"What if they find it?"

"They will not find it. It is amongst all my socks in a drawer."

"What about our radio?"

"They will never find that. It is in our chicken pen disguised as a laying box. You know I only rig up the aerial when I listen to the broadcasts from the Reich. I have no worries about that. They can pull the house apart but will not find the radio. Even if they manage to find one or two sets in Sarona we still have others so we can still get the proper news they want to suppress."

"I just hope you are right. I do not want you to get into trouble and be sent off to Acre again."

"You know Sophie, this is just a ploy. The French and British will soon suffer an humiliating loss. They cannot win on the battlefield so instead they attack interned civilians who cannot offer any resistance. It is just too much of a coincidence that this is happening here at the very time our Wehrmacht is pushing them into the English Channel. We are just the victims of the British offensive in Palestine."

The internees were held in the hall for several hours. It was already dusk when they were allowed to return to their homes, hungry and thirsty, their small children stressed and fidgety. The Bergerles were quite unprepared for the scene that greeted them at their home: cupboard and wardrobe doors had been left open; clothes lay strewn over the floor or in untidy piles on tables and beds; the beds had all been stripped and the bed linen and doonas left lying on the floors; items had been tipped out of drawers. Not one room had been left unscathed - even the cellar had been rummaged.

"They have taken my camera," Wilhelm said angrily. "they are thieves and vandals; worse than gypsies. Just look at the mess. How would they like it if I just went into their homes and pulled everything apart, scattered the contents and then just walked away. "

"You should see our meal! I left it on the stove and now it is totally burnt. Uneatable! What a waste! I just don't know where to start to clean up. We will have to remake our beds so that at least we can sleep in them tonight. I am so disgusted – I expected better of the British but it is if savages have been through our home. They even took the pictures off the walls. Anyone would think we are dangerous. Can you imagine how something like this will affect our elderly?"

"Yes, I know Sophie. I am also furious but we will clean up, and one day soon the boot will be on the other foot. Believe me, their day of reckoning will come!"

ROMANIA JUNE 1940

At the outbreak of war Romania had declared itself neutral in the conflict that was about to engulf Europe. Nevertheless, it was a hotbed of political intrigue as the Allies and the Axis powers competed for influence. Romania's neighbours, understanding the weakness of the Romanian government stood poised to claim territory that they coveted. The German government successfully applied pressure to force the resignation of the Romanian Foreign Minister and a new Foreign

Minister, friendlier to Germany, was appointed as well as several other ministers. A German military mission was invited to Romania and the King abdicated.

In May 1940 the German offensive against France and Britain commenced and in just a few weeks the British were forced to evacuate their forces at Dunkirk. These Blitzkrieg victories were greeted with great celebration by Erich and his comrades, especially the signing of the armistice with France in June at the same place where the armistice was signed at the end of the Great War. This time, however, Germany set the surrender terms. Erich lamented that he had yet again missed out on the real action - firstly in Poland and now France – but it had been a testing time for the *Brandenburgers* in Romania and they were not found wanting as several attempts to sabotage the production of oil and to disrupt oil deliveries to Germany had been foiled.

In June 1940 the Soviet Union occupied Bessarabia, a large northern province of Romania, Transylvania came under Hungarian rule, and Bulgaria annexed part of the Dobruja region. The occupation of Bessarabia was of major concern to the Germans as it brought Russian forces to within 200 kilometres of the Ploesti oilfields.

The *Brandenburgers* had successfully mingled with the local workforce and gathered valuable information on foreign and Romanian workers who could not be trusted. When the German ground offensive began against England and France they received intelligence reports that the British were planning to destroy the oil loading port facilities on the Danube River near Bucharest, the *Brandenburgers* were called in. The British planned to pull a barge laden with explosives into the port where they would blow it up causing major damage and serious fires at the oil loading dock. Erich was part of the group to mount a surprise night-time counter-attack by boarding the boat hauling the barge. It was a risky plan, especially in the middle of the fast flowing Danube River, but it was a complete success - the British crew was captured and the explosion averted, allowing the oil supply to Germany to continued without disruption. Most importantly, only those intimately involved in the mission ever knew about it.

When the German government started sending troops into Romania in September 1940, the *Brandenburgers* were withdrawn as the troops moved in to protect the refineries, the ports and the railways.

MONTEFIORE NOVEMBER 1940

Erich had been absent from Palestine for more than a year; Miriam was already six months old and people, strangers, often remarked on her daughter's beauty to Ruth. She had a photographer in Tel Aviv take portraits of Miriam alone and with her and wished with all her being that she could send one to Erich. Several times Ruth had taken a walk with young Miriam in the pram to Jaffa and along the waterfront overlooking the old port. She always paused at the spot from where she had waved farewell to Erich, and looked forlornly westwards hoping for Erich's eventual return. On each occasion she had lifted Miriam from her pram, directed her gaze to the west and whispered to her, "That's the direction your father went. One happy day he will come back to us, lift you tenderly in his strong arms and give you a big kiss." Despite her optimism that Erich would return, Ruth became melancholy whenever she thought of him, far away and at war. But on this grey November day, she determined to clear the doubt – she decided to write to Erich's parents in an attempt to obtain some news of him.

*   *   *   *   *

In Palestine the violence continued to increase without respite. The Jews were particularly unsettled by the news of the swift German victories in Western Europe which placed large areas under German control, trapping family members and friends in Europe. This led in turn to increased hostility toward the British and their policy restricting Jewish immigration to Palestine; had the British been more accommodating, many more Jews could have escaped and found shelter in Palestine. Despite these laws, the *Yishuv* and the *Haganah* had been able to smuggle hundreds of refugees into Palestine where they were placed in Jewish settlements and communities throughout the land. The British conducted regular searches for these illegal immigrants and anyone who was unable to produce the required papers was imprisoned.

BRANDENBURG NOVEMBER 1940

After the Romanian mission was successfully completed, Erich and his comrades returned to their home base barracks at Brandenburg-an-der-Havel, just outside Berlin. His hopes of a posting to the Middle East were dashed: two of his comrades were posted, undercover, to Cairo; and another two to Syria where the Vichy French and Free French were fighting each other. For each posting, the determining requirement was the ability to speak French as well as Arabic.

His disappointment was tempered by receiving news of his parents; although the words were few he was reassured that they and his sister were all well. But as the letter cards had been censored by the British, stamped with an official internment camp stamp and posted free via the Red Cross he realised that they must be interned and felt sad at the thought of the restrictions and privations they must be enduring.

"I wonder what is happening to all the oranges - it's harvest time. What a busy time that always is in Sarona!" He recalled the hustle and bustle throughout the entire settlement as the oranges were picked, mainly by Arab workers, and placed in mounds in the packing sheds where the packers wrapped each piece of fruit and placed them into boxes. His mind's eye conjured a vision of the colourful wrappers that proudly proclaimed *"Aus deutschen Siedlungen in Palastina – Feinste Jaffa Orange – Sarona Wilhelma"* (From the German Settlement in Palestine – the finest Jaffa Orange – Sarona Wilhelma) with the logo of a boat laden with orange boxes being taken to a ship against a background of Jaffa with the sun rising behind the arabesque skyline. During his earlier sojourn in Germany, his parents had sent him a few boxes each year and he had shared them with his comrades who always marvelled at the sweetness and quality of the oranges. What he would give now in the cold northern late autumn for the sweet juiciness of Sarona oranges – and for that matter, a few bottles of the famous Sarona wines or a bottle of Arak from the distillery. Yes, at this time of the year the winery would be working at full capacity to process the grape harvest and he remembered the sight of the long line of wagons in the shade of the large eucalyptus trees outside the Sarona winery waiting to be freed of their heavy loads of grapes. No doubt, if she was able whilst interned, his mother would already be baking some *Gutsle* (Christmas cookies) - how his saliva flowed at the thought of her other Christmas recipes - *Bauernbrötle, Ausstecherle, Butter Ess, Lebkuchen,* and *Zimmtstern.*

His longing for the comforts and routines of home also brought Ruth into his conscious thoughts. He treasured her photo and each time he looked at it his heart beat faster. He was wracked by the uncertainty - did she still love him? Had she transferred her love to another man – most likely a fellow Jew? He wouldn't blame her if she did - she was so beautiful and full of life that he was certain that she would be eagerly pursued by many young men. He thought that if they couldn't have each other then each should allow the other to find happiness elsewhere, but he was not about to relinquish her – he adored her and wished only that he could hold her in his arms, have her scent fill his nostrils, gaze into her soft dark eyes, kiss her tenderly, lovingly stroke her hair and feel her warm, soft body against his own. Her absence caused him a pain that was almost physical.

SARONA DECEMBER 1940

It was a cool showery day in December 1940 when the Bergerle family was disturbed by a knock on the door as they were just finishing their breakfast.

"I'll get that, Sophie," said Wilhelm rising from the table, "it can't be anything good at this early hour."

"Dr Feldmann? Good morning to you. What brings you here – we have no animals requiring a veterinarian."

"Good morning, Mr Bergerle. I have come to deliver an envelope on behalf of a young woman; she asked me to deliver it by hand as she did not want her letter to be censored by the camp authorities as it would if sent through the post. She knows that I am a regular visitor to the Sarona compound and pleaded with me to deliver it to your hand – she says it is important. Please, I must now ask you not to divulge to anyone that I have breached the rules of this camp by bringing you this letter," Dr Feldmann said as he handed a neatly hand-written envelope to Wilhelm.

"Thank you, Dr Feldmann. Don't worry - it will go no further. You know how important it is for us to keep some unofficial channels open."

"What was all that about?" asked Sophie when Wilhelm returned to the kitchen.

"It was Dr Feldmann. He handed me an envelope from a young woman who told him it was too important to send through the post and begged him to deliver it. He didn't say who she was. Well, I suppose we had better open it and see for ourselves," he said reaching for the letter opener.

Still standing, he unfolded a neatly handwritten letter that enclosed three photographs and read aloud:

"Dear Mr and Mrs Bergerle,

It has been with great difficulty that I have written to you.

My name is Ruth Stein - I am unknown to you and live with my family near the Jewish settlement of Montefiore. I have known your son, Erich, for more than five years – we are not just acquaintances, we have been deeply in love since our first meeting, even through the three years that Erich was in Germany for his military training and further schooling. While we would have loved to have shared our bond with our families, this was impossible in the prevailing circumstances, and instead, we had to keep our relationship a secret.

Just before Erich departed for Germany in August last year, we did not restrain our love as we said good-bye - we didn't know whether we would ever see each other again. As an entirely unintended consequence, I became pregnant to Erich and in May this year gave birth to a beautiful baby girl who I have named Miriam. The photos I have enclosed were taken only last week. I see so much of Erich in her little face.

I know that this news must come as a terrible shock to you - believe me when I tell you that I pondered for a long time how and when I should tell you this news. I hope that I have not offended you.

As I am sure you do, I worry about Erich all the time and have heard nothing from him since he left. I hope and pray that he is well but I would be most grateful if you could let me know how he is - just a few words would be so reassuring. Perhaps Dr Feldmann will be kind enough to bring your reply to me. Also if there is any opportunity, please tell Erich about Miriam and reassure him that I still love him dearly and that he is always in my thoughts.

With my utmost respect

Ruth Stein"

With a pale face, Wilhelm sat at the table and handed the letter to Sophie who read it silently while he looked at the photographs. Neither spoke for several minutes, their thoughts racing until Wilhelm broke the silence.

"What do you think about all of this, Sophie?"

"I cannot believe it. Our Erich becoming so deeply involved with a total stranger? But a Jewess? No! It cannot be true!"

"I can't believe it either. If only Erich was here, we could ask him directly, but we can't even write to him about it. In fact, we haven't heard from him for some time. His last letter, if you can call twenty words a letter, arrived more than seven months ago. I don't know why we get no news - it is probably a ploy by the British and the Jews to withhold news about our loved ones to make us anxious and break our spirit. Well they won't succeed, we know that Germany is winning the war and we will soon be free again." Wilhelm was becoming agitated.

"Wilhelm, don't get so excited. Just think this through rationally," Sophie said quietly.

"You know Sophie, this letter is part of a clever plot. Before the war the Jews pressed us constantly to sell our land outside of Sarona proper but we all steadfastly resisted. The Jews need our land to allow Tel Aviv to expand to accommodate the thousands of illegal immigrants that have flooded into Palestine. The British just seem to turn a blind eye to all of this. But we know whose side they are on. Now that we are interned, the Jews think they can continue to apply pressure on us through subtle means. They know full well that Erich is in the army in Germany and that it is impossible for us to corroborate any story they put to us. We do not know who this Ruth is, or whose baby is in the photographs. She could be anyone but I am sure that our Erich would never have gotten into a bed with a Jewess.

"However, if we agree that this baby girl is our grand daughter then we fall straight into their trap. It would give her some claim over our land. We are getting older and who knows for how long we will remain in good health? Meanwhile, Erich is away fighting as a soldier for the Fatherland – I pray that he will come home safe and sound but we must face the reality that as a frontline soldier he is in great danger.

"We should destroy this letter and the photographs – just pretend that it was never delivered. I cannot accept this situation without some proof.

102

"Even if this was true, how could this woman and her child live in our family and community? Surely Erich knew that any relationship could never work out - it would be against German law - he could never marry this woman and the child would never be Aryan. It would bring shame and even ridicule on us - to say nothing of Erich. The situation is quite impossible."

"You know, I also have some doubts about it. But it could just be true and there may be no plots - just a genuine desire by the young woman to let us know and through us to let Erich know if we should have the opportunity to do so," Sophie replied. "When I think back, there were so many times when Erich would just disappear, or say he had to go to Tel Aviv for some reason. Whenever I asked him he always had some excuse and would tell me that I worry too much about him, that he was an adult, able to look after himself, and that I didn't have to mother him so closely.

"You know, Wilhelm, he never had a girlfriend in our community. There was never any talk that he was seen dancing with someone or seen out with anyone in particular. Several times feelers were put out whether he might be interested to meet some young lady from a respectable German family, but he never was. He never asked if he could even bring a young lady home for a meal and he often found excuses not to go to dances or socialise much within our Sarona community. I know he had his close circle of friends, especially those from school, and he participated actively in sport, but he didn't join in many other social community activities. He always had an excuse."

"Perhaps, Sophie, but I still don't believe it of Erich; if it is true, then all will be known when he returns to us. In the meantime we must not only ignore this letter but destroy all trace of it. Can you image what would happen if this became known in our community? What a scandal it would cause! We would be outcasts! The anger was mounting in Wilhelm's voice. "I'm just glad that Helga is out so she knows nothing of it."

"Wilhelm, we should keep one of the baby photos - just in case it is our granddaughter."

"Sophie, believe me, it is all a hoax," Wilhelm retorted forcefully, "this trash must be destroyed. It is our only possible course of action – we cannot write to Erich as all the letters are censored and we are certainly not going to respond to the letter."

"All right, Wilhelm, but before you destroy them just let me read the letter and look at the photographs once more. I want to remember as much of it as I can and fix the photo in my memory. Somehow, I feel that she could be our granddaughter. Both the young woman and her baby have beautiful faces with clear complexions and striking eyes. I still think we should keep at least one photo of the child," Sophie said as she stared intently at the photos.

"Come on, Sophie, you are weakening! Soon you will believe that the letter is real. Don't be duped by nice words and photographs of attractive people. Do you really think they would have sent a picture of an ugly person? When Erich returns, he can tell us exactly what took place, if anything. We must not be drawn into this extortion attempt."

After Sophie had finished with the letter and photographs, Wilhelm took them to the wood-fired kitchen stove, opened the lid of the fire grate, dropped them onto the glowing coals and watched as the flames reduced them to ash.

CHAPTER 5 - 1941

BRANDENBURG FEBRUARY 1941

Many of Erich's friends from Palestine returned to the Brandenburger Barracks in high spirits. Most had been involved in the successful offensive in the west. These young but now battle-hardened warriors had been instrumental in securing key installations, particularly bridges and transport facilities, to allow the unimpeded German thrust through the Low Countries. After the fall of France, they were assigned to establish and control the new border through France, which separated the German occupied zone of northern France from Vichy France in the south. They told Erich of their battle experiences and close escapes at the front - it was a great reunion and they were now eager for their next assignments.

Rumours constantly swept the barracks particularly when it became known that General Rommel had been appointed to command a new unit - the German Africa Corps, which was to save the Italian forces from total annihilation in northern Africa where the British had forced them to retreat from Egypt, Libya and the Cyrenaica. Rommel would surely need some personnel who were fluent in Arabic and familiar with the customs and practices of the Middle East. The young Palestinian Germans believed that they would be the natural choice for that sphere of the war.

However, when only a few of their comrades were assigned to the Africa Corps, Erich and the remaining Palestinians were bitterly disappointed. They had all yearned for this posting, which would have taken them close to their home and families in Palestine, out of the cold misery of the European winter and into the warm Mediterranean climate. They all longed to be part of the campaign that would expel the British from Egypt and Palestine, but they were reassured that a major mission was being planned for them elsewhere that would involve them in active front line service.

MONTEFIORE MAY 1941

It was Miriam's first birthday and Ruth had decorated the living room with some flowers and a few coloured ribbons as streamers. She had covered the table with a bright cloth and placed the cake, made and decorated by Mrs Gold, in the centre of the table. She was determined to mark the happy occasion with a little party. Miriam seated in her high chair at the head of the table sensed that something special was happening. She laughed and squealed with delight as the family gathered around and fussed over her.

She had grown into a delightful little toddler – still unsteady on her feet but lively and inquisitive. Her combination of curly hair, deep dark eyes and clean olive skin complexion made her attractive indeed - people often commented to Ruth that her child was beautiful. Both Ruth and Miriam had found complete acceptance in the neighbourhood. Within the family, Miriam was an inexhaustible source of joy and laughter amidst the dismal news of German successes in Greece and the Balkans. Crete had been taken by an assault of German paratroopers and in North Africa the German Africa Corps were pushing back the British forces in Libya. In nearby Syria, the Vichy French and the Free French were in armed combat. Suddenly the war was extremely close to Palestine which had previously seemed to be a haven far removed from the war.

Throughout Palestine there was considerable anxiety about the possibility that the German armed forces might reach Palestine. Ruth had overheard her brother talking to their father about joining a new military unit, formed to combat any German invasion of Palestine.

Known as the *Palmach*, meaning strike force, it was jointly established by the British military and the *Haganah* in May 1941. It consisted of several assault units and placed high value on mutual responsibility, sacrifice and contribution to the greater good amongst its members. The British provided expert training as well as equipping them with arms, explosives and equipment. *Palmachniks*, dressed as Arabs and speaking fluent Arabic, were assigned to launch pre-emptive strikes in Syria and Lebanon, carry out sabotage activities and gather intelligence about the Vichy French.

Amid the excitement of Miriam's party Ruth's thoughts kept turning to Erich. "If only he could be here and celebrate his daughter's first birthday," she reflected sadly. She did not doubt he would accept and love his little daughter, but she longed to know that he was safe and felt assailed by fears that he may have come to harm. She was also feeling greatly disappointed that she had received no reply to her letter to Erich's parents; not even an acknowledgement that they had received it. Dr Feldmann had assured her that he had placed the envelope in Erich's father's hand but although he had seen the Bergerles several times since, they had never mentioned it. As the war continued to unfold, all manner of thoughts raced through Ruth's mind: what if Erich was with the German army in North Africa and that army reached Palestine and he had to fight against her brother and the Jewish people here? She just couldn't bear that thought! But with an effort, she put on a brave face so as not to allow these thoughts to spoil Miriam's celebration.

EASTERN EUROPE JUNE 1941

During April and May, those Palestinian Brandenburgers not in North Africa underwent another strenuous training program at the completion of which they were moved to Przemysl in southern Poland in June 1941. The San River which flowed through Przemysl had become the border between Germany and the Soviet Union when Poland was partitioned in 1939. It was not until 21st June that Erich and his comrades received the details of their mission in the course of a secret briefing. Hauptmann Schmidt addressed the assembled troops, "My fellow Brandenburgers, our Führer and Germany expect you once again to be the spearhead of an important mission in the Soviet Union. Just as in the campaign against France and England, your mission will be vital to the success of imminent action by our army. Your mission is dangerous and you will be exposed to considerable risk, however, your unshakable trust in each other, your hard training, your tenacity and your unwavering faith in the Führer and the Great German Reich will all stand you in good stead.

"Tonight you are to cross the San River and in secret enter the Soviet Union. You are to position yourselves to secure the two main bridges over the San. You will wear full German army uniforms but these will be covered by long Russian Army coats. You will operate as several separate small units, each of which will have two Russian-speaking soldiers, fellow Brandenburgers from the Ukraine. Your unit leaders will be given precise orders regarding the commencement of the operation. You must be ready to strike as soon as the order is given because we know that explosive charges have been placed by the Russians in order to hinder our advance by destroying the bridges. We must capture both bridges intact. When the bridges are securely in our hands, you will discard the Russian coats and fight in German uniform. Several other Brandenburger units will also cross into the Soviet Union tonight - they have other targets chosen to cause havoc and confusion on the Russian side. Brandenburgers, wear your emblem – the mask and dagger – proudly! I look forward to the success of your mission and your safe return."

* * * * *

In the early hours of 22 June 1941 the world held its breath as Operation Barbarossa, the surprise German attack on the Soviet Union, was launched. The Brandenburger units were amongst the first German troops to enter the Soviet Union before the general offensive began. They crossed the San undetected in small inflatable boats; their objective, the bridge, loomed large before them against the night-sky. Although challenged several times, they were able to get very close to the bridge because their Russian-speaking members answered the challenges. It was still dark when they launched the second stage under cover of a barrage of artillery fire from the German side. They moved quickly to overpower the Russian guards and cut the detonation wires to the explosives. The shells whistled overhead and the ground shook as the shells exploded nearby but within only minutes German aircraft could be heard flying over and the unmistakable rumble of approaching tanks and other motorized units was clearly audible.

The Russians immediately attempted to wrest the bridge from the Germans and destroy it to prevent the German advance; they directed a barrage of small arms fire at the bridge as they marshalled their troops. Erich and his small unit were pinned down as they had only small arms and hand grenades to defend themselves. Several fell to Russian bullets and a number were wounded and it appeared that they could hold out for only a short time, so it was with considerable relief that Erich saw the rapidly approaching German infantry and armoured vehicles in the early dawn light. For Erich it had been his baptism in field warfare.

SARONA JULY 1941

Since the German attack on the Soviet Union four weeks earlier, the Sarona internees had been in extremely high spirits and their confidence had grown that they would soon be liberated by the victorious German army. A meeting called by the camp commandant in the Community Hall dampened their spirits considerably; once again, all internees in the Sarona perimeter camp were summoned to the meeting. The hall which was filled to capacity was stifling in the late July heat and many had to stand outside in the blazing afternoon sunshine and strain to hear the proceedings. The commandant read a list of names of internees who would be deported to an unnamed destination; he told them that they had to be packed and ready to move in seventy-two hours, that the luggage they could take was strictly limited to forty kilograms per adult and twenty per child, and that any piece of luggage that exceeded the limit would not be taken. He gave them no clue as to their destination except to say that they would be going into springtime, which gave rise to speculation that the destination was southern Africa. The selected deportees, who included Wilhelm, Sophie and Helga, were told they would undergo medical examinations to ensure that they were in good health and free of the eye disease, trachoma.

The stunned internees milled around the lists of deportees that had been posted to check the names once again. The silence was oppressive. Many left in that gloomy silence to begin the melancholy task of picking what of their belongings to take and what to leave behind and to make arrangements for the care of their pets, livestock and the possessions they would have to abandon. All were angry at the apparently random selection of individuals and families for deportation - there seemed to be no logic in the process.

Erich's mother and sister were both in tears as they entered their home. "This is just awful," Sophie despaired as Wilhelm hugged her and Helga, "we don't even know where we are going and we have to leave all our keepsakes and memories behind to say nothing of our dishes and linen. What will we do with all our things? Will someone agree to look after them? We don't even know for how long we will be away! And what will happen to our livestock and our pets? What about all the perishable food, and the preserves and fruits and vegetables in our cellar? We just can't leave everything to rot! Why were we chosen and others not? We haven't done anything wrong! It is just so unfair!"

"Don't cry my dear ones," Wilhelm said quietly. He was as shocked and angry as his wife, but felt that he needed to take control at that point. "We must think this through logically. We have to be strong and not panic. We have to choose carefully the things we need to take and make sure that we don't exceed the weight limit. The official was not joking when he said overweight luggage would be left behind. As for those items we cannot take we will speak to our friends and relatives who are staying behind to look after them or use those things that will not keep. Let's first sit down, have a cup of coffee and get our thoughts in order.

"The British know that it won't be long before Rommel and his Africa Corps reach Palestine and they are feeling very uneasy about having us in their midst. Maybe they want us as hostages interned elsewhere so they can use us as possible bargaining chips for the ceasefire terms when Rommel takes Palestine."

The next few days were an extremely difficult period in Erich's parents' house. It was so difficult choosing clothing and what other items to pack and what to leave behind.

Wilhelm decided to hide most of the family jewellery; he wrapped each piece and some gold coins in cloth and placed these in a small metal box which he coated with grease. He then dug a hole under the foundations of the steps to the back door, wrapped the greased box in a cloth and placed it in the hole, just as he had done with his pistol two years earlier and encased it with the concrete. He then backfilled the hole with soil and watered it in. He was sure that it would be safe there until they returned and that even if the house was ransacked it was unlikely that their valuables would be found. The process of sorting and weighing their belongings and deciding what should be packed, what left and what discarded was slow and difficult for Erich's family.

On the day before their scheduled departure, the deportees had to present themselves for their medical examination. Helga, who wore glasses, was recovering from an eye ailment which was not trachoma, but for which she had to use drops which inflamed her eyes. When her eyes were examined the British Army Medical Officer immediately said she could not go because he suspected the inflammation in her eyes to be trachoma. Despite arguing and trying to convince the authorities that it was not trachoma the British doctors would neither relent nor agree to check with the Jewish ophthalmologist in Tel Aviv who had been treating her for several years. Their decision was final – Sophie and Helga would have to remain in the Sarona perimeter camp but Wilhelm would still have to go. The separation was a devastating blow to the Bergerle family.

Several other families were separated because of the medical examinations and, like the Bergerles, cast into despair. The Sarona community leaders protested to the authorities and each family pleaded its own case, but the British administration would not relent – families would be separated. Consequently, on the night before the deportation almost no-one in Sarona slept; the prospect of deportation had been dismal but the thought of enforced separation was almost too much to bear, although most families affected had no time to think as they undertook the re-packing of the luggage which had been so painstakingly packed.

It was the thirty-first of July when the deportees took their luggage to the collection point to be weighed and loaded onto military trucks. The deportees then assembled near the Community Hall where a fleet of buses awaited them. "Wilhelm, I have made sufficient food for you for twenty-four hours – nothing fancy, just sandwiches and fruit, and I have filled your water flask," Sophie said as they were about to leave the house.

"Thank you, my dear. It will be more than enough; they have to provide for us, especially for the many families with young children," Wilhelm replied.

Every Sarona internee had come to the Community Hall to farewell their family and friends. It was a heart-wrenching scene; people weeping and embracing, some angry, some accepting, some hopeful and some fearful because everyone knew that the deportees were being taken far away, probably into the Southern Hemisphere, and they wondered when, or if, they would see each other again and if this was the end of the Sarona community, their home, that they loved.

In typical military fashion, the British and Jewish police and military personnel quickly moved the deportees away from the crowd, checked their names against the lists and directed them aboard the buses which then drove slowly towards the main gate. Hands waved and final farewells were called from the windows to the crowd that followed on foot. Wilhelm had managed to secure a window seat from where he could see his wife and daughter in the crowd outside. "Good-bye, good-bye, my dear ones. Stay strong and stick together. Don't worry about me - I will be alright and will try to get word to you as soon as I can. I am sure we will all be together again soon, in better times," he shouted to them above the noise from many voices. He wasn't sure if they heard him but they waved back – two forlorn figures with tear-stained faces. He kept waving for as long as he could see them.

As each bus passed through the camp gate, an eerie silence descended inside cabin; the sombre mood did not lift at all as they drove through Tel Aviv and out along the road to Jerusalem. Some passengers sat quietly, deep in thought, some whispered to one another, muffled sobs could be heard from time to time and many people dabbed tears from their eyes. Only the young children, unable to comprehend the seriousness of the situation, talked and laughed in normal tones. Wilhelm, who had worked so hard to keep up Sophie's and Helga's spirits, was unexpectedly overcome with a profound sense of loss and loneliness as his wife and daughter disappeared from view. In common with many of his fellow deportees, he clung to the belief that his absence from Sarona would not be long, that Germany would soon vanquish Britain, France and the Soviet Union and he would come back home to Sarona.

It did not take long for the buses to cover the short distance to Lydda Railway Station where more buses carrying internees from the other perimeter camps were already discharging their passengers. The men had to transfer the luggage from the trucks to rail wagons while the women, children and elderly boarded third class carriages that were in a filthy state. Consequently, most family groups became separated but when the luggage was all loaded, the heavily armed Palestinian police refused to allow the men to try to find their families and insisted that they board any available partly filled or empty carriage.

The train did not depart immediately but sat in the hot afternoon sun – the police refused to explain the delay but as a precaution against any escape attempts, they refused to allow any windows to be opened. Inside the carriages, conditions rapidly became unbearable – clothing quickly became soaked with perspiration and the limited water supply was soon exhausted but not replenished. After a wait of several hours, the reason for the delay became obvious when a train arrived, bringing

German deportees from northern Palestine. The carriages were quickly coupled to the train and the journey began.

Wilhelm shared his food with a friend whose lunch was with his family in another carriage and he gave most of the water in his flask to a family with small children who were distressed with thirst. "I never thought we would be treated like this or that our women and children would have to suffer," Wilhelm said to his friend. "In one way I am grateful that Sophie and Helga do not have to go through such humiliation and degradation."

The train headed south. When night fell, there was no relief from the heat as the windows remained closed under the watch of the heavily armed guards stationed at each end of each carriage. Nevertheless, most of the passengers dozed fitfully. The rhythmic clicking of the wheels, normally so soothing, kept Wilhelm awake as Sophie and Helga filled his thoughts. With no relief from the heat, the stench of perspiration and stale breath became overpowering, but the guards denied all requests and pleadings for relief until it was obvious that the children were quite distressed, at which point they allowed the windows to be opened a fraction. Wilhelm felt immediate relief as the cool fresh night air flowed into the carriage but there was no relief from the raging thirst - only a small amount of water was provided for the young children who were becoming dehydrated.

The train travelled through the long uncomfortable night. Shortly after dawn the train pulled into the Kantara Railway Station. They had reached Egypt. Immediately, the guards began shouting orders, "All women and children must leave the train. Take your hand luggage with you." Many of the children had still been asleep and stumbled out onto the station. Much to their relief they were given a drink and a sandwich before being ferried across the Suez Canal. Wilhelm noticed that all the hand luggage had been left on the station. The women gesticulated that they wanted their bags and some even tried to retrieve them but the guards forced them away, causing distress and shouting. Wilhelm watched all of this and wondered how much more their group would have to endure, when he was called, with the other men, for a hasty breakfast of a sandwich and a cup of tea before being taken across the canal.

Another train stood waiting for the deportees but those who had been separated from their families were given time to find them before boarding the cramped and uncomfortable third-class carriages. The hand luggage was nowhere to be seen and the numerous requests and pleadings received no response. Wilhelm's anger rose with his growing concern that his personal hand luggage had been left behind.

The train moved at a maddeningly slow pace through the sandy desert towards Suez. Despite the blazing heat, the journey was not without visual interest: the shipping traffic on the canal was visible most of the time and the train passed through several oases, their tall palm trees and unexpectedly lush greenery in sharp contrast to the generally desolate countryside. Again, no water or food was provided for the deportees, many of whom were in a state of exhaustion when the train moved off the main line into a siding. From the train window Wilhelm and a few others called out to some Arabs nearby to bring some water. When a senior British official saw that they were bringing dirty water from a nearby ditch, he ordered them away and called for clean water to be given to the passengers from a military water tanker.

The train made another stop for the evening meal of mashed potatoes and stew served from a military field kitchen. The internees had to queue for their meal, but none had plates on which the meal could be served; some found scraps of cardboard, others used handkerchiefs or anything that would hold the food. Wilhelm had kept the wrapping paper from his lunch and he folded it into his cupped hands to receive his meal which was too hot to hold; he placed the paper on the ground and ate his meal with his fingers. Several people who had nothing on which to receive their food tried to hold it in their bare hands and dropped it on the sand; Wilhelm shared his meagre ration with one such friend.

Before boarding the train for another uncomfortable night, the deportees were much relieved to learn that their hand luggage had not been left behind but had been loaded onto a separate wagon. There was an undignified scramble as the internees retrieved their items; Wilhelm was pleased to locate his bag after a lengthy search.

The following morning, the train arrived in Suez, its destination. As in Kantara, the men were held back to unload the luggage while the women and children walked to an awaiting ferry. The men toiled for hours in the hot sunshine, transferring the luggage from the train to the ferry – many had no hats and used handkerchiefs, knotted at the corners as protection from the searing sun. The Palestinian Police guards kept threatening that any luggage not transferred in time, would be left behind and Wilhelm and a number of the older deportees worked themselves to exhaustion trying to meet the deadline. When the task was completed, the weary men joined the women and children aboard the ferry which cast off and headed south into the Red Sea.

Before long, an enormous ship loomed ahead; it was the liner "Queen Elizabeth" converted for troop transport. Still unaware of their destination, the exhausted deportees boarded the ship.

MONTEFIORE AUGUST 1941

Ruth and her parents were having lunch when David returned home in high spirits after an absence of almost a week. He joined them at the table.

"Well, we have finally started to get the Germans out of Palestine," he announced.

"What do you mean?" Ruth asked.

"I've just come back from escorting over six hundred of them to Egypt where we handed them to Australian military officials. It looks as though they will be going to the other side of the world. In Egypt we saw army units from so many different countries – England, Australia, New Zealand, and India. There are military personnel everywhere as well as vast quantities of military equipment especially around the port of Suez. I have never seen anything like it in all my life. I just hope they can stop Rommel and his army reaching us here. Anyway at least the British are moving the Germans out from here."

"Who did you escort from here? The Germans have done us no harm in Palestine, and they were all interned at the outbreak of war to prevent any problems." Ruth persisted.

"They were mainly family groups with a few single men. They were deported and had no choice but to go. They came from all over Palestine - Haifa and the German internee camps in the north, Sarona /Jaffa, Wilhelma and even Jerusalem. We took them by train to Kantara in Egypt, ferried them across the Suez Canal and then again by train to Suez. It wasn't the most comfortable ride for them, we made sure of that. Why should they be allowed to travel in comfort? It is war time and they are the enemy!"

"But what will happen to the ones that are still here?" Zara asked.

"Imma, I really do not know what the British have in mind. They were no doubt concerned about the number of Germans in Palestine and have now moved most of those of military age away from here. I haven't heard anything and assume that the camps will continue to function for the time being. The camps were overcrowded and the deportations will alleviate that problem. The authorities were also keen to reduce numbers in those camps that were entirely dependent on British army supplies to feed them. In Sarona at least, the internees were still able to produce much of their own fresh food from their gardens and dairy herds.

"But there is something I want to tell you while we are together. Seeing all the military activity in Egypt really brought home to me just how close the war is to us and the serious threat we are facing here in Palestine. I have made up my mind: I am going to resign from the Palestinian Police Force and join our *Palmach* unit which is looking for recruits. The entry standard is high but I think I have a good chance of being selected because of the training and experience I already have with the police force. I've discussed this with a few people, including you, Abba.

"The situation in Europe is grim; the Germans are occupying more and more of Russia and no-one knows how far they will be able to advance into the Ukraine. At present, they seem to be unstoppable - they may even try to get to the Middle East through Turkey.

"Meanwhile, in North Africa Rommel's forces are also pushing forward towards Egypt; the Germans now control the Balkans and Greece and have taken Crete. Who knows what the Vichy French will do in Syria? But if they start something we will have the war right on our doorstep.

"I think, as do many of our people, that war may well come to Palestine. If it does, then the future of our entire people is threatened to say nothing of our dream and hopes of a Jewish homeland. Just think of all those unfortunate people who fled here and once again face the same enemy. And what about the thousands of Jews like us, who have lived here for several generations and called Palestine our home? I'm not prepared to give up without a fight. At the very least we must prepare for the worst case scenario and, if necessary, fight the common foe alongside the British forces. If it means joining forces with the British to defeat the Arabs and Germans, then so be it! We must defend ourselves!"

"David, you have our whole-hearted support," Avraham said as he embraced his son. "We have spoken before and you know that I admire your bravery and idealism. If I were a few years younger I would join you. It is a noble cause and you are right - we cannot yield if we want to realise our dream and that of our people. Yes, I also think that our whole future is at stake now. Our best wishes go with you. But whatever you do, be careful. We want no harm to come to you - our family needs you and we all love you."

"I agree with your father, David. He mentioned your intentions to me some time ago and I want you to know that I also support your decision. But please, my son, take care. Don't put yourself at risk unnecessarily. I love you dearly and I am proud of you, but we want you back home with us again," Zara hugged her son and bade him goodbye.

"I will be alright, Imma. Don't worry – I will be back but I must do this," David replied, trying to reassure his mother as they clung to each other in silence for another minute.

Before leaving, David turned to Ruth whose glum looks betrayed her anxiety. They stood looking at each other before he stepped towards her. The aggressive and abrupt manner he had adopted towards her was gone. Tenderly he said, "Ruth, we have had our differences and arguments in recent times, but now I'm doing this for all of us, including you and Miriam. Our destiny is at stake. I hope you know that I love you as my sister and want nothing to harm you or Miriam." He hugged her and kissed her cheek. These were the first kind words he had spoken to her for more than eighteen months. Ruth knew that he meant them.

"I love you too, David" she replied quietly, "Goodbye, and take care of yourself."

Before he left, David bent down, gathered Miriam in his arms and said, "Good-bye, little one. I will see you again soon. Be good for your *Imma* and *Safta* and *Saba*." He gave her a kiss and departed.

UKRAINE AUGUST 1941

The German forces had penetrated deep into the Soviet Union; their eastward advance was relentless and seemed unstoppable as they forced the Red Army back. Thousands of Russian soldiers were taken prisoner as vast territories, and numerous cities and towns were captured and occupied. Erich could not understand how the Red Army was still capable of fighting after the capture of so many thousands of Russian troops and so much military equipment; on the contrary, the further the German advanced into the seemingly endless Russian territory, the more resolutely the Russians fought. "Surely," thought Erich, "their reserves will soon be exhausted."

Erich and his Brandenburger comrades had been in the vanguard of this advance. Over and over again, masquerading as Russian troops and using captured Russian vehicles and equipment, they had infiltrated the Russian lines to secure and hold strategic infrastructure targets until the regular German units arrived. After several months of these special operations, Erich had become battle hardened, but at considerable emotional cost. All too often comrades fell - some had been his friends since childhood - and it was always a grievous and heavy task to dig a grave and bury a friend so far from his home and family. The only comfort in those times was the knowledge that the fallen friend had received a proper soldier's farewell and lay in a place marked with a wooden cross.

At such times Erich reflected on the happy and carefree times of his youth in Sarona and of course, wondered about his family and what they were experiencing. He had heard nothing from them for a long time although he had learned that they had been interned in Palestine - at least it wasn't like World War 1 when they had been deported to Egypt.

And Ruth - even though two years had passed since he had last seen her and spoken to her – was always in his thoughts. He yearned to hold her again, to see again the love in her dark eyes, to bask in her brilliant and warm smile and hear her soft voice. The memory of their last time together – when they had made love at their own secret place, high on the sand dunes of the South beach, and looked so deeply into each other's eyes – sustained his spirits in the vast, alien Soviet Union and the war, that like Russia itself, stretched far into the distance.

When Erich's unit was assigned to take and secure the bridge over the Bug River near Vinnitsa, they had already carried out so many missions like it, that it seemed routine: use the cover of darkness to cross the river; wear Russian army overcoats and caps to infiltrate the enemy lines; work a way to the bridge; overpower the guards; cut the detonation wires and hold the bridge until the German infantry and motorized units arrived. After crossing the river undetected in inflatable craft, they quickly and silently made their way towards the bridge. Suddenly, tracer bullets split the night just above their heads, and forced them all to the ground. Quickly they discarded their coats - to be captured in disguise would have meant certain death. Erich reflexively checked his pocket to be sure he had his suicide pill with him - the pills were issued whenever they went into combat to ensure that if captured they could avoid torture.

Despite their early discovery, their objective was unchanged, but they had to fight their way to the bridge. They still had the cover of darkness but there was already a glimmer of light in the eastern sky and the main German attack was not due to commence for another hour. The group split into smaller groups of twos and threes in order to provide covering fire to each other. Painstakingly they approached their objective from different directions, breaking cover to quickly run a short distance before taking cover again. Erich and his two companions reached the end of the natural cover; they considered their difficult final advance which would be over open terrain providing only scant cover. From the firing, they knew that at least one machine gun was pointed in their direction, but they refrained from returning fire so as not to reveal their position. Fortunately, they knew that other small groups had spread further to provide a diversion for the final assault.

The darkness of the night was rapidly fading and the bridge appeared to be only a stone's throw away when it was Erich's turn to dash a few metres forward. As he stood to cover the short distance, he could clearly see Russian soldiers moving on the bridge. Sporadic gunfire greeted him as he ran. Suddenly, he felt a hot jab in his upper left arm; he felt no further pain but his arm hung limply at his side and blood oozed through his grey uniform and dripped from his hand. He felt another hot jab in his left thigh and fell heavily.

He heard the sound of several small explosions on the bridge; "Hand grenades," he thought, "obviously some of the boys have made it to the bridge and are now engaged in hand to hand combat with the Russian guards." Then he heard a much larger explosion and slumped in disappointment to think that the bridge had been destroyed; he feared that he and his comrades would be trapped on the Russian side of the river. Almost immediately, a huge barrage of artillery fire started from the German side directed at the Russian defensive positions and strongholds. Around the bridge the gunfire continued only for a short time and then subsided as the Brandenburgers secured the bridge, which had sustained only superficial damage in the earlier explosion. Soon the welcome sound of the approaching German motorized units was clearly audible in the cool morning air.

Using his right arm and leg only, Erich had painfully dragged and pushed himself towards some tussock bushes on the river bank where he lay exhausted listening to the nearby conflict. Both his left arm and left leg were limp. When the noise of battle subsided, he called for help and after several cries, Hans and Paul arrived.

"I've been shot," his voice was very quiet and without panic.

"Stay calm. You are safe now. We'll dress your wounds," Hans said reassuringly, "but we'll have to roll you onto your back so that we can get to them." Erich groaned as they rolled him over. The pain had intensified and was particularly sharp when they moved his injured limbs.

"We'll have to cut away your uniform to see the wounds properly and apply a dressing. Just remain calm you will be alright. Proper medical help will be here shortly and we'll get you to a field hospital," again it was Hans's reassuring voice.

"How bad is it?" Erich asked after Hans and Paul had inspected his wounds.

"Not too serious. Your arm is still bleeding and we will apply a temporary tourniquet near your shoulder to stop the bleeding. It looks as though the bullet passed right through without hitting the bone. It's a flesh wound," Paul reassured him, "I will clean it with my field dressing. You will be alright, try not to worry."

"Your thigh also has entry and exit holes, so it has missed the bone," said Hans. "You have been extremely lucky - 20 centimetres higher and it might have hit you in the stomach or shattered your hip. There is only a little bit of bleeding, so it must have missed your artery. When you dragged yourself here you got some dirt into the wound, but I will try to clean it with some antiseptic and then dress it for you."

"By the way, Erich, we captured the bridge and fought off the Russians. They all backed off when our shelling began and they fled when they heard of the advance of our motorized units."

"Yes, I heard the loud explosion when I got here – there was even a light debris shower – and I thought they must have blown the bridge. Did we have many other casualties?" Erich asked.

"Because we were spotted as we approached the bridge, we didn't have time to fully defuse the explosives. Only one charge was detonated and that partially damaged one span, but the bridge is still standing and can be used for the time being - I'm sure our engineers won't take long to have it repaired. Anyway, the damage won't hold up our advance further into the Ukraine, especially after we take Vinnitsa. I don't know what our losses were this morning – Paul and I came over to look for you as soon as the Russians retreated and that was when we heard your calls," Hans answered.

"Look Hans!" Paul yelled, "Our troops are nearly at the bridge. I can see our infantry, several panzers and a whole column of motorized personnel carriers making straight for it. I bet our comrades up on the bridge are feeling relieved. Actually, there hasn't been a squeak out of the Russians - I wonder where they have retreated? Maybe they have pulled back to Vinnitsa proper rather than fight us here. Lie still Erich; help is not far away now. You'll soon be in good hands."

"Thanks for your help. Do you have any water? I am so thirsty." Erich whispered as the pain intensified.

"Yes I have some here in my flask. Just sip it - don't drink quickly or take too much," Hans said, opening his flask and handing it to Erich's right hand. "I'll just prop you up a little while you drink."

"Ah, that was good," Erich sighed as he lay down, pleased to no longer have to make the effort to sit.

"The troops have reached the bridge and the first ones will be on this side in just a few minutes. I'll go and see if I can find some medical orderlies to take proper care of you," Paul said.

"I'll stay with you until Paul comes back, Erich."

"Thanks, Hans - I feel so helpless not being able to walk or do anything."

"You will be OK. Just thank your lucky stars that it was not a lot worse. Just be patient - rest until help arrives. There is nothing else to do right now."

After resting for a few minutes, Erich asked, "Is my arm still bleeding, Hans? I'm starting to feel a little dizzy."

"Yes, but only a little. I loosened the tourniquet a while ago and it started to bleed again but now it has virtually stopped. You are probably in shock, so the best thing is to lie still. Help is not far away."

After an absence of an hour or so, Paul returned with two stretcher bearers.

Erich was roused from his dozing by the calm reassuring voice of one of the stretcher bearers - "Hello Erich, we've come to take you to the field doctor who will ensure that you are properly attended but first we must put you onto the stretcher. We'll try not to cause you any pain - we have done this many times before." Expertly, they placed him on the stretcher so quickly that Erich's grimace of pain was fleeting. The four men each took one handle and set off toward the bridge with the stretcher. There were still some Brandenburgers on the bridge and they called words of encouragement to Erich as he passed. When they reached the field dressing station, Hans and Paul left Erich in the care of the orderlies and returned to their unit. In the meantime, the sounds of a fierce battle, only a few kilometres from the bridge, could be heard clearly – evidently, the German advance had run into strong Russian defensive positions around Vinnitsa.

The orderlies confirmed that none of Erich's bones had been shattered and they referred him to a more senior medical officer who assessed Erich's wounds and ordered that he be repatriated to Germany for proper medical treatment as his left thigh had been severely damaged. Erich was taken by ambulance, with several other wounded soldiers, to a hospital train, waiting at a nearby railway station to carry the wounded back to Germany.

Erich was placed in a window seat from where he could observe the never ending line of ambulances bringing the wounded to the train. As others were brought into the carriage - blinded, severely burnt, amputees, grown men crying and groaning in pain, some with blank faces, others bandaged so heavily that their faces were obscured, yet others with abdominal or chest wounds lying motionless - he saw at once how relatively fortunate he had been. This was an aspect of war he had not before encountered – an aspect concealed also from the home population which was euphoric with the news of German victories. He realised with a shock that each wounded man was a loved son, brother, sweetheart, husband or father and he wondered what their families would feel when they saw their loved ones so reduced.

It took fully another twenty-four hours before the train had a full complement of wounded and began its long journey back to Germany. From his seat, Erich could see the destruction - rural villages ruined, the buildings destroyed, the men killed or away fighting, the fields churned to dust by the passage of heavy military equipment. In each village he saw the women with head scarfs and young children moving about aimlessly. Almost no livestock or horses could be seen in the ravaged landscape. The trip was slow because the hospital train was often shunted onto a siding in order to clear the main line for military transports – long trains heavily laden with fuel, military supplies and armoured vehicles – and Erich gained an appreciation of the difficulties of providing for an army fighting so far from home, and how critical it was to the front line that supplies arrived on time and in sufficient quantities.

The orderlies and nurses seemed never to rest - changing dressings, providing reassurance and comfort, tending to the personal needs of the seriously wounded and amputees, and feeding those unable to feed themselves. Unfortunately, some of the wounded succumbed to their injuries before reaching home. The train passed through the Polish cities of Brest, Warsaw and Poznan and the mood of the wounded lifted noticeably when they learned that they were back in Germany. From Berlin, the train turned south and travelled through Dresden to Würzburg, where the wounded were admitted to a large hospital.

Erich's bandaged arm was in a sling and, although his thigh was heavily bandaged and throbbed with pain, he could get up with the aid of a crutch. The hospital staff placed him in a wheel chair for the trip to the assessment centre where he waited several hours to be seen by a doctor because his wounds were not life threatening. It was an elderly doctor who examined him – most of the younger doctors had been conscripted for service at the front.

"You are a very lucky young man. The bullets passed through your arm and leg without hitting a bone or a vital artery. Your arm wound is clean and should heal quickly but the wound in your leg has become infected so you will have to stay here until we have the infection under control. After that, you'll be moved to the rehabilitation centre where they will help you to walk freely again. You should make a full recovery once your muscles heal and regain their strength."

WÜRZBURG SEPTEMBER 1941

After two weeks in hospital Erich was transferred to a nearby rehabilitation centre. He was glad to be leaving the hospital where he had found it most depressing to see so many young men severely injured, many of them permanently disabled or disfigured.

At first, Erich was unable to walk without the assistance of another person, but slowly his mobility improved and he was able to walk alone using a walking stick. One of the members of staff at the centre was a young war widow, Hildegard, who was tall with a trim figure, pale blue eyes and long fair hair tied in a bun. She had a delightful warm nature - her cheerful smile and genuine care for the soldiers made her popular. Every one of the patients hoped every day she would attend to him, but many soon became quite jealous of Erich because Hildegard visited him every day to help him with his walking and exercises.

Erich learned from her that she married in July 1939 and just after their return from honeymoon her husband, Gunter, had been called up for active duty. Only a few weeks after the invasion of Poland, she received notification that he had been killed in action in Poland. Devastated by the news, she had moved back to her parents' home in Würzburg and when, in early 1940, the Government established the rehabilitation centre, she volunteered to work there. She wanted to help young men recover from their wounds and reclaim their physical and mental wellbeing as a meaningful contribution to Germany. Her good looks also lifted the morale at the centre.

"I so look forward to seeing you each day - it makes my day to see your happy face and to talk about things other than fighting a war," Erich greeted her.

"And I look forward to seeing you too - you remind me so much of my Gunter. You cannot know how much you resemble him in both appearance and mannerisms - I have to pinch myself sometimes to remember that it is you and not him.

"I'm also glad that you are getting better. Your arm in particular is looking fine and has excellent movement and flexibility."

"Yes, the arm is much, much better. Of course, it is still sore if I try to stretch it above my head or if I attempt to lift something weighty. The doctor believes that I will soon have full use of it again. He is also most positive about my leg; the infection is gone and the wound has healed really well. My mobility has increased greatly and he tells me to be patient, to keep walking and doing my exercises. He is confident that when the muscles have regained their strength, the leg will function as it did before the injury. I was actually quite surprised when he told me that he expects me to be able to return to active service again. Who knows? Hopefully the war will be over by then; with all the advances we have made, we should have defeated the Russians by then and can then make peace with England."

"I think you are a bit too optimistic but I hope you are right," Hildegard answered. "Russia is a vast country with enormous resources - it is not as easy to conquer as France or Greece or the other countries we have occupied.

"Remember, Erich, it is not as if our victories have come at no cost. Since early 1940 I have seen hundreds of young wounded soldiers, many of them will never be able to do anything again. Everyday we receive more cases. It's heart-breaking; these fine young brave men in their prime of life; fathers, brothers, sons and friends. Sometimes I console myself by thinking that it is better to die, like Gunter, than have to live and suffer constantly for the rest of your life. It must also be a terrible burden for the families when someone comes back severely maimed, or blinded, or badly burnt, or scarred, or with his mind destroyed. I have seen some horrifying sights and some nights I just go home and cry."

"Why do you continue to do this work if it affects you so badly?" Erich asked.

"I feel it is my duty. I care for our people. Someone has to give these brave boys hope, love and kind words; they need to feel wanted. They have suffered enough already. Anyway, if I wasn't here I wouldn't have met you, Erich," she said with a smile as she pecked his cheek. "You are so special to me."

"I admire your dedication, Hildegard, and you have been wonderful to me."

SARONA CHRISTMAS 1941

Christmas was subdued and sad in Sarona in 1941. Since July, when 200 people, mainly families with young children, were deported, many of the houses had stood empty. Although some of the deserted houses were occupied by the British authorities and police, much of the life of Sarona had been snuffed out, having first been reduced in vitality in September 1939 when the perimeter fence had been erected.

Nevertheless the remaining internees where determined to celebrate Christmas in the traditional German way - with family get-togethers on Christmas eve, lighting a Christmas tree and the singing of carols and the giving of presents. As always there would be a church service in the community hall on Christmas day.

On the last Sunday in Advent, the remnant Sarona community gathered in the hall where a cypress sapling had been erected and decorated. The candles on the Christmas tree were lit, giving the darkened hall a warm festive atmosphere. A brief religious service, highlighting the significance of the birth of Jesus and the message of goodwill amongst men, was held and the congregation joined the depleted choir in singing hymns. After the service, the children of the settlement, small in number, also sang and presented a nativity scene, after which Father Christmas arrived and distributed small wrapped gifts to them. The youngsters were, of course, oblivious to both the war and the implications of the internment, displayed the exuberant behaviour of children at Christmas time. The evening ended with communal singing of traditional German carols.

However, on Christmas Eve the festive atmosphere was not nearly as evident as the thoughts of the Sarona internees were for their loved ones and friends now far away: in Australian internment camps and in Germany, where several holidaying families and the teachers attending a seminar had been trapped, unable to return to Palestine, when war broke out. They prayed for the young men fighting for Germany in the bitter winter deep inside Russia or in the desert of North Africa. For those families that had been separated by the British authorities, Christmas was particularly difficult; the future was so unclear and the possibility of reunion seemed so remote as the war entered its third year.

So it was for the Bergerle women, Sophie and Helga; as tradition demanded, they had made an advent ring out of cypress branches, decorated it with red ribbon and four red candles, and placed it on a large plate on the table in their living room. On each of the four Sundays of Advent they had lit a candle. For Christmas they had cut a small cypress from their garden as a small Christmas tree and decorated it with candles, tinsel, stars, bells and coloured balls. As they had done all their lives, using the figures which had been in the Bergerle family for generations, they arranged the Nativity set on a small side table in the living room. Together, they had also baked some Christmas cookies and gingerbread and a "Stollen". And finally, to complete the feeling of Christmas in the house, Sophie had purchased a few small items through Dr Feldmann as presents for Helga, wrapped them and placed them under the tree.

On Christmas Eve, which was cool and wet, Sophie and Helga sat talking in their living room - their mood was subdued as their thoughts naturally turned to Erich and Wilhelm. They had received a Christmas greeting letter-card from Erich which he had written two months earlier and a letter, heavily censored, from Wilhelm. These meagre items provided a link between them and brought comfort and reassurance that at least Wilhelm and Erich were alive and well. Nevertheless, they longed for the war to end so that their family could be reunited.

Early in the new year, Hasso, Erich's dog, became ill and Sophie asked the camp officials for a veterinarian to come and examine him. When Dr Feldmann called, Sophie explained, "Hasso just has not been himself for the last week or so. He has been going downhill ever since my husband was deported in July, but now he just hobbles about and has difficulty getting up the back steps."

"I'll see what is troubling him. Animals, especially dogs, are very sensitive and they will pine for their master. How old is Hasso? He must be getting on in years by the look of him."

"He was still a tiny puppy when we gave him to Erich for his 12th birthday in 1929 so that would make him nearly thirteen years old."

"That is a very good age for a dog. There is probably nothing I can really do for him - he's old and his joints have stiffened, but he doesn't appear to be in too much pain. Just keep an eye on him and call me if he gets any worse. Have you heard anything from your husband and Erich?"

"Yes, we received Christmas greetings from both of them. As you probably know, Wilhelm is interned in Australia, on the other side of the world, with the others that were taken from Sarona last July. Our Erich is in the army fighting somewhere in Europe or Russia. The main thing is that they are both alive and wrote to us. But we do worry and miss them terribly! How much do I owe you for your visit to-day?"

"There's no charge - I didn't have to do anything for Hasso, and anyway I have several other calls in Sarona to look at livestock, so I didn't have to make a special trip," Dr Feldmann replied. "Good-bye Mrs Bergerle, and I wish you all the best in the coming year."

"Thank you Dr Feldmann, and all the best to you also. 1942 can surely only improve on the dreadful year we have just endured."

"Yes, it certainly has been a very difficult year for everyone here in Palestine."

*   *   *   *   *

The next day Dr Feldmann caught up with Ruth as she was taking Miriam for a walk. After exchanging pleasantries he said, "You have asked me several times about the Bergerle family. Well, I spoke with Mrs Bergerle

131

only yesterday; she and her daughter are both well. Her husband was part of the group deported to Australia in July. I still can't understand that he was deported and his wife and daughter were left behind; a number of families in Sarona were split and it has created a lot of anxiety for them. Anyway, that was not our doing, nor our decision. She told me that she had received Christmas greetings from Mr Bergerle and from her son Erich who is somewhere in Europe. I just thought I'd pass it onto you."

"Thank you for letting me know, Dr Feldmann. We've often wondered what had happened to the Bergerles. We knew the family before the war and they were always helpful to us. Erich in particular was a fine young man."

After Dr Feldmann had moved on, Ruth cuddled Miriam and whispered in her ear. "Your Daddy is alive but he is far, far away." Miriam looked wide-eyed at her mother, not knowing what all the fuss was about, but Ruth's thoughts were racing,

"At least I know he is still alive! Wouldn't it be wonderful if somehow he came to Palestine and we could meet again and he could see his gorgeous little daughter. Your daddy is such a wonderful person – I know he would love you dearly," she whispered to Miriam as she hugged and kissed her.

BRANDENBURG NOVEMBER 1941

Having regained his mobility and once again able to walk without assistance, Erich was discharged from the rehabilitation centre in Würzburg. Although he was still unfit to return to active service at the front, he returned to his home base at Brandenburg where his knowledge, experience and skills were put to good use in the training of new recruits.

He was pleased to be back at his barracks. As he checked through his personal belongings, he turned up the photographs of his family and the one small photograph of Ruth. He held it for a long time; it was just as he remembered her, beautiful, young and charming. When he realised that it was more than two years since they had last spoken, he wondered what she was doing and if she even cared for him any longer. So much had taken place in those two years: could she sustain a love for some-one who she had neither seen nor heard from? A soldier fighting for Germany, the arch-enemy of her people? Yet despite his fears he felt the passions for Ruth deep inside; truly, he had never really cared for anyone else.

His thoughts also turned to his family and the internment they were enduring. He hoped that they were not suffering and were being treated with respect and dignity. He longed to return to Palestine to see his family again – they didn't know that he had been wounded!

Winter came early to Europe in 1941 and dreadful reports of the suffering of German troops in the freezing open wasteland before Moscow and Leningrad circulated in Germany. The *Wehrmacht* had been unable to capture those cities before winter set in and the soldiers were completely exposed to the elements without proper winter uniforms in the abnormally severe Russian winter.

Since leaving Würzburg, Erich had spoken to Hildegard several times by telephone. It was clear to him from the tone of her voice that her feelings for him were deep and genuine, although it had also been evident in the attention she had paid him whilst he was in her care and from her letters since. In mid-November he received a letter from Hildegard inviting him to join her and her family for Christmas; Erich needed no persuading and his request for three days of leave was granted without delay: "It will do you the world of good after what you have been through," the commanding officer told Erich. "It is always nice to be able to spend a Christmas with a family rather than here in the barracks. We have always encouraged that."

"Thank you, sir. Yes, I am looking forward to it as I have not celebrated Christmas with my family for three years now, and I am glad to be joining another family for the holiday even though it is hard to be fully joyous in these difficult times. I wonder how our comrades are in the terrible conditions in Russia and hope that they may have found some shelter to protect them from the worst."

"Ah, yes. We have done everything we can to get some winter supplies to them but the transport and supply problems are extraordinarily difficult at present. Communications with some of our advance units are also spasmodic, especially with those that had penetrated into Moscow and beyond to prepare for the advance of our armies. Their fate is unknown and we can only hope that somehow they maybe able to fight their way back to our lines. We certainly cannot reach them."

"If I had not been wounded I may well have been with one of those advance units," Erich said philosophically. "It is strange how the hand of fate works sometimes."

"Yes, we never know. Although you probably would not have been assigned to the units we deployed at Moscow and Leningrad - most of those Brandenburgers were Russian speaking. Most of your friends from Palestine were recalled after their sterling service in the Ukraine. Some companies had taken a high number of casualties and were no longer a viable fighting unit. They have all been given a well deserved rest and leave. No doubt next year we will need all their skills and bravery again."

WÜRZBURG CHRISTMAS 1941

As Erich's train passed through the beautiful German winter landscape, it was difficult to believe that many German families were enduring difficult times - millions of men were far from home, fighting valiantly against the enemy while having to cope with the fury of nature. All such thoughts were pushed from Erich's mind when he alighted from the train at Würzburg to receive Hildegard's welcoming and warm embrace. "I am so pleased you could come and share Christmas with us, Erich. My parents are keen to meet you - I have told them so much about you."

Hildegard lived with her parents in a neat old brick house only a short walk from the station. Its tiled roof was covered with white snow and in the surrounding garden the narrow snow lines on the leafless branches of the shrubs and trees and the long icicles hanging from a wire fence line provided a classically lovely wintry backdrop.

Hildegard's parents greeted Erich warmly and showed him to their guest room. Erich unpacked quickly and returned to the lounge room where he placed the presents he had brought under the wonderfully decorated Christmas tree where there were already some other presents wrapped in Christmas paper. In the fire place, a red-glowing coal fire added warmth to the festive Christmas atmosphere provided by the hand-carved nativity scene and festive candles.

It was still only late afternoon but darkness had already fallen outside when Hildegard's father announced, "Now that we are all gathered together, I will light the Christmas candles and we will sing a few of our beautiful traditional German carols; Mother will accompany us on the piano."

After the carol singing the presents under the tree were distributed. Hildegard was visibly delighted when she unwrapped the silver brooch from Erich. "Oh! Erich it is beautiful," she exclaimed as she hugged him and kissed him affectionately, "you are observant to have noticed that I like silver jewellery more than gold. Please pin it to my dress for me."

Erich opened his present and gaped at the shining wrist watch with a strong leather band. The card made clear that the watch was a gift from the whole family. He was quite stunned.

"Do you like it?" Hildegard asked.

"I certainly do! I really didn't expect such a generous gift. I am quite overwhelmed, speechless. Thank you all very, very much."

"It is a pleasure," Hildegard's mother said. "We did not know what to buy for you, a stranger to us, but Hildegard told us that you often asked her the time, so we decided to give you a watch."

"I do need one. During our campaign in the Ukraine earlier this year, I lost the watch my parents gave me for my confirmation, nearly ten years ago. As you can imagine, I was upset because it had such sentimental value. But now, this watch will always remind me of your kindness and this memorable wartime Christmas in Würzburg."

"I have something else for you," Hildegard said handing Erich another wrapped package, this one is from me alone."

"My goodness," Erich exclaimed as he unwrapped the present to find a silk tie and a tie clip. "Oh, I am being spoiled!" Erich rose and gave Hildegard a kiss. "Thank you. I like your taste and look forward to wearing it when I am out of uniform and in civilian clothes again."

For his hosts, Erich had wrapped his last bottle of fine red Sarona table wine. He had brought three bottles with him from home and had kept this one for a special occasion. Hildegard and her parents were intrigued by the name of the wine, *"Hoffnung der Kreuzfahrer"* (Hope of the Crusaders), and the wording, *"Deutsche Weinbau Gesellschaft Wilhelma-Sarona, Sarona Deutsche Kolonie"* (German Winery Co-operative Wilhelma-Sarona, Sarona German Colony), on the colourful label.

"Well this is really something special - we will always remember your stay with us at Christmas 1941," Hildegard's father said holding and turning the bottle and re-reading the label. "I really haven't heard much about Germans in Palestine. Isn't it amazing - before the war we sometimes bought oranges that were wrapped in paper that was printed to the effect of Jaffa oranges from German settlements. If only I had taken more notice. But what I do remember clearly is that the oranges were very sweet and juicy - we loved them but they were very expensive."

Erich laughed, "They were probably grown in our orange grove back home. Growing and exporting oranges was my family's main source of income. We also grew grapes and some of them probably finished up in the wine I gave you. Back home, the main orange harvest would have just finished by now."

Over dinner, the conversation continued with its focus on Erich, his early life in Palestine and his home town of Sarona. The evening passed very quickly. Just after eleven o'clock, the family prepared to go to midnight mass in the local Catholic Cathedral and asked Erich if he wanted to join them. He agreed to go, as he had never been to a Christmas mass as he was not Catholic. Although Christmas is generally a time for joy part of the service was devoted to prayers for the soldiers serving far from home and for those who had made the supreme sacrifice for their Fatherland. Many tears flowed as members of the congregation mourned their sons, brothers and fathers. Erich was moved and wondered about how his family was spending Christmas scattered across three continents. When they had last celebrated Christmas together in 1938, no-one could have foreseen what had come to pass.

After breakfast on Christmas Day, Hildegard and Erich took a short walk through the medieval town of Würzburg. Dressed in thick winter clothing for protection against the bitter cold, they crossed the Main River and strolled up the hill to the ancient Marienberg Fortress, which overlooked the town that had been settled since 1000 AD. Covered in a heavy winter mantle of snow, the old town looked pristine - the roofs and trees white and the river flowing smooth and quiet. The spirals of white smoke rising into the sharp and clear air from the chimneys added mystique to the view of the town. The couple lingered, entranced by the view, and Hildegard took the opportunity to ask Erich about his plans for the future and what he thought about settling down after the war.

"I really have not given it much thought," Erich replied. "I still dream of returning home to Sarona one day to be with my family and friends. You know, my parents are getting old and my father, in particular, always planned for me to carry on our farming business there; it is what our family has done for several generations now. Land is now so scarce and expensive in Palestine, that unless I take over from my parents, it will be impossible for me to buy land. I don't have a trade, so staying in Germany would not really offer me many opportunities except to work as a farm hand or a factory worker, neither of which appeals to me. Even before the war, finding work in Palestine was becoming a real problem for our young men; a number of my friends went to Germany to train as apprentices and find work as there was nothing for them in Palestine."

"Perhaps I could talk with my father - he knows a few business people in Würzburg and maybe able to find work for you if you stayed on after the war. Given that so many young men have fallen or been permanently maimed in combat, I am sure there will be many opportunities for you here."

"I really haven't given it much thought, Hilde - I suppose my immediate goal is to survive the war. I've already had one lucky escape. I expect that next year will be an important year for Germany when we finally defeat Russia. But who knows what the future holds for us? When Russia is defeated I hope that we will have peace again and then we can plan in a more stable environment."

When they returned to the family home, wonderful aromas greeted them as they opened the door. They were in plenty of time for the magnificent Christmas lunch Hildegard's mother had prepared: for starters a thick vegetable soup; an entrée of smoked *Schinken* with pumpernickel; followed by roast chicken with dumplings and vegetables as the main meal. Dessert was baked apples covered with a thick custard sauce.

Hildegard's father insisted that the bottle of Sarona wine, Erich's gift, be opened to accompany the meal. "The wine is worthy of such an occasion as today! Erich, you never know when you will have your next drop of Sarona wine, so let us all enjoy it," he declared as he opened the bottle. After letting it breathe for a few minutes he poured some into four crystal wine glasses. The four clinked their glasses and drank to each other's well-being and for better times ahead. The wine had matured well - it was rich in colour and Hildegard's father noted that it was not as dry as the local German wines.

Erich enjoyed the family meal without reserve. It had been so long since he had eaten a tasty home cooked meal – and this one had the added glow of Christmas. The conversation over dinner was free-flowing and stimulating, enabling him to forget, for a brief time at least, the ravages and misery of war. Using silver cutlery, fine china plates and crystal glasses in a family setting made Erich feel at home – certainly, he had been welcomed as one of the family. On reflection, he realised that he had never before experienced such hospitality and was glad that he had come to Würzburg for Christmas.

The hours passed quickly and lunch extended into the late afternoon. As darkness fell outside, Erich realised with a thump that he had to pack his case to catch the overnight train back to Berlin. With sadness, he took his leave of Hildegard's parents and thanked them repeatedly for their hospitality and kindness. "You made me feel as if I were at home. We celebrate Christmas exactly as you do, but of course, in Sarona, we have no snow. This has been a very special Christmas for me," he said sincerely. In turn, they reassured him that they were pleased to have been able to give him such joy a long way from home and family, and they invited him to stay with them over his next leave.

Hildegard walked with Erich to the railway station, holding his hand. The train was approaching as they arrived, but they still had enough time to say goodbye.

"Erich, you don't know how much you mean to me - we must see each other again," she said, looking him straight in the eye as they embraced. "You are someone very special. My parents were also impressed by you and quite amazed by your life in Sarona."

"I admire you too, Hilde. You are unforgettable - kind-hearted, warm and caring, with a genuine laugh and a ready smile. I'll be in touch with you whenever possible. I don't know where my next posting will be, but if I get anytime off, I hope we can meet somewhere. Your parents were so good to me - I really felt at home at your place. It has been a memorable Christmas, one that I will cherish forever. I really don't know how to thank you sufficiently for inviting me. It was wonderful to be able to forget the war for a few days, and now it is time to return to reality. I don't know what the next year will bring, but I'm sure we will see each other again very soon." He kissed her passionately before dashing for the train which had started to move.

"Good-bye my dear one!" he called, waving from the open door of the carriage.

Hildegard stood silently on the platform and returned his wave, her eyes fixed on him as the train gathered speed.

CHAPTER 6 – 1942

The casualty rate of the Brandenburgers was markedly higher than that of other military units because of the high risk of their special missions. The Russian campaign of 1941 had taken a particularly severe toll on the original complement of the Brandenburger Battalion - some units had been decimated as the severe Russian winter had added frostbite and exposure to the customary risks of heavy fighting and covert operations.

The German High Command was gravely concerned that the German offensive in Russia had been brought to a halt in December 1941 before achieving its key objective – the defeat of the Soviet Union. This setback was compounded by the entry into the war of the United States in December 1941 and the increasing harassment of German forces in occupied countries by partisan units forcing the Führer and his strategic military planners to completely revise their plans for the continuation of the war.

In April 1942, the German High Command directed that there would be another summer offensive against the Soviet Union, although a new offensive along the entire eastern front was impossible after the heavy losses incurred during the 1941 offensive and during the harsh winter of 1941 - 1942 when the Wehrmacht lost almost a quarter of its original strength. A two-pronged offensive was planned – to capture Leningrad in the north and, in the south, to destroy the Russian war economy by capturing the Donets and Donbas industrial complexes, the large railway and waterway networks, Stalingrad with its substantial armaments factories, and the Caucasian oil fields. The Maikop and Grozny oil fields were the prime objectives as their seizure would alleviate Germany's chronic shortage of oil. If the southern Russian objectives could be attained, then ultimately an unbreakable link could be forged with Rommel's advance through North Africa and into Asia Minor.

BRANDENBURG AND DRESDEN
MARCH/ APRIL1942

By the end of the first week of January 1942 all of the Brandenburger soldiers had returned from leave to their barracks. Over the next few weeks their units were replenished with newly trained recruits and together the veterans and the newcomers prepared to receive their orders for their next missions. The waiting period offered the men an opportunity to renew acquaintances with colleagues from whom they had been separated as they undertook diverse operations. Erich was pleased to have the opportunity to catch up with a number of his Palestinian colleagues and some from other countries with whom he had served in Romania at the beginning of the war. There were many stories to share of the experiences of the past twelve months – unfortunately though, many of their comrades had fallen in battle and some were absent, serving in North Africa with Rommel.

Erich had been medically certified as fit once more for active service. He was glad to have regained full use of his arm and leg and to be assigned to a company that was bound for the front line.

Between Christmas and April, Erich had exchanged several letters with Hildegard who suggested in each letter that they should meet again. However, he was unable to obtain leave to travel to Würzburg and there was no suitable accommodation for Hildegard in Brandenburg. In any case, both were kept busy with their wartime commitments.

In mid-April, Erich's company was told that it would be deployed to the Russian front within the next two weeks; they were assigned to the Southern Army Group A, which was under the command of General

List and comprised the I Panzer Army and the XVII Army. As in the previous summer offensive, their role was to spearhead the offensive – infiltrate enemy lines; capture and secure strategic bridges and transport centres and create confusion in enemy lines.

*   *   *   *   *

Before their departure to the East, the men were granted two days leave; Erich telephoned Hildegard and they were able to arrange to meet for a weekend in Dresden, the capital of Saxony, situated in the large region that separated Berlin and Würzburg. Erich caught an early train and, having arrived two hours before Hildegard, took the opportunity to book a room for two at a comfortable-looking hotel. The elderly reception clerk didn't ask many questions as he had made similar reservations many times before for young soldiers and their girlfriends. But his face displayed a big grin while Erich made the reservation. When Hildegard stepped off her train from Würzburg, Erich was waiting. They greeted each other affectionately before Erich took the suitcase from Hildegard's hand and linked his arm with hers for the short walk to the hotel.

"I am so happy that we can spend a few hours together before you leave - I've missed you so much! I begged my supervisor to give me some time off - she must have realised that it was for something special because she allowed me two days – today and tomorrow. We are just swamped with work at the rehabilitation centre; most of us are working twelve to fourteen hours a day treating those poor boys from the Russian front with amputations due to frostbite. But, darling, I am not here to talk about the war or the wounded but just to enjoy a couple of good days with you."

"Yes, Hilde, it is very sad that our summer offensive ended so tragically, especially after its promising beginning. You know, several of my comrades fell at the gates of Moscow. As I told you on the phone, we will be posted to a new front region - but of course, I cannot divulge where. I do hope that we will achieve final victory in the East this year because that will change things dramatically for us - it may even bring about a ceasefire with England and the United States, which in turn will end the bombing of our cities and the killing of our civilian population. But you are right, Hilde – we are here to enjoy some time together, not to brood on the war. As it is already afternoon, why don't we take a short stroll around Dresden and drop your case at the hotel on the way?"

Neither of them had ever spent any time in Dresden, renowned as "Florence on the Elbe" because of its fine examples of baroque architecture. The city was untouched by the war and the atmosphere was serene - the tulips, harbingers of spring, were in bloom, forming blocks of bright colours in the garden beds under the trees that were heavily in bud. With their arms about each other, they strolled happily towards the *Zwinger*, Dresden's most famous landmark, entering through the Crown Gate and visiting the many ornate pavilions and galleries within. From the Zwinger, they went to the theatre place, the opera house and the *Schlossplatz,* relishing the peace and quiet of the beautiful old city. When they reached the Elbe, they walked out onto the *Marienbrücke* and stopped at its mid-point, their arms around each other's shoulders, to gaze wordlessly into the clear water flowing silently below; it was a reflection of life itself, unstoppable, ever-changing, now bright, now dark.

Erich and Hildegard chose a romantic restaurant, with candles twinkling on the tables, for their dinner. A string quartet, comprised of two elderly men and two young amputees, war casualties, played background music and romantic melodies. Other tables were occupied – a family group including a young man wearing an officer's uniform, and several other young couples. It was clear that all were enjoying a rare moment in those troubled times to savour a meal together in an untouched pre-war setting. After a delicious meal and an expensive bottle of fine wine, Erich and Hildegard entered a world of their own, dancing gently into the night, exchanging tender kisses and embraces.

MONTEFIORE MAY 1942

It was Miriam's second birthday – she was blissfully unaware of the deep uncertainty that weighted every moment in the lives of all around her. The adults knew full well that 1942 would be a decisive year for them: if Germany defeated Russia then German influence would spread to the Middle East and Palestine through Asia Minor; and if Rommel continued his relentless thrust in North Africa, Egypt would soon fall and it would be inevitable that he would continue through Palestine to join the German forces advancing through Asia Minor. The Germans had made no secret of their aim to wrest control of the Middle East from the British. If the Suez Canal was captured by Rommel, Britain would be deprived of its lifeline to the eastern realm of its Empire.

But Miriam's sunny and carefree manner, her animation and her musical laughter spread happiness throughout her family and beyond, to their friends, and lifted the gloom. Certainly, no-one thought that Miriam's birthday should pass without celebration and accordingly the family, including Mrs Gold, gathered to celebrate. As she had done the previous year, Mrs Gold provided the birthday cake which she had decorated and crowned with a large number two. "I had no children of my own, so Miriam is very special to me," she told Ruth, when regularly chided for bringing all sorts of small gifts. "I know her father and despite all that has taken place I still respect him as a fine and decent man. Oh, he is now so far away at war - only God knows if Miriam will ever meet him."

"Oh! Mrs Gold, how can you say that? I know that one day Erich will return - he promised he would."

"I'm sorry, Ruth. I certainly did not mean to cause you any anxiety - probably my words poorly chosen, but on the other hand, we must face reality. The war has now been going for several years and it has spread worldwide with Japan and the USA now fighting in the Pacific and Far

East. I too hope that nothing happens to Erich and that he will be able to see and meet his beautiful daughter one day, but that day is still a very, very long way off."

"Yes, I know, but I think of him often and will not give up hope. If only he could have the joy of watching Miriam grow up and the celebration of her birthday."

SOUTHERN UKRAINE JULY 1942

Erich had been tormented ever since his return to the barracks in Brandenburg after his tryst with Hildegard in Dresden. She had been forthright – she thought that they should get married. Erich was in no doubt that he respected, liked and even desired Hildegard, but he hadn't given her a direct answer, telling her instead that he would consider it and talk to her about it when he next had leave. Hildegard's attraction for him had been growing ever since their first meeting at the rehabilitation centre, but he couldn't deny the deep and insistent longing, even after three years, for Ruth, the girl he really loved. Despite the difficulties, he had taken care to keep her photo with him and while she was rarely absent from his thoughts, she came to the fore whenever he was on dangerous missions – like a subconscious inspiration to survive in order to fulfil his promise to return to her.

The 1942 German offensive opened on 28 June; the German advance broke through the Russian defensive lines and rapidly advanced deep into Russian territory. Erich and some of his comrades from Romania in 1939 and 1940 were not in the vanguard of this initial onslaught as their knowledge and experience of oil refineries were held in reserve for the capture of the oil fields; first at Maikop, then further south at Grozny and ultimately, Baku, on the Caspian Sea.

Despite the intense summer heat, the German front moved steadily forward through the vast Kalmyk and Kuban steppes. Erich had never seen such vast, flat countryside - he and his comrades were overawed by the treeless steppes, almost devoid of distinguishable landmarks. Orientation was difficult, but by late July the Maikop oil fields were within reach of the German forces.

Knowing full well that the oilfields were vital to Germany's ability to continue to fight, Erich and his comrades readied themselves for a mission into the oil fields and refinery. Dressed in Russian uniforms and travelling in captured Russian vehicles they set forth under the cover of darkness to penetrate the Russian lines. The Russian speaking members of the unit were dressed in officers' uniforms. They found total disarray behind the Russian lines as many units had been decimated during the month-long German advance and all the Russian forces were in retreat. Without much difficulty, Erich's unit reached the perimeter of the main refinery and readied themselves to secure it before the direct German assault. Their mission was only partly successful. The Russians had adopted a "scorched earth" policy of destruction as they retreated - parts of the refinery were destroyed by the fleeing Russians and the rest was in flames when the German forces captured it. Nevertheless, the German command was optimistic that much of the refinery would soon be restored to near-full production.

With Maikop now firmly in German hands, Erich and his comrades were ordered to join into the next thrust south, towards Grozny. In only two months the German forces had already penetrated 500 kilometres into the Azerbaijan Soviet Socialist Republic as the panzer army set a rapid pace, meeting little resistance from the Red Army. Maikop is situated on the steppe just north of the western foothills of the Caucasus Mountains, which blocked the southward thrust of the German Army. The advance did not stop, it merely changed course, east-south-east through the scenic foothills towards Grozny. Erich had never seen such majestic and formidable mountains, with their snow-capped peaks rising high from the steppe.

On 21 August, the advance paused at the base of Mt Elbrus, the highest peak in the Caucasus range, where a party of German troops decided to ascend to its summit and raise the German flag. With the lull in the fighting Erich and some of his colleagues decided to climb to a vantage point from where they could take in the magnificent scenery; when they looked out, they stared with amazement and pride over the huge territory which was now part of the German Reich.

When he returned to base, Erich was aware of a distinct tremor in the air - the mail had been delivered to the camp just before his return. At the front, hundreds of kilometres from home, the infrequent mail was the only link to family and friends, and the arrival of a single letter was a joy for its recipient. Before the letters were distributed, each soldier was in a heightened state of anticipation: would he receive a letter, and if he did, would it contain good news or sad news; what was happening at home; how were his loved ones coping? Letters were often read over and over again – whether the news was good or bad, or induced homesickness – and thus the enlisted men were involved at a distance in the ebbs and flows of family life. Erich received two letters - the usual twenty-five word letter card from his mother, dated two months earlier and uncensored, and a letter from Hildegard. He read his mother's card first and was reassured to read that she and his sister, Helga, were both well and still in their home in Sarona.

Then he opened the envelope from Hildegard and unfolded her letter. "At least," he thought, "in Germany, people are allowed to write full-length letters to their loved ones in the war zone." He skimmed the letter before deciding to find a quiet place to sit and read it in detail in order to fully comprehend the contents.

"My dearest Erich

I was so pleased to receive your letter a few weeks ago and hear that you are well. I think of you everyday and pray that no harm has come to you. We have all been following the news reports of the gigantic advances of our brave troops in Russia. All the news is good and we hope that at long last victory will be achieved soon.

I have some wonderful news for both of us - I am pregnant. The doctor has told me that I should have a healthy child in January. I know this probably comes as a shock to you, but I am delighted that we are having a child. When I told my parents they were surprised but have been very supportive and understanding and say that they are looking forward to the birth of their first grandchild. They like you very much and think very highly of you. Mother has already started knitting baby clothes and I have started buying some of the things that I'll need when our baby is born. I have not had any sickness and am continuing to work at the rehabilitation centre were every pair of helping hands is desperately needed.

Erich, you know that I have wanted to marry you for a long time – we spoke about it when we had that lovely weekend in Dresden - but now, for the sake of our unborn child I believe we must marry; our child should not have to grow up with the stigma of illegitimacy. A traditional wedding at home is virtually impossible to arrange because it is so difficult for the Army to grant sufficient leave to allow you to return to Germany. I have spoken with our local priest and he is willing to arrange a field marriage for us. I would make my vows in our local church and at the same time you would make them wherever you are posted at the front. He told me that these marriages are now quite common with so many young men away on war service and their brides back in Germany. Just think though, Erich, how wonderful it would be if when we next meet that we would be husband and wife and have a baby to love as well.

Erich I know this has come as a shock to you, but please answer as quickly as you can so that the necessary arrangements can be made. Please remember that I am already four months pregnant and there is so much to arrange and the postal service from the front is usually slow.

I love you deeply Erich and you mean so much to me. Do look after yourself.

With a very tight hug and a kiss from the bottom of my heart

Your Hildegard

PS. I nearly forgot – my parents also send their love and best wishes."

149

Erich read the letter over and over. His jumbled thoughts raced through his mind - he was in a quandary. What about Ruth who remained the true love of his life? He had loved her from the moment he first saw her and she was constantly present in his thoughts. And he knew that she also loved him passionately. They had promised eternal love to one another - could he still love her as a person if he married Hildegard? Would it break her heart if she ever found out that he had married another? Yet they hadn't seen each other or communicated for three years - perhaps she had married in the meantime? And given the hatred that had developed between their peoples, the Germans and the Jews, could she still care for him? And, he also thought with dismay, that when Germany finally won the war he wouldn't be able to marry her anyway, because German laws forbade such marriages.

On the other hand, he was very taken by Hildegard – it was not like his bond to Ruth, but he did feel deep affection for her. His initial doubts about her attention towards him at the rehabilitation centre had been completely dispelled by his Christmas stay with her family, and their tryst in Dresden had convinced him that she truly cared for him and that her love for him was genuine. Hildegard was German but also a Catholic - her parents had made him, a Protestant, welcome in their home and he did not doubt their sincerity. But would his parents be as understanding and tolerant? And what about the closely knit Sarona community - how would Hildegard be received there? He knew only too well the suspicion with which outsiders were regarded.

But the overriding consideration was that Hildegard was carrying his child. He understood that he had an obligation to both Hildegard and their unborn child – as it was, he knew that Hildegard would have a very difficult time caring for the baby while he was away at the front, although it was fortunate that she was living with her parents who would help her. The summer offensive had been very successful and a German victory in southern Russia appeared to be imminent - he knew that the baby would need a father in peace time. Finally, he felt compassion for Hildegard who had already experienced much grief when her husband had been killed early in the war. Could he cause her more anguish by refusing to marry her?

After spending a sleepless night, agonizing over his situation, Erich decided to discuss the issues with the chaplain. He did so the same day and then composed and sent his reply to Hildegard.

SARONA SEPTEMBER 1942

Sophie entered the house clearly agitated. "Helga!" she called to her daughter, "I need to speak to you." Helga hurried into the kitchen, "What is it, Mother? I can see that something is wrong."

"Yes, my dear. I have just heard that more of us are to be deported. After the first deportation that took Father away, I didn't think that there would be any more. But then, last December, some more of our people were deported to Germany."

"What will happen to us?" Helga asked her mother, her voice rising with anxiety.

"Surely they will not move us even further away from Father? Why are they doing this to us? We haven't done anything bad."

"If you remember, the group sent away last December was much smaller than your father's group – apparently they were swapped for British prisoners of war. Now, who knows? But I have thought about it, my dear - I have heard that the British will ask people if they want to go to Germany and I thought about our situation. At present, our family is in three different places: Australia, Sarona, and Germany. We haven't seen Erich for three years - he is in Germany, and even if he is fighting at the front, we can be there whenever he has some leave. If we can be transferred to Germany, then we will be in just two countries."

"Oh, Mother! I don't want to go anywhere - Sarona is our home. We have lived here all our lives, and despite the war, many of our friends are still here or not far away, in the other internment camp at Wilhelma. And anyway, where would we live in Germany? We have no relatives or friends there so everything would be strange to us and we would be arriving into the middle of the war! Right now, we are hearing about German cities and towns being bombed and the huge loss of innocent lives – the elderly, women and children being killed and their homes destroyed. Really, Mother, I think we should stay here and see what develops. Just look at the houses here in Sarona of the people that have left; all their belongings had to be packed and stored in the wine cellar and now although some of the houses stand empty, many are occupied by the military and police. I don't want that to happen to our home. In the past, you often told us how everything was ransacked in Sarona when you had to leave during the last war and how you all had to restart afresh. I'm sure the same would happen again if we left."

"Helga, I understand your concerns and I even share some of them. But at least in Germany we wouldn't be interned - we could move about without being confined by a barbed wire fence and having to front up for a roll call everyday. We might even get an opportunity to see Erich. The two of us will have to decide - we can't ask Father for advice."

"I'm sure that Father would tell us to stay to look after our things and those of the families that have gone. He was born here and grew up in this house – he would never leave it or Sarona voluntarily."

Only a few days later the rumour was confirmed when British military officials announced that Sarona internees who wished to go to Germany could apply to do so. The numbers would be limited and in the selection process, those applicants whose husbands or close relatives were already in Germany would be given preference. It was to be part of an exchange process negotiated through the Swiss Protecting Power to allow Germans to be exchanged for Jewish internees being held in Germany. The offer was not limited to internees in Sarona - Germans in other internment camps in Palestine would also be given the opportunity to participate.

After lengthy discussion, Sophie and Helga opted to remain in Sarona - to continue to occupy their family home.

SOUTHERN RUSSIAN FRONT
SEPTEMBER 1942

Late in September, Erich and several others from his unit were asked to report to their commanding officer. After the initial formalities he came to the point, "We have now largely achieved our objectives in this theatre of war. The resistance we are meeting from the enemy is minimal and I have just received the orders for your next deployment. Your knowledge and skills are highly valued and you will be sent to serve where your skills are most needed. Army Group B, under General Paulus is making steady progress. When Stalingrad is securely in our hands we will control the Volga and push forward to the vital ports downstream from Stalingrad. It is particularly important to capture Astrakhan where the Volga flows into the Caspian Sea. Your knowledge of ports, particularly those with oil loading facilities such as those you secured along the Danube in Romania in 1939/40, will be required in the next phase of this offensive to secure these port facilities along the Volga so that we can control the shipping on the river. Then, once we have taken Grozny and its refineries, the Wehrmacht will advance to Astrakhan. I'm sure I don't have to remind you that it is vital that your special mission remains absolutely secret. I wish you success and expect to see you all soon in Astrakhan."

By the end the month, Erich and the other members of the new unit had been redeployed at a Luftwaffe base near Oblivskaya, which was also a railway head for supplies to the front. From the airstrip at Oblivskaya the Luftwaffe flew daily sorties into the Gumrak airport in Stalingrad; while some were bombing missions against Red Army strongholds, most were for ferrying supplies to Stalingrad, which on the return journey airlifted the severely wounded soldiers from the battle zone.

SARONA OCTOBER 1942

The internees of Sarona gathered at the community hall to farewell relatives and friends. Unlike the departure of the deportees in July 1941, the leave-taking was not particularly traumatic because almost all of the one hundred and thirty people departing had applied to be included in the exchange of internees with Germany; most were looking forward to an unfettered life in Germany and to a reunion with their husbands and other relatives. Furthermore, no families were separated as had happened in 1941. They were not daunted by the prospect of the long journey overland - by bus to the camp at Atlit, the staging point for all the Palestinian German internees to be exchanged; then by rail through Syria, Turkey and Eastern Europe to Germany. Their spirits were high - they were certain that Germany already had the upper hand in the war and felt that they would be far better off living inside the Reich until they could return to Sarona after the inevitable German victory. The area in front of the community hall resounded with cheerful farewells and last minute reminders and requests. Smiles and waves were everywhere to be seen.

But as the last of the buses left the gates of the Sarona camp, a deep despondency settled over the people left behind. The deportations were transforming the formerly vibrant colony into a ghost town. It was not simply that more homes stood empty, but the unavoidable knowledge that the viability of the settlement was now seriously threatened – certainly it had none of its former vitality.

"What do you think will happen to us next?" Helga asked her mother that evening as they glumly ate their evening meal.

"I really don't know, Helga, dear. We are at the whim of the British and they don't disclose their plans for us."

"You know, Mother, I bade farewell to Erna and Elsa, my two best friends, today. You remember, we went to school together – but during the last two years we grew extremely close, sharing our problems. I trusted them to the extent that we often freely discussed personal issues with one another. Now, there is no one of my age left in Sarona. We are so few in number but we are not allowed out past the barbed wire fence – not even to buy clothes or just see what is happening outside! Father was taken far away; we cannot write proper letters to him and we only receive the briefest of postcards from him every now and again. The same with Erich; all we know is that he is fighting somewhere in Europe. I'm so sick of living like this, I just hope this war finishes soon," she said despairingly.

"Oh, Helga, I know, and feel for you. I miss Father and Erich just as you do – and we are not unique in Sarona – many are in the same situation. We just have to be strong and hopeful until we can be together as a family again. It's so important in these difficult times that all of us remaining in Sarona stick together and support ourselves as best we can. At least we still have each other – there are many here, especially the elderly, who have no family left here. I am sure that you have noticed how depressed some of them have become."

SOUTHERN RUSSIAN FRONT
OCTOBER/NOVEMBER 1942

It was late October when Erich married Hildegard; he took his marriage vows at the Luftwaffe Base near Oblivskaya as Hildegard took her vows at the same time in Würzburg. The army chaplain officiated – he was already an old hand at such marriages – and Erich's marriage witnesses were his good friends, Lazlo, a Hungarian and Sepp, an Austrian, both of whom had served with him in Ploesti in 1940 and on numerous missions since. Under the difficult circumstances at the front, Erich had not planned a celebration, but after the formalities, the chaplain produced a bottle of wine and a plate of *Schwarzbrot* and cheese open sandwiches. He explained to Erich that he always tried to hold a small celebration for the groom – after all, it is a wedding. He filled the glasses and proposed a toast to Erich and his bride faraway in Germany.

From the time that they had arrived at the base four weeks earlier, the three Brandenburgers had been subjected to endless questioning, verging on hostility, as to what they were doing at the base. It was obvious to the Luftwaffe personnel that the trio was not involved in any combat role - they just lounged around at the base. As the weeks had passed, the questioning became more insistent and hostile and they were constantly asked why they were having a holiday when everyone else in the Stalingrad theatre was fighting hard every day. Some said contemptuously that they must know people in high places to be exempt from combat; others challenged them asking if they were afraid. Erich and his comrades held firmly to the line that they were awaiting further orders.

Gustav, a pilot who had befriended Erich, asked him more than once to fly with him to Stalingrad. "Why don't you fly with us on one of our sorties? We could put a medical orderly arm band on you and no-one would know. We would only be gone for three to four hours: an hour to fly in to Gumrak; another hour or so to unload and then take aboard the wounded - the number is larger if they can be seated but smaller if they are on stretchers; then we fly home again. Nobody would miss you in that time and our medical people always need help with the wounded."

"Gustav, I would actually love to accept your offer, but I can tell you nothing about my function, even though you are my friend. My orders were to wait here for further orders and under no circumstances speak about my role. You know, I would probably be court-martialled if my superiors found out I had left the base for an airborne jaunt to Stalingrad. You too, Gustav, would probably be in serious trouble for taking me on a flight without proper authorization."

When it became widely known that Erich had married, the taunts became more hurtful and Erich had to restrain himself from striking back physically:

"Now we know why you're here – for your honeymoon! What a location! When does your bride arrive?"

"Do you want us to fly you and your wife to Stalingrad so you can take a cruise on the Volga?"

"As your wife is in Germany, maybe we can arrange for a young Russian lady to share your marriage bed here!"

The intense heat of summer had quite suddenly given way to the cooler weather of autumn; the nights were freezing and heavy frosts covered the ground every morning. As the daylight hours shortened noticeably, many remembered with trepidation the harshness of the previous winter. "Surely," they thought, "we won't be caught out in the open again."

The battle for Stalingrad was not yet over; the German forces had fought their way into the city proper against stubborn resistance, but the Red Army still held pockets of the devastated city and was defending its positions fiercely. The Germans suffered heavy casualties as they pushed the Russians back, street by street and building by building. Despite the heavy German bombing and artillery shelling, the Russians were clinging tightly to the banks of the Volga. Meanwhile, because the overland supply routes into Stalingrad were so long and arduous, the demands on the Luftwaffe to bring the supplies for the front-line troops were increasing steadily.

Almost as a matter of form, each time he saw Erich, Gustav repeated his invitation to Erich to fly with him to Stalingrad to see the battle front at first hand. But after a full month of sitting idle, Erich and his colleagues had become bored and restless - it seemed that they had been forgotten and the Army's focus concentrated on the continuing battle for Stalingrad. So Gustav was stunned when he repeated his offer to hear Erich reply, "If you are flying to Gumrak tomorrow, I will come with you - just as long as it is not a bombing raid."

"Am I hearing correctly? Do you really want to come along?" Gustav was stunned.

"Yes, I mean it. I will come if you have room on your plane."

"OK. We will take off for Gumrak at ten o'clock tomorrow morning, just as we do everyday, weather permitting. We are in the second flight for the day - you know, three planes leave every two hours from here. It won't be a bombing raid - we haven't done any of those for some time now - our mission is to fly in supplies, as much as we can safely load. Be here by ten o'clock and you can join us - only the crew will know you are onboard, nobody else will need to know."

The day dawned with clear skies. After breakfast Erich made his way to the hangers beside the runway where three Junkers JU-52 bomber/transport planes were being loaded and fuelled for their morning mission. Erich looked at their dull frost-covered fuselages glistening in the weak rays of the morning sun; he had seen these grand planes, affectionately known as "*Tante Ju*", one of the mainstays of the Luftwaffe, fly overhead many times. They had been completely reliable since the beginning of the war whether on bombing raids, carrying supplies or taking paratroopers to their destined jumping zone. His reverie was cut short by the arrival of Gustav and his co-pilot, Erwin, who had come early to check their aircraft. When all the goods had been loaded, a small fleet of ambulances arrived bringing medical orderlies, three of whom were assigned to each aircraft.

Erich was introduced to Erwin and the medical orderlies as they boarded. He was amazed at the way every available square centimetre had been packed with boxes of food, medical supplies and mailbags. Gustav explained, "I see we have many mailbags on board today. A large amount of mail arrived here yesterday, and now we have to take it on its last leg. The fighting in Stalingrad is chaotic and I don't know how they will distribute it but that is not my problem. I just hope that the poor devils at the front are still alive to receive their mail and I also hope that those who receive a letter from their loved ones will feel better for it. I often wonder when we carry mail back from Stalingrad how many of the letters will be the last one written by a soldier - that's why I always take extra care with the mail bags. We have a full load today, so buckle in for the flight. The visibility is good, but the temperature is very low. We will be flying along the Don and onto Gumrak. Our flight is entirely over German held territory, so we will not encounter any anti-aircraft fire. I expect our flight to be uneventful, as they have been in the past few days. OK! We are away!"

One by one, the heavily laden JU-52s roared down the runway with engines at full throttle, lifted slowly off the ground, climbed higher and set an easterly course. Erich had seated himself in the gunner's seat – as no problems were expected, there was no gunner aboard - and Erich had an uninterrupted three-hundred-and-sixty-degree view of the vast treeless countryside below: the mighty Don river was clearly visible; only a few buildings were still standing; some military vehicles were moving on the roads but the entire area was devoid of civilians. It wasn't long before the urban sprawl of Stalingrad came into view. Large areas of blackened ruins and heaps of rubble stood starkly as reminders of the fury of bombing and warfare. The devastation of residences and industrial sites spread over many square kilometres. Along the distant horizon palls of smoke were rising as the grim struggle for control of Stalingrad continued. As the aircraft banked on its approach to Gumrak, the Volga came into view.

Erich alighted from the plane and watched as the supplies were quickly transferred into the waiting trucks. He was struck by the haggard, weary bodies and sullen faces that greeted him – "These soldiers have quite obviously experienced some harrowing times," he thought, "maybe they have some foreboding!" As soon as the plane had been cleared of supplies, the medical orderlies swung into action, bringing the wounded to the plane. Stretchers were carefully manoeuvred into the aircraft and carefully placed on the floor and fastened. In all, ten stretchers were loaded and another six walking wounded were assisted aboard for their repatriation to Germany via the field hospital at Oblivskaya.

Some of the stretcher-bound wounded were writhing in severe pain, others just lay silently with their eyes closed, a couple smiled weakly and pressed Erich's hand when he offered comforting words. Erich's thoughts flashed back to the time he had been wounded at Vinnitsa and was evacuated from the front on the hospital train – he had no doubt that they were relieved to be homeward-bound and moved away from the hell fire of the front.

The turn-around at Gumrak airbase was smooth and fast - it was obvious that both the flight crew and the airbase personnel were well-practised in the routine. Altogether the stay on the ground was less than two hours and as the plane took off for the flight back to Oblivskaya, Erich was sure that he would be back before he was missed. This time, he sat in the radio operators seat, just behind the pilot.

Thirty minutes into the flight, without warning, the plane was raked with machine gun fire, the bullets penetrating the thin fuselage. A roar was heard above the drone of the engines as two Yakoulev Yak-1 fighters swept past the lumbering transport planes. Gustav led the other two JU-52s to a lower altitude in an effort to avoid the next attack which was imminent as the Yak-1s executed a one-hundred-and-eighty-degree turn ahead and returned to attack again. "Hold on!" Gustav shouted to his crew. "We're in big trouble; we can't defend ourselves because the Yak-1s can fly twice as fast as we can. Our best hope is to fly as close to the ground as possible."

As expected, the next attack came within minutes. With some alarm, through his window, Erich saw the aircraft immediately to their left explode and disintegrate. Cannon fire from the fighters ignited a fuel tank in their port wing and the plane began to spin uncontrollably, thick black smoke trailing. The Russian attack continued - its fuselage shuddered as the Yak's 20mm cannon immobilised its front engine, and the Russian machine gun fire claimed Erwin, the co-pilot, one medical orderly and several of the wounded. Gustav struggled to control the aircraft but with only the starboard engine, insufficient to keep the plane aloft, it continued to lose altitude and veer to starboard: Erwin's lifeless body was slumped in the co-pilot's seat next to him; acrid smoke, billowing from the port engine, was permeating the interior of the plane; the rudder had been damaged in the attack; the port and front engines had been shut down. As the mortally damaged aircraft continued to fall, the Russian fighters withdrew, having already counted it as a "kill".

Now free of Russian harassment, Gustav was able to steady the aircraft although it continued to veer to starboard and he knew that he could only keep it airborne for a limited time – it was only a few hundred metres above the ground. He was way off course and could not tell if they were over German occupied territory or had flown into Russian-held country. Desperately, he looked for a place to crash land - a field ahead offered the opportunity to put the plane down in one piece. "Hold fast," he shouted. "Everybody hold on, brace yourselves as we touch down!" The field was rough - the plane bounced then slewed, the left wing-tip bit into the ground and the burning wing was torn off. The fuselage remained intact, careered across the field, gouging a deep furrow before finally coming to rest with its nose partially buried.

When Erich opened his eyes, his head throbbed and his chest ached with every breath he took. He became aware of blood running down his cheek and neck; reaching up he found a deep cut on his head; his hair was soaked with blood. The oppressive silence was broken occasionally by soft moans from behind him. Looking forward he saw Gustav slumped over the controls, pieces of the broken windshield lying scattered about. Slowly he became aware of the intense cold and the heavy smell of fuel and gradually began to recall the flight, the attack by the Russian fighters and the crash landing. Although he didn't know where he was, he knew, by the smell of the fuel, that he must leave the plane before it exploded. With considerable effort he pulled himself from the seat, his chest heaving painfully as he gasped for breath. His right leg was too painful to carry his weight, but he pulled himself from his seat to see how Gustav had fared. Alarmed, he looked at his friend's ashen face but felt relief when he found a weak pulse in the pilot's neck. His relief was short-lived - Gustav was quite unresponsive to his yelling and slapping.

He was anxious to leave the plane, to secure his own safety but he had to make his way through the cabin to the door which had sprung open on impact. As he reached the bulkhead he was confronted by hideous chaos: the medical orderlies, who had been moving about the cabin attending to their patients had been hurled forward against the bulkhead; the stretchers had ripped free of their fastenings and landed, with the patients still strapped to them, onto the pile of bodies. He discerned heads and limbs protruding from amongst the stretchers but saw no movement; however, when he heard a few moans coming from this pile of misery, he weakly attempted to separate the tangle. He had neither breath nor strength, but discovered that one of the heavily bandaged stretcher-cases was, by some miracle, conscious. He reassured the distressed man, "I will go and get help. I am also injured and can do nothing for you by myself."

As he left the plane Erich felt his tension subside instantly but a new fear arose in his breast when the cold, desolate and featureless landscape greeted him; no buildings were visible, and because the sun was blotted out by a low and heavy cloud cover, he could not find his bearings. He had no idea if he was in German or Russian-held territory. He dragged himself away from the crash site, his progress excruciatingly slow as his leg could not support him. He needed frequent stops to catch his breath. The bleeding from his head wound had stopped but, whether from loss of blood or because of his other injuries, he blacked out.

When he regained consciousness, it was still daylight. His vision was blurred and it was only with effort that he could focus. Erich raised his head and looked around; only one hundred meters behind him lay the wrecked aircraft, its nose partly buried in the ground, its tail section, with the large swastika symbol, clearly visible against the dull sky. Further back he saw more wreckage. He shivered in the intense cold and was painfully aware that the ground was hard and uncomfortable.

From the jumble and confusion of his thoughts, he envisioned himself sitting with his parents and sister at the family table. He smiled at the familiar scene: a bunch of flowers in the corner on a small table next to the piano; a white cloth, embroidered by Mother with bright flowers, covering the solid wooden table; Father seated at the head of the table; a delicious aroma steaming from a casserole on the table; the sweet fragrance of an apple cake baking in the wood-fired oven for afternoon coffee.

The words of the Sarona song drifted through his mind;

> *"Where the Audsche waves are flowing is my home, my parents' house. Like God's wonder garden, like a golden paradise."*

He was swimming with friends - racing each other across the Audsche - where the old mill stood shaded by the towering Eucalyptus trees on the bank - or were they washing the salt from their bodies after an afternoon at the beach? Then back in the settlement itself, the tall, angular trees casting welcome shade in the heat of the summer afternoon; the soft feathery foliage of the jacarandas, which in spring sprinkled a purple carpet of petals on the ground; the white, pink and red oleander bushes adding riotous colour to the imposing stone houses; the green belt of orange groves, neat market gardens, vineyards and pastures around Sarona.

> *"Through the sparkling green leaves, dreaming oranges are glowing. Through the sweet air, overwhelming flows the magical orange scent."*

He smiled at the sight of the orange groves, the branches bent almost to breaking point under the weight of the Sarona oranges which glowed like nuggets against the green velvet of the foliage. The Arab workers busy picking the fruit and carrying them in baskets to the packing shed where they stood in heaps for sorting, wrapping and packing for export. He began to peel an orange, the waxy stippled skin coming away readily, releasing juice that ran over his hands and forearms, its luscious flesh like nectar in his parched throat.

When he sang the last verse of the song,

> *"Would like to see you one more time, to enjoy myself in your splendour,*
> *to wander under your sun and to rest only in your soil's lap*
> *Oh you home of my youth, my thoughts are with you all the time,*
> *all my longing, all my hopes, but you are so far, so far away."*

The Russian cold intruded, and the pain: "Oh, God! Please let that not be an omen! I have never before thought of the words like that!" I must return to Sarona: to swim in Lippmann's basin; to ride with the Sarona Bicycle Club; to participate in the *Deutscher Sportverein Sarona* at the annual *Sportsfest* for the Bismarck Cup; to enjoy the ambience

163

of Kuebler's Bar where I earned a few piasters with my friends picking up the skittles in the *Kegelbahn*. Oh, my Sarona. will I see you again? I don't want to perish alone in this godforsaken Russian steppe. I must find help."

The sky was darkening when he looked back at the aircraft. He found it difficult to focus in the low light; there seemed to be some movement around the plane. He lay still, pressed against the ground, waiting for some sign. Suddenly, the frosty air was pierced by the distinct sharp crack of a shot, quickly followed by several others; with a sickening shock, Erich understood that someone was shooting the wounded survivors. Gripped by fear he lay perfectly still in the furrow determined not to be captured - he had heard of prisoners of war being transported to remote labour camps and underground mines in the vastness of Siberia and the gruesome stories of German soldiers captured by the partisans or the Red Army. He began to check his pockets; he had left his suicide pill in the barracks but when he reached into his jacket pocket, he was reassured to feel his pistol and remembered that it had been a last-minute decision to take it from the barracks. "At least," he thought, "if the enemy finds me I will fire one shot at them and then shoot myself – that will be an honourable way to die."

As the night enveloped the plane, Erich's thoughts returned to his own condition. He could no longer feel his right leg. His fingers were beginning to freeze. He was hardly able to breathe as he sucked the icy air into his aching lungs.

"I must see my family again. My parents need me to manage our orange groves and vegetable gardens. Who will look after them in their old age if I die here? How I yearn for the warmth of the Palestinian sun. No, I cannot die here …

Ah, Ruth, my darling. What are you doing here - how did you know where to find me? … Yes, I have your photograph with me and look at it every day. But more vivid are the memories I carry: your beautiful face; those sparkling dark eyes that communicated your love; our last time together, high up on the sand dunes overlooking the Mediterranean; the touch of your lips when we kissed; your warmth, your kindness, your understanding - oh, how deeply embedded you are in my soul ... How sad that we could not enjoy our love openly. But now we can leave our hiding place - I will introduce you to my parents and you will take me to meet your family. Forgive me, my darling - though I married someone else, you know that my heart is entirely and eternally yours.

Ah, Hilde, you are here too? It is so cold – how will you give birth to our baby in this wasteland? We have spent so little time together, to really know each other – but those fleeting moments were so precious. I want so much to consolidate our love and family after this horrible war is over. Forgive me; you know I never had a chance to write about you to my parents, to tell them that we are married."

A cold breeze assaulted Erich's face and he found himself alone. He summoned his determination, "I must remain still until it is fully dark. Then I will set out to find shelter and get help."

CHAPTER 7 - 1943/44

WÜRZBURG JANUARY/FEBRUARY 1943

It was a most unsettling Christmas for Hildegard; she had heard nothing from Erich since their marriage in October; although she had sent him several letters with photos of their wedding day she had received no acknowledgement. The uncertainty and worry was greatly magnified by the steady stream of disturbing news from the southern sector of the Eastern Front. Early in January, the entire German nation was overwhelmed by sorrow when it learned, officially, that the 6th Army had been defeated at Stalingrad; several hundred thousand German soldiers had been either killed or captured by the Red Army. The national grief was compounded by the widespread understanding of the bleak fate that awaited captured German soldiers in Russia; the chances were slim indeed that the captives would ever return to them.

Hildegard knew only that Erich was stationed somewhere in the southern sector of the Eastern Front but she couldn't know whether or not he was at Stalingrad. She prayed endlessly that he had been spared the fate of those lost in that terrible battle. "Surely," she prayed, "I will not lose another husband within a few months of marriage? What of our unborn child - will it ever see its father?"

Uncertainty nagged at her constantly, "Is my Erich alive in that vast icy wilderness?
"Perhaps he has been wounded again?

"Is he cold and hungry? Is he being carried even further from me? "What will happen to him if he falls into enemy hands and they should discover that he is a Brandenburger?"

She was well advanced in her pregnancy and despite her parents comforting words Hildegard had a frightful premonition that Erich had met with a catastrophe. Her main concern was that he should not suffer.

In mid-January, Hildegard received the dreadful news she had for so long feared - official notification that Erich was missing.

Two days later she gave birth to a son whom she named Heinz-Erich.

SARONA JANUARY 1943

"I am so worried about our Erich," Sophie said to Helga in a subdued tone. "It is the first time in four years that he has not written a letter or card for Christmas."

"Maybe the mail has not got through; perhaps it has been withheld by the censor. Who knows what is going on these days," her daughter answered, trying to sound bright.

"Now that the war seems to be going bad for Germany, it seems that our guards are only too eager to let us have newspapers again – and the news just gets worse all the time. In North Africa, the English have stopped Rommel's advance at El Alamein and the Americans have now landed in Morocco to open a second front against him. I don't think he will be liberating us here in Palestine now. The newspapers report that more than 300,000 German soldiers have been lost at Stalingrad – a whole army - even if the reports are a exaggerated, I think that Germany has suffered a huge loss. I no longer think that it is just English propaganda - although I hope for our victory but I am no longer sure of it. I just hope our Erich is safe. I know I shouldn't complain because we are secure while the Allies bomb our fellow Germans in their cities with the loss of so many innocent civilians."

"Yes, Mother, the outlook is discouraging. At least Father seems to be safe even if he is far away; he can at least write long letters to us now. I must have read his last letter, the one that arrived just before Christmas, about ten times. It is reassuring to read that he is coping but I miss him so much and think of him often – just as I think of Erich and miss him."

"I miss him too, Helga, especially at this time of the year, after the autumn harvest, which he so loved. How wholeheartedly he celebrated *Dankfest*, the highlight of his year, when he felt rewarded for his hard work. And he was right - how blessed we were here! The entire Sarona community gathered for a religious service to give thanks for the abundance of our crops, which were displayed in the hall – citrus fruits, vegetables of all kinds, sheaves of grain crops, grapes, wines and even cheeses. He took pride in the whole display, but especially the vegetables he had grown himself. That was our day of celebration after the hard work of the harvest. Do you remember how we all gathered outdoors near our *Wäldle* (little forest, wood) for a community lunch. In the afternoon, the celebration continued – the band played, the choirs sang, we danced and then shared coffee and cake. There were so many sweet grapes and juicy watermelons left from lunch that we ate all afternoon. The *Dankfest* we celebrated this year in camp was a pale shadow of the good years – we haven't been able to work our fields and groves and we have nothing to celebrate.

"I am sure he thinks of us at this time of the year and wishes that he could be here, just as he must miss us at Christmas. I so miss his company and wise counsel - he always knew what to do. But I'm so grateful that I have you, Helga - at least we can share our thoughts and feelings and give comfort to one another. How dreadful it would be to be alone!

"How quickly Sarona has changed from a thriving happy place, full of life; the happy calls of children all around – running, playing, swimming; our brass band and choirs; trips to the beach; Jewish and English visitors coming to enjoy coffee and freshly baked cakes at Günthner's patisserie; our men enjoying evening *"Medschles"* at Kuebler's Bar; others playing skittles; the excitement of football matches against the other Templer settlements; young people's Saturday night dances; the concerts and the humorous Swabian plays. You know, for such a small community, we had a great deal of talent.

"Before our numbers were so reduced, the gardens around the houses were well tended, a perfect reflection of the pride we all felt in our settlement.

"But now our community life has been almost completely snuffed out - everything is quiet and subdued, most of the children have gone, no-one laughs. Most of our houses are empty - although some are occupied by the English authorities - the community bake-house sits unused and only a few pets remain. At least the furniture and belongings of the deportees are stored safely in the wine cellar."

"Oh, Mother, you are right – it is dismal here. There are so few people of my own age, almost all having been deported or sent to Germany as part of the exchange last year. I feel insecure because I don't know what will happen to us, and bored because we are not allowed to go anywhere or buy new things. I don't know why they won't allow us to go out for just a few hours, say once a week – we pose no danger to anyone. It is all so frustrating and makes me angry."

"I know how you feel, Helga, but this is war – I have lived through it before. I know we are no threat but I think that the English are keeping us behind wire as much because they are concerned for our safety. There are many people outside the camp who so despise Germans that they could well harm us - or worse. At least we are still in our homes - not like the last war when we were deported to Egypt and interned at Helouan."

"True – you and I haven't been forced to leave our home but our family has been split – Father, who was forced to leave, is in Australia, and Erich is fighting somewhere in Russia. Meanwhile we are imprisoned here and hardly hear from them. My life is wasting away: I can't learn anything; I can't buy any new clothes; I can't go out and enjoy myself like most young ladies; my friends have all left and there is nothing for me to do in Sarona. Life is just so dull and boring: we can't go dancing, to see a film, to the beach, to eat in a restaurant, or go on excursions like we used to on our bicycles or those good fun donkey rides. All the young males have gone and I am spending what should be the best years of my life cooped up in an internment camp.

"We are treated like criminals everyday – I mean, we have to stand at our front door and be checked off against a list to see if we are still here, and the few remaining men have to assemble near the community house to be counted. It is crazy! What on earth do they think we would do? And where should we go, even if we escaped? Start a revolt? How? They have already confiscated all firearms, radios, cameras and other personal belongings. They have searched our homes from top to bottom several times - what more do they want? Why can't we be given just a little freedom? How very generous of them to allow us to visit friends and relatives in other settlement camps every now and again! What a big deal! Or their "generous" concession to grant a "land pass" approval to leave camp with a guard to look at your own land outside the fence! How depressing it is to see the overgrown and neglected orchards and market gardens. Perhaps they are trying to slowly break our spirits and resolve. Well I'm sick and tired of it all. If only this stupid war would end so that we could get on with our normal lives again," Helga wailed in despair.

MONTEFIORE APRIL 1943

Another spring had arrived, signalling the approach of Miriam's third birthday. Because Ruth had the support of her family, she had been able to devote herself almost entirely to Miriam as she had grown from babyhood to a toddler to the lively, fun-loving little girl who lifted the spirits of her loving family. Although she had never known her father she didn't miss him because her adoring grandfather had always been the dominant male in her life.

She was, of course, too young to understand the impact of the far-off war or the political turmoil around her as the Jews and Arabs continued to clash violently with each other and with the British who were desperately trying to maintain law and order and were consequently suspected by both sides of favouring the other. The Arabs, who feared that they would lose territory to Jewish interests, pressured the British to restrict Jewish migration; while on the other hand, the Jews generally felt totally betrayed by the British policies which appeared to them to be biased towards the Arabs and frustrating their desire for a homeland. The Jewish inhabitants were becoming increasingly impatient and the militants were even more determined to pursue their goal at any cost, including armed conflict.

Warfare and politics notwithstanding, Ruth often took Miriam for a long walk and almost always followed a route that skirted the high barbed wire fence. Miriam registered that her mother would stop to look sadly at some apparently empty two-storey houses inside the compound and then bend down to hug her and, with a tear in her eye, point to one particular house and say that the family that had lived there was a decent one. The armed soldiers and police stationed here and there around the wire fence and at the large gates, knew Ruth and Miriam well through this frequent contact; they often chatted with them as they passed and they always had sweets or chocolates for Miriam.

The regular walk was especially enjoyable in April when the pink and white blossoms of the fruit orchards added life and colour to the enclosed settlement. The flowering season of the citrus groves was almost at an end but the sweet scent of the waxy white orange blossom, almost luminous against the dark green foliage, still permeated the air. Ruth could not help but notice that the orange groves, once so carefully tended, were seriously neglected: without irrigation, some branches had died and the foliage had become dull and somewhat pale in colour; branches which should have been pruned had intertwined; weeds were growing uncontrolled underneath the trees amongst the fallen fruit rotting on the ground. The vineyards and vegetable gardens were likewise neglected – unpruned, choked with weeds and invaded by prickly pear. What Ruth knew to have been the pride of the diligent farmers of Sarona, had been allowed to revert to wilderness.

On her return with Miriam from a walk one morning early in April, Ruth found that her brother had come home for a short break after a tour of duty of several weeks. He was in a buoyant mood and it was infecting the entire family.

"At long last," he whooped, "the war has taken a turn for the better: the threat of a German invasion of Palestine has passed; Egypt is already safe, and now that the Americans have landed in Morocco, Rommel will be defeated in North Africa. Meanwhile, the news from the Russian front is also encouraging - the German advance has been stopped so they won't be able to attack Palestine through Asia Minor. That is all good news for us. Now with Germany in retreat, our struggle for our homeland can be intensified and even realized. If only the British were true to their word and give us what they promised in the Balfour Declaration. It's not as if that promise was made so long ago – it was after the Great War, but since then the British have become extremely supportive of the Arabs."

"Exactly, David! So I don't think that we'll get our homeland quickly or easily," Avraham replied.

"I certainly see that, Abba, but I think we can hasten the outcome by continuing the armed struggle. I do not know why the British are so intransigent - well before the war they were considering a partition of Palestine but they never went ahead with it. Closer to home, it would be good if we could get Sarona into our hands; it is right in the middle of Tel Aviv and surrounded by new suburbs and we need that land to build homes for our people. Because so many of the German settlers have been deported, their land is not being farmed properly and has become overgrown with weeds with the loss of many fruit trees. It doesn't seem likely that they'll ever return – in fact, they may not want to – so I can't understand why they won't sell given that a German defeat is almost certain now that the United States has joined the fight against them. You know, even before the war we offered them good money for some of their outlying fields but they refused to sell. Then, only a few years ago, they were approached again and offered payment in American dollars or Swiss francs deposited into a Swiss Bank account but they wouldn't budge - we were prepared to pay realistic prices for their land but they refused. They are stubbornly clinging to the hope that they can all come back to their former homes, farms and businesses as they did after the last war but they don't realize that the world is changing. Perhaps soon, when they realize that Germany cannot win the war, their attitude will change."

"David, what will you do with their properties if you get them?" Ruth asked.

"We will put them to good use," David replied. "If the British deport the rest of them, we will use their homes for our people and develop some of their land for housing. We might continue to use some tracts of land for agriculture, especially some of the fertile and irrigated fields they developed, to grow vegetables. We could also continue to run their factories and workshops to produce items for our needs and provide employment as the population continues to grow. But before we can do any of that, ownership of those properties will have to pass to us."

SARONA JUNE 1943

One morning in June, the somnolence of the Sarona perimeter camp was shattered by a loud explosion. As their houses shook, the startled internees ran from their homes to see what had happened; in no time at all, British military and police officers were on the scene. It soon became apparent that a bomb had been detonated in the assembly area – the place where the daily roll-call of the interned men took place. The stunned Saronians looked with dismay at the devastation – one house had been completely flattened, the fronts of several houses had been destroyed, many windows shattered, and debris strewn over the ground. The spot where the bomb had been placed, under a bench seat, was marked by a large crater in the ground.

"Oh my God!" Helga exclaimed, holding her hands to her cheeks. "Look at the houses! They might collapse! Oh, Mother, what is happening? The war has come to Sarona."

"I don't know my dear," Sophie replied, her face ashen. "Nothing like this has ever happened here. Just imagine though if the bomb had gone off half-an-hour earlier, when all the men were here for roll call. They would have all been killed! This could have been a terrible tragedy!"

"Who could have done this? And why?"

"I can only guess that it is because we are German, and the enemy. Maybe it is an attempt to frighten us. But who knows the motive for this?"

"We might be the enemy, but we have been interned ever since the war started, we have done nothing wrong. So why bomb innocent people and destroy our property?"

"Helga, neither of us can resolve this. Come, let's just go home."

Later that day, Mrs Bergerle answered a knock on the front door. It was the friendly British orderly from the office of the Camp Commandant.

"Hello, Mrs. Bergerle. We received a mail bag from the German Red Cross today. I have a letter for you."

"Oh, thank you! I hope it is from our son, Erich - we haven't heard from him since last year. I thought you had come because of the bomb blast," Sophie said.

"No," the orderly replied, his face serious, "it looks like an official letter, so I brought it around straightaway."

A quick downward glance revealed the insignia of the German government, and Erich's mother's face turned pale.

"Are you all right, Mrs Bergerle?" the orderly asked.

"Yes, thank you, my daughter is here. And thank you for bringing the letter."

She closed the door and turned to Helga, who had joined her at the door, before opening the envelope, which had already been opened by the British camp censor. It contained a single typed sheet, folded once. She read aloud the short message it contained, only the word "missing" making an impact. Mother and daughter embraced as tears sprang from their eyes. After some minutes of silence, Helga asked her mother on what date the letter had been written.

"It is dated 20 February 1943. The mail always takes three to four months to reach us from Germany. I must write immediately to Father to let him know – this letter was addressed to both of us – and that will be a further delay of two months.

"With the turmoil on the Eastern Front, who knows where our Erich is? I just pray that he is still alive - even if a prisoner of the Russians. I have felt so uneasy about him since Christmas. Oh, Helga darling, please pray for your brother every day.

"What a horrible day it has been – it began with the bombing and now this terrible news from Germany. I am just so glad that you are here with me, my dear - I would be completely lost without you!"

The two women sat together at the kitchen table, their arms about each other as they wept for their son and brother.

SARONA AUGUST 1943

The memory of the bombing of the previous June was still very much on the internees' minds when the settlement was shaken a second time. They hurried to the site of the explosion - the new school building, which had been occupied by the British police since the establishment in 1939 of the perimeter camp. The anxious internees could not be sure if the bomb had been targeted at them or the British police. Fortunately, no-one had been killed or injured, but the building was extensively damaged.

The effect of the two bombings was to unnerve most of the internees who grew quite concerned for their own safety, fearing that if the British guards could not prevent the bombing of their own police headquarters they would be powerless to protect their charges, who were disarmed and predominantly elderly and female. The Saronaians understood that they were still enjoying greater safety and security than the residents of German industrial cities but they became aware for the first time that their own safety was tenuous. Having suffered two bombings in three months, they began to wonder when the next would occur and at whom it would be directed.

MONTEFIORE OCTOBER 1943

"At long last the British have given us a ray of hope that we will be able to acquire the land around Sarona," David excitedly told his sister and parents as they sat eating their dinner.

"What do you mean, David?" Ruth asked.

"After long months of negotiations the British have agreed to force the Germans to give up at least some of their land. The British knew that they could not delay any longer because we would fight openly for that land which we desperately want and need in the middle of Tel Aviv. So to avoid unnecessary violence they have proclaimed an ordinance called "Land (Acquisition for Public Purposes) Ordinance", which will allow them to issue an order to compulsorily acquire land and transfer ownership to the Municipal Corporation of Tel Aviv. It is a huge step forward for our people to get more land."

"But David, what if the German owners object to this new law?" Avraham enquired.

"They are unable to. If the British agree to our request, they will issue an order for the compulsory acquisition of the land. It will be an administrative process and the owners will be advised." He continued with a note of sarcasm, "As we know, the British are scrupulously fair, and will allow a short time frame for the landowner to lodge a compensation claim with the Director, Department of Land Settlement, and provide details for their compensation claim. We know that will be a difficult enough task for those landowners still living in Sarona, but it will be quite impossible for those interned in Australia or those who were sent to Germany. In any case, the matter of compensation is quite separate from the actual transfer of the land. I've been told that once the order has been issued to acquire the land, ownership will pass to the new owner – no ifs, no buts."

"So when will the transfer of land begin? Will all the German land be transferred in one lot?" Avraham enquired again.

"It will be done bit by bit, Abba. For each parcel of land, we have to explain to the satisfaction of the British authorities just why we want it and what we intend to do with it. The first orders will be issued soon. At this stage we can only try and get land on the perimeter of Sarona, that is, the agricultural land. The British have made it quite clear that claims for any land within the Sarona settlement itself and the Perimeter Camp will be rejected out of hand. The land we need right now is all outside the settlement anyway. We should all be happy with the outcome so far. As I said before, it is a big step forward for our people and for Tel Aviv especially."

Ruth was dismayed. "David," she asked, "is what you're saying really fair? It sounds to me as if the settlers' land, land they have developed and worked for more than fifty years, will just be taken."

"Ruth, just because you had a German boyfriend, you shouldn't rush to defend the interests of the German settlers. To begin with, we are at war. But secondly, what do you think is happening to our people in Europe? Do you think they have any say over what is happening to their properties and possessions? Anyway, the transfer of property ownership here is a matter for the British to determine as they are the governing authority. We Jews have no say in the transfer of land or in the compensation. All we can do is to submit proposals for any allotments of land we wish to acquire – and, in fact, we are the only party to have submitted realistic purchase proposals to the Germans only to have them all rebuffed - the settlers would not even sell us small unviable plots outside the camp."

"David, my stand has nothing to do with Erich! I am not supporting the Germans, but I do think it unfair to take property from any people and give them nothing in return - especially here in Palestine where the Germans bought the land and have worked it for several generations. I know that our people are being treated harshly in Europe, but that is no reason for us to do the same here. It is neither right nor fair!" Ruth replied with some conviction.

"We could argue for hours, Ruth, but in the end it is not our decision and we can't change it anyway. There is however, something else I wanted to speak to you about. You know my passion for a Jewish homeland here in Palestine, where Jews can live together, free of persecution, where we can practise our religion in peace, where we can speak our own language and live according to our own customs. I am not alone – many of our people share my passion. There is now an opportunity for our dream to become a reality.

"As the war continues, the news reaching us from Europe confirms the need for a Jewish homeland, yet despite our pleas to the British to allow Jewish refugees from Europe to enter Palestine, they have become even more intransigent and imposed totally unrealistic immigration restrictions on Jewish refugees. Despite the Nazi persecution, they will neither lift nor ease the restrictions they imposed before the outbreak of war. Britain is now the main obstacle to the fulfilment of our dream; Britain has become our enemy with its pro-Arab policies; and that is why we now have groups like the Stern Gang that openly challenge and fight the British.

"In the ongoing struggle and in the inevitable future war, the Jews here in Palestine will be hopelessly outnumbered. We therefore need every one of our able-bodied men and women to help us reach our goal, and that includes you, Ruth. We all have a role to play!"

"Do you expect women to fight like soldiers?"

"Yes - if worst comes to worst, but not at present. Women however can play a vital support role in the conflict that is inevitable sooner or later. Whether it be in a combative role or in a supportive role such as caring for the wounded; providing shelter for our warriors on the run from the British authorities; storing arms; providing supplies; assisting with communications – these are just a few of the roles for women. Believe me, in the coming years we will all be involved in some way in the fight for our rights and independence – for our very existence."

"I hear you, David, and I understand what you are saying. I have thought so much in recent months. I do not know if I will ever see Erich again or if Miriam will ever meet her father. I don't even know if he is still alive – you know, it is now four years since we last saw each other - but I truly feel that the bond between us is as strong as ever. I have no bitterness towards him, quite the opposite I love him with all my heart. But I also know that I must move realistically towards the future and think of the future of my dear, innocent and dependent Miriam.

"I am more than willing to play my part, but I don't know in what way. Maybe you could suggest how best I can assist."

"Thank you, Ruth," he said, giving her a hug and a sloppy brotherly kiss. "I knew that you would come through. The next few years will be so important for us all. I will let you know how and when you can help our cause."

SARONA NOVEMBER 1943

"I am not looking forward to Christmas this year, Helga. Nineteen-forty-three has been the worst year of my life," Sophie said sadly. "Since August we have had no further word of Erich's fate – from neither the Red Cross nor the Wehrmacht - I just fear the worst. I haven't even heard from father since August - I wonder if he received my letter about Erich.

"To be fair, as the war is not going well for Germany, the Wehrmacht must have more important issues at hand than the fate of one missing soldier. According to the British, hundreds of thousands of German soldiers have been killed or captured in the last twelve months in Russia and Africa. What a tragedy for our country to lose all those young men! And as if that is not enough, our beautiful German cities are being relentlessly bombed with further loss of life and destruction.

"Oh thank goodness that in Sarona we are at least out of the war zone, and fortunately, there have been no bomb attacks here since August."

"I'm sad too, Mother. Everyone is despondent and walking around with their own worries and concerns. It is just awful here. I just want to get out and have some freedom and do something with my life. Christmas is approaching and we have always made an effort to keep things normal, but there is no hint of Christmas spirit here."

"Helga, never mind Christmas!" Sophie spoke sharply to her daughter. "I have to finish this letter to tell father about the new law that allows the British to take our land. Our local leaders here are most concerned and are urging our people interned in Australia to give Power of Attorney to family members here so that compensation claims can be lodged when the compulsory acquisition orders are issued. What a mess! Father always looked after our business affairs, so I don't even know where to start. The few leaders left here will be snowed under with work and I admire their energy and diligence to do it all without pay. Their devotion to our community is quite amazing as they have more than enough with the ongoing work in our camp, let alone compile multiple compensation claims in a very short time. It is brazen theft - our enemies are stealing the land that our forefathers bought and cultivated. It is just so wrong! If we lose the war we will have nothing left at all! Everything we have worked for will have been taken from us and we are helpless to resist! It makes me so mad!"

"I know how you feel, Mother," Helga tried to calm her mother, "I have heard other people say the same things. They are also angry and upset. Why does this all have to occur in the middle of the war, when we are all interned, and nearly all our friends and relatives are on the other side of the world? What more will they do to break our spirits? To humiliate us? I suppose they will eventually move us from here and take our homes and belongings as well."

SARONA JULY/AUGUST 1944

In June the British authorities offered the Sarona internees another opportunity to be exchanged for internees held in Germany. Fourteen people accepted the offer - they had become totally disillusioned during their four years of internment in the Sarona perimeter camp. Some had family members in Germany, but all went of their own free will notwithstanding Germany's precarious position in the war and the news that the Allies had invaded Normandy in France. Those who opted to go to Germany saw the only opportunity to be free and the hope of family reunion.

As the small group assembled to board the bus that would carry them away from Sarona, the farewell was difficult. Those remaining behind felt the loss keenly, even of only fourteen people. The elderly, in particular, were aware that they were unlikely ever to see their departing friends again, especially if Germany lost the war. Over all of them hung the knowledge that none dared express – if Germany lost the war, then their remaining in Palestine would be problematical, especially after the loss of all the agricultural land.

Only a few weeks after that tearful farewell, the Sarona community gathered in shock and grief for a memorial service - six of their friends, within days of arrival in Germany, had been killed in a bombing raid on Stuttgart. This loss was felt deeply by everyone in the diminished community.

The British began issuing land acquisition notices to the internees in August 1944. Sophie and Helga were determined to remain in Palestine; Wilhelm had written from Australia urging, even commanding, them to stay on the land, and had sent Sophie Power of Attorney to authorise her to deal on his behalf with any land acquisition notices that might be issued for any part of their property.

Late that month, Sophie opened her front door to a young British policeman who had knocked. "Are you Sophie Bergerle?" he asked.

"Yes, I am."

"Please sign here to acknowledge receipt of this envelope," he said, handing her a manilla envelope and a pen with which to sign. With a quick glance, Sophie saw that the envelope was from the Land Registry Office in Jaffa and knew immediately what it contained - other internees had already received similar letters. She signed the sheet and went inside.

"Well, Helga, now it is our turn to be dispossessed. It does not come as a surprise - the Land Ministry is methodically issuing notice after notice." She opened the envelope and unfolded its contents – a short letter attached to an official notification. The letter, typed on Land Ministry Office letterhead, was addressed to Mr and Mrs Bergerle, C/o Perimeter Camp IV, Sarona. She read the body of the letter:

> *"I am instructed to inform you that the parcel of land described above and in the attached notice, owned by you in whole, has been acquired by the municipal Corporation of Tel-Aviv under the Land (Acquisition for Public Purposes) Ordinance, 1943.*
>
> *You are hereby requested to surrender your title of the property to this office as soon as possible.*
>
> *I have the honour to be,*
>
> *Your obedient servant*
>
> *Signed*
> *Registrar of Lands"*

She handed the letter to Helga who asked, "What do we do now? The land they are taking is our orchard and our fields. They are not only taking our land, but our livelihood. How will we make a living?"

"I know, my dear. There is nothing we can do - it has happened to others already. Because we are enemy subjects, they can intern us and do whatever they wish; they can confiscate our property but we are powerless to stop them. Our leaders are doing their best to obtain some compensation but I don't think that will be successful. I had better go to the office tomorrow and let them know that we have received our notice. There was talk of engaging a solicitor to challenge the notices, but there are so few of us left here and we are in a weak position both in numbers and financially – I am starting to believe that the British want us away from here.

"Sarona as we know it is fast coming to an end. Without our orange groves, fields and market gardens our community cannot continue to exist. Sarona will be swallowed up by Tel-Aviv and settled by Jews."

"Mother, let me look at the notice; I think my English is good enough to read most of it." Helga studied the document for a few minutes.

"Well, what does it say?" her mother asked.

"It is a legal document saying that the High Commissioner has authorized the Municipal Corporation of Tel-Aviv to acquire our land. Their right to do so has been published in a Gazette. It also says something about us having the right to claim compensation in the next two months, but we have to provide proof and much other information. The trouble is that it is written in very complicated English which I don't fully understand. It shows all the details of our land and that it will be used by Tel-Aviv Council for water supply. It also says something about giving up our land straight away.

"You know Mother, I think it is best if we go to the office first thing tomorrow – they'll be able to explain it to us."

"Thanks, Helga. Yes, we'll learn more tomorrow. From speaking with others, it looks as though our hands are tied. If only Father was here to handle it - he always dealt with official matters. I will write him a letter straight away to let him know what has happened and we can post it tomorrow when we are at the office. He will despair when he receives the news - all the hard work invested in the land by his parents, by him, and in more recent times by Erich is now worthless."

TEL AVIV SEPTEMBER 1944

After a rigorous security check, Ruth was admitted to an intensive training program at a secret location in Tel Aviv and had become a competent radio operator, proficient in sending and recording coded

messages to units of the *Haganah*. It was exacting and trying work
to decipher messages, often in Arabic, over the crackling static;
the tension was considerably heightened by the need for utmost
secrecy.

She was on duty at the *Haganah's* secret central communications centre,
having been called at short notice earlier in the evening. Whenever she
was rostered for duty her mother took care of Miriam. Her workplace
was a sparsely furnished room in a nondescript building in suburban
Tel Aviv. The walls of the operations room displayed several large maps
of Palestine; the operators sat, wearing uncomfortable headphones, at
bare wooden desks.

In the past few weeks Ruth had often been required to work through the
night when illegal shipments of arms were being smuggled into Palestine
for the Jewish fighters. The fighting, against both Arabs and the British,
had spread throughout Palestine and had grown increasingly bitter. The
British, in an attempt to stem the fighting, were increasingly vigilant
and had intercepted many arms shipments; as a result, many Jewish
fighters and their supporters had been imprisoned at the formidable
old stone jail in Acre.

On this night, an arms cache that had been smuggled in through
Aquaba and carried on camels through the Negev desert by a unit of the
Palmach, disguised as Bedouin and led by David, had reached the south
east outskirts of Tel Aviv. In this final risk-laden, stage, the shipment
was to be sorted and distributed to a number of hiding places, such as
kibbutzim all over the country. After a long and tense night, when the
sky was already streaked with light, Ruth was relieved to receive the
coded message in Arabic *"mish mish mistoui"* (ripe apricots).

Ruth was exhausted when she reached her home in the dawn hours and
quietly opened the door to the room she shared with Miriam. As she
gently leaned over the sleeping child to plant a tender kiss on her forehead,
her heart thumped as she recognised Erich's features in miniature. "Oh,

Erich!" she thought. "You have never seen your beautiful daughter. I wonder if you even know you are the father of this wonderful child?"

Despite her exhaustion, Ruth lay wide awake in her bed thinking of Erich whose presence in her thoughts had not diminished at all despite his absence of five years – sometimes she could almost feel him at her side. Her only tangible reminders of him were the single photograph and the bracelet he had given her as a parting gift, yet her memories of their intimate moments remained intense. She could summon at will the physical sensation of his arms holding her as they danced together near the pump house simply by humming the tune he had crooned softly into her ear - *Du, du liegst mir im Herzen* (you, you lie in my heart) *Wenn, wenn ich dich liebe, dann dann liebe auch mich* (When, when I love you, then, then love me too). Lying in the darkened room, listening to her daughter's regular breathing, she hummed softly to herself and felt his heart beating against her chest, his hand softly stroking her hair as they shuffled in the sandy soil of his father's orange grove.

She thought of their times together at their secret spot, high on the sand-dunes above the south beach where they had spoken freely, shared kisses and on their last visit, shared their bodies in true love. She had never revisited the spot - it was far too dangerous for her, a Jewess, to travel through Jaffa, an Arab area. Wondering if she would ever again see Erich, the only man in her life, she dozed restlessly.

SARONA NOVEMBER 1944

In October 1944 the worst fear of the remaining internees in Sarona became real when the British ordered them to pack their belongings for relocation to the nearby Internment Camp at Wilhelma. While it was not unexpected, the order caused sorrow, even anguish, to the internees because it meant that their Sarona would soon cease to exist. The elderly were particularly agitated at the prospect of relocation and the knowledge that their life-long labours had come to nothing.

The order had been given at a meeting of the Sarona residents in the community hall. When they were dismissed, they dispersed in silence – no groups formed to discuss possible ways of avoiding the end – a feeling of despondency, of defeat, hung over the entire settlement.

"Where do we start?" Helga asked her mother as they entered their home and closed the door. Sophie had suspected for some time that they would be moved and some large wooden trunks she had ordered for this eventuality stood ready in their living room.

"We will just work our way through the house room by room. At least we have more time for packing than when father was deported although I really don't know what to do with all of his things. We also still have almost all of Erich's possessions here, because he only took one suitcase with him in 1939. He planned to come home as soon as the war was over - we all thought that would be no more than a year, yet here we are five years later and it is still dragging on."

"That reminds me, Mother. Erich's motorbike is still in the cellar – and all of Father's tools - what will we do with all of that? What about our good furniture?"

"Ah, Helga! We can't take everything so we will have to be carefully selective. We can't even sell anything – firstly, because we have no contact with the outside world and secondly, because we would get almost nothing in a forced sale. It makes me feel sick that so many sentimental possessions, and so many goods for which we worked hard and saved money, will have to be abandoned. I wish your father was here to help me but, on the other hand, I know that it would break his heart to have to choose what to leave."

Despite their heavy hearts they worked solidly for two days during which they packed their personal possessions and decided just what they would have to leave. They had been told that they could take no animals, that any pets would have to be put down and any remaining livestock would have to be given away. Sophie took control, "I will give our hens and rooster to whoever wants them, but our loyal Hasso will have to be put down. He is so old - I am sure no one will want him – and he was always at Erich's side. I'll ask Dr Feldmann for his advice and assistance."

"What about Mittzi, Mother? I don't want to part with her! Maybe I can take her with me - I have been thinking that we could smuggle her out with us in our hand luggage. Surely we can keep our pet cat! She'll do no harm. But I couldn't bear to have her killed – I would rather just leave her if we have to, and I don't think she would starve in that case."

"Alright, Helga – we'll give it a try. I have some material and my sewing machine is still here so I can make a cloth bag – we'll put her into it just as we leave and you can carry her in your large handbag. Let's just hope that she doesn't meow or put up a struggle."

The instruction to the residents was that all luggage was to be placed outside their front doors for collection and transportation to the Wilhelma Camp and that they should then assemble near the community hall to board the buses. Sophie and Helga took a slow walk of final leave-taking through their home. As they looked at the empty shelves and bare walls in each room, countless happy memories were triggered in their hearts. With heavy hearts, the two women left the only home they had known to face the uncertain future.

At the front gate, Helga stopped with a shock, "Mother, we have left the house without locking the front door. Shall I go back and lock it?"

"No, my dear - I deliberately left our front door unlocked. I noticed that when people left in the earlier deportations, many people left their doors unlocked as a symbolic gesture. Locking the door gives the impression we will not be back again. Of course, I don't know if any of us will ever return, but if you or Erich should return, our door will be open to welcome you."

Without a backward glance and in silence Sophie and Helga walked to the assembly place where several buses awaited them. The small crowd was sombre and silent – there were no greetings – as they waited to be called to board the bus. When their names were called, the two boarded the bus with Mittzi concealed inside Helga's handbag. That small act of defiance enabled them to hold their heads high as they took their seats.

The silence was almost eerie as the buses slowly made their way down the straight, narrow streets of Sarona, past the imposing houses, the once-splendid gardens, the towering trees - planted decades earlier by the pioneer families - their branches swaying in the slight breeze as if waving goodbye, and the huge winery and cellar building which had come to be the Sarona landmark. As they passed through the gates, the terrible realisation that they would never return to their homes confronted the deportees. Tears flowed silently down every face.

PART THREE

SARONA GARDEN

CHAPTER 8 – 2009

INTERVENING YEARS 1944 - 2009

After the German internees had been cleared from the Sarona Perimeter Camp, the British occupied it as a military and police base, thereby making the entire Sarona settlement the *Haganah's* primary objective in the Tel Aviv region during the struggle for independence. After several armed clashes, the British withdrew from the camp in late 1947 and the *Haganah* took control on 16 December 1947. They renamed it Camp Joshua, in honour of Joshua Globerman who had been killed at Latrun on his way back to Tel Aviv after a secret mission to Jerusalem. Eventually the site became known as Hakirya because it was the area where the government and military headquarters were located when Israel became an independent nation. Although Tel Aviv was at that time the temporary capital of Israel; the government and military operated out of Sarona.

At first the *Haganah*, later known as the Israeli Defence Forces including the *Sheruat Avir*, the Israeli Air Force, used the Templer buildings as their headquarters. Later the fledgling Israeli government departments also established their offices in the large buildings there. During the early struggle for independence, the *Haganah* had installed radio transmitters in well shafts in the Sarona orange groves to conceal them from the British. These secret transmitters remained in use after the British withdrawal and one of them may well have been used to broadcast the proclamation of the new State of Israel by David Ben-Gurion, the first Prime Minister.

In the early 1950s the large German school and sporting complex was renovated and became Hakirya Maternity Hospital, the largest maternity hospital in the Tel Aviv area. It was demolished in the 1980s. Another of the buildings became Ben-Gurion's Ministerial Office and later in the 1950s a library was also established. The Hakirya complex, with its sensitive defence force and other government offices was closed to the Israeli public. Hence, the old buildings and their surroundings remained largely intact although of course, some renovations were carried out and some smaller buildings fell into disrepair. Gradually, the agricultural land which surrounded Sarona was developed for housing and commercial use.

Beginning in the 1970s, the military and government agencies began to relocate their offices and administrative centre away from the southern sector of Hakirya. The extremely high land value of former Sarona, now in the very heart of Tel Aviv, attracted the keen interest of developers; the City Council also wanted to develop this former German precinct. The initial proposal was to widen Kaplan Street, a major thoroughfare in Tel Aviv, and clear the whole area south of Kaplan Street where a large part of Sarona had stood. When tenders for the development of the area were invited, the proposal was challenged and opposed by prominent historians and academics who, with the strong support of the Society for the Preservation of Historical Sites in Eretz Israel, brought to the attention of authorities the historical significance of this area The Preservation Society was particularly vocal; it organized public rallies and lobbied for the preservation of some buildings. The historians gained the support of sufficient prominent people who lobbied for the retention of some of the former Sarona settlement and presented carefully researched background material on the rich history of Hakirya and the significant role this area had played in the development of modern Israel.

TEL AVIV MAY 2009

After a smooth and uneventful three-hour flight from Frankfurt, Heinz-Erich landed at Ben-Gurion Airport, a short distance from Tel Aviv just before midday. After collecting his luggage and clearing customs and

immigration he travelled by taxi to his hotel located on the coast just north
of the prominent Jaffa headland. He had eaten during his flight and chose
to retire to his room to refresh himself and take a rest. To orient himself, he
took a Tel Aviv city map and several brochures from the reception desk.

It was a perfect spring day – the sky was clear blue from horizon to
horizon although considerably warmer than the weather he had left
behind in Germany. He was particularly delighted with the view from
his hotel window – in front of him the sparkling blue Mediterranean
stretched as far as the eye could see and along the beach was the band
of colourful beach umbrellas that provided shade for the chairs and
tables where people could be seen relaxing. The aroma of freshly-brewed
coffee seemed to waft up to his air-conditioned room even though the
window was closed.

Two hours later, he was dozing when he was awoken by the telephone.
It was the receptionist. "I have your tourist guide here and she was
wondering if she could speak with you."

"Yes that will be fine. I will be down in a few minutes - just ask her to
wait in the lobby."

He tidied himself and took the elevator down to the reception area
where the receptionist pointed out the tourist guide. She was a middle
aged lady well dressed with well groomed hair with just a tinge of grey.
She rose to greet him as he approached.

"Shalom and welcome to Israel, Mr Bergerle! I am Miriam, your Tel
Aviv guide. You were probably not expecting me until tomorrow," she
said, her hand outstretched. Her greeting was warm and her smile
genuine but what caught Heinz-Erich's attention were her deep dark
eyes – what a lovely striking feature they were.

"Hello, and thank-you. I only arrived this morning. But please call me
Heinz," he replied, shaking her outstretched hand. "Please sit down."

"How was your flight? Did you have any difficulty at the airport?"

"Everything was fine: the flight was smooth and uneventful; security before boarding in Germany was extremely strict but my travel agent had forewarned me that flights to Israel are subject to tighter security. Everything else was just fine and I had no trouble at all with the airport officials. It was quite chilly in Germany when I left and the weather here is noticeably warmer."

"Yes, this is a good time of year to tour Israel. Of course, for us locals, it is still quite cool. The people you can see on the beach are probably all holiday makers.

"I always try and meet my clients before their tours start so that I can gain some idea of what they are interested in. I think that it is far better to have an individually focussed tour rather than to hope that a general tour will include what the client really wants to see or experience. Your travel agent in Germany indicated that you wanted a guide who was familiar with the former German Templer settlement of Sarona, which is now known as Hakirya."

"Yes, that is right. My father and his forefathers and my paternal grandmother's family all lived there long ago. I have done some research into the settlement and a recently published book aroused my interest even more. If at all possible, I would like to see for myself what remains of the settlement and I particularly want to see my grandfather's house if it is still standing."

"Fortunately, I know the area and its history well. The southern area of Hakirya has undergone some major changes in the past few years – part of it is being redeveloped and the name "Sarona Garden" has been given to the section where part of the former Sarona settlement stood. I'll explain more tomorrow when we are actually on location. Are there any other parts of Tel Aviv that interest you?

"Yes there are a few other areas I would like to see. I read about the other nearby Templer settlements in Jaffa and Walhalla which were closely linked with Sarona. I am also interested in the old port of Jaffa through which all my grandparents' oranges were exported. I really have no idea if any trace of these places still exists and I have only two more days here before moving onto Jerusalem. I thought I might take a city tour on one of the days, but perhaps you can show me more of Tel Aviv as I have no idea how long the visit to Sarona will take."

"Let's see how much ground we can cover tomorrow. There are still a few old houses remaining from the Jaffa/Walhalla settlement, and the old port of Jaffa still exists although it is no longer a commercial port. In its day it was far more than just the port for exporting oranges - it was the only port in southern Palestine and your forefathers probably came ashore there in the 19th century. It was one of the main ports in Palestine. Many pilgrims disembarked there for their journey to Jerusalem and other Holy sites for Easter and Christmas. It was also the port through which thousands of Jewish immigrants passed. During the British mandate period the port facilities were improved and it was a strategic shipping facility along the coast.

"I will plan tomorrow with a focus on Sarona Garden. If we get to Jaffa it will be only a brief visit. Now, tomorrow will be a long and full - may I suggest that we start at eight o'clock. Can I pick you up here in the lobby?"

"It all sounds fine to me. I have been looking forward to this day for a long, long time and I'm quite excited to retrace my roots. If you wish, we can start even earlier, I don't mind getting up."

"No need for that – an eight o'clock start will give you time to enjoy a good Middle East style breakfast, and we will have plenty of daylight hours.

"You mentioned that your father lived in Sarona before the war. Is he still alive?"

"No. I never knew my father - he didn't return from the war. My mother, who has also passed away, knew only a few sketchy details about his family and the settlement he came from. Evidently his family was one of the pioneering families who came to the Holy Land in the 19th century. It is only in recent years that I became really interested in finding out more about my father and his family. I spoke with the people at the Temple Society in Germany and they were very helpful with family background and the history of the Templer settlements in Palestine. They also referred me to some interesting literature which they thought might interest me. One book in particular really aroused my interest – it is very detailed, well-illustrated with old photographs and a plan of Sarona with all the homes and communal buildings identified. It was published only a few years ago and although written in English, my school English was adequate."

"I think I know the book - it is called *From Desert Sands to Golden Oranges* and I have a copy of it. I agree with your assessment and I am pleased that you already have some background and understanding for our tour tomorrow. I often have tourists from Germany who have absolutely no idea of the history of the Hakirya district. They are usually quite astounded when I tell them about the historical significance of a former German settlement right here in the middle of Tel Aviv."

"Oh, so do you get many people visiting the area?"

"The numbers are increasing all the time, especially now that Sarona Garden has been established as a park and historical precinct. Several of my colleagues take their clients to visit Sarona Garden because of its historical significance. And in recent years, many descendants of the former settlers, like you, are curious to see the places where their forefathers lived."

"I'm really glad you called, Miriam. I am looking forward to our tour tomorrow."

"I am too, Heinz. I'll see you tomorrow morning at eight o'clock. Oh! I forgot to mention that you should wear comfortable walking shoes as we will be on our feet for most of the day."

"OK. Thanks, Miriam. I'll see you tomorrow."

*   *   *   *   *

Heinz-Erich awoke to another glorious day. When he drew back the curtains he was greeted by a cloudless blue sky and the sparkling Mediterranean Sea. He felt upbeat and after a hearty breakfast he was ready and waiting in the hotel lobby at seven-forty-five. He didn't have to wait long because only a few minutes later Miriam arrived to collect him.

"Good morning, Heinz," she greeted, "did you sleep well?"

"And good morning to you, Miriam. Thank you, I slept very well. I had an early night and have enjoyed a good breakfast and am ready to go."

"Great! We will begin in Jaffa, then briefly visit the old Jaffa/Walhalla settlement site, travel through Tel Aviv to the Yarkon River and I will show you the site of the old mill which was a popular and well known recreation spot for the Sarona settlers. We won't spend too much time at these places so that we can spend the rest of the day in Sarona Garden. My car is just outside."

As Miriam drove south along the coast towards old Jaffa she began her commentary -

"This long beach on our right, the one you can see from your hotel room, was known to the settlers as the North Beach. In the 1860s that whole area stretching north and for more than a kilometre inland was just an arid expanse of sand known as the White Sands.

"In 1909, the Jews of Jaffa, who had been living in squalor in overcrowded housing in the old city decided to establish an independent Jewish neighbourhood – Achuzat Bayit. They purchased a tract of sandy arid land just on the northern outskirts of Jaffa and sub-dived it into 60 plots. After 12 months the area was renamed Tel Aviv, meaning the Hill of Spring. From its inception the planners of Tel Aviv envisaged a well planned European style garden town with wide streets and boulevards not like the unruly, unplanned maze of alleys and laneways of Jaffa. It was from these humble beginnings this large modern city developed and grew in a northerly direction. This year we are celebrating the centenary of Tel Aviv.

"In the 1920s and 1930s Tel Aviv expanded into a large city that completely overtook Jaffa in commerce. The beach has always been a popular spot for the residents of Tel Aviv and also for the Sarona residents for whom it was a walk of only a few kilometres."

Miriam drove through Jaffa to the Crest Gardens surrounding the Summit Hill near the 19th century St Peters Church. From this high point, Heinz-Erich could see for kilometres along the coast line and turn for a panoramic view of Tel Aviv's imposing skyline.

"Over there, where you can see those two distinct towers, is Sarona," Miriam explained to Heinz-Erich pointing in a north easterly direction. When they returned to the car, Miriam explained, "I will drive a little further, then we'll walk through the narrow winding cobblestone alleyways of old Jaffa to the port. This was a rundown and derelict Arab quarter after the establishment of the State of Israel."

As they walked, Heinz-Erich admired the tasteful restorations and the proliferation of boutique shops, popular eating places and expensive apartments. When they reached the port, Miriam explained, "This is the spot where your forefathers landed when they came to Palestine. If you look down there you can see some old stone steps which the passengers of the nineteenth and early twentieth centuries had to negotiate. The breakwater you see was not there in those days - it was built by the

British during the Mandate period. The Jaffa port had some protection from the headland but it was a rather exposed port and you can see that all those dark nasty-looking rocks made it a dangerous task to load and unload passengers and goods from ships. The Arab boatmen lined up along this narrow strip of foreshore ready to ferry people and goods to and from the ships which anchored out in the deeper water. But they could only work in relatively calm seas. Over there is the old Customs House which also housed the immigration officials. It was modernized and expanded by the British."

"Could my forefathers have landed anywhere except here?"

"Not unless they travelled overland from the northern port of Haifa, or further north, Acre.

"We will take a quick walk up to the promenade – from the seawall you will gain a good perspective of the whole port. It was along this raised walkway that people stood to wave goodbye to departing family and friends."

"I wonder if my grandparents waved goodbye to my father when he left in 1939 to go to war?"

"They may well have," Miriam replied.

"As you can see this is no longer a commercial port as it is quite unsuitable for modern shipping and wharf handling needs. The main port for Tel Aviv is located further north along the coast near the estuary of the Yarkon River."

From the old port they drove past the old Jaffa railway station to the site of the former German settlement of Jaffa/Walhalla.

"We won't stay here for long. You can see some of the old buildings are badly dilapidated. Over on that corner is the old Breisch's store which was a large shop that sold a large range of goods. It was well patronised by the Germans settlers and most of the Saronians. As we walk around the corner, you can see the old wooden houses that were part of an American Christian church settlement that was abandoned in the 1860s. The buildings were bought by the Templers when they arrived in 1869. As you can see, only some of the houses have been restored, the others are falling apart.

"It was in this locality that Baron Ustinov, the grandfather of the famous actor, Peter Ustinov, built a hotel with a large and beautiful garden, stocked with exotic plants, in which he kept monkeys and parrots. See that wooden building over there - it is probably the place where your father was born. The Templers ran a little hospital here and many mothers from Sarona came here to give birth. It was a general hospital staffed by German doctors."

"I almost cannot believe that after all this time some of these wooden buildings are still standing - many look as if they are about to collapse, but those that have been restored look so neat and tidy."

"The land has become so valuable that it is inevitable that much of what you see will be redeveloped. The high rise building in front of us stands on the site of the renowned Wagner Brothers foundry and engineering works."

"I read about the factory. Wasn't one of the Wagners assassinated in the 1940s?"

"Yes, that was Gotthilf Wagner, a director of the Wagner Company and the last mayor of Sarona. During the war years, when the Germans were interned and many deported, he diligently and tirelessly looked after the commercial and financial affairs of the settlement and of the many deportees. He was a highly respected leader of the Sarona community—and not just them, he was awarded an MBE by the British authorities for his community and industrial work in Palestine during the mandate period. He was however, a staunch German national and fiercely opposed to the sale of any German-owned land to Jewish interests. It seems that he steadfastly hoped for the return of the deported settlers and therefore wanted to retain German ownership of the Sarona settlement and the land necessary to its existence. As such he was seen by some Jewish leaders as a major obstacle to the development and growth of Tel Aviv. Sadly, he paid for his strongly held views with his life – he was assassinated in 1946 by members of the Jewish underground.

"From here we will now drive north through central Tel Aviv, along the Rothschild Boulevard as we head to the old mill on the Yarkon River."

As they drove along the wide tree-lined boulevard Miriam pointed out the many Bauhaus-style buildings of the 1930s that flanked the boulevard. She explained that the precinct, known as the White City because of the characteristic white render finish and the clear symmetrical lines, had significant historical and architectural significance – in fact it was being preserved under the protection of UNSECO after having been declared a World Heritage site. She pointed out Dizengoff House, where David Ben-Gurion, Israel's first Prime Minister, declared the State of Israel in May 1948, after the withdrawal of the British following the United Nations Partition resolution of the previous November.

"From the enquires I've made, it seems that my grandmother and my father's sister were deported from Palestine in 1948," Erich ventured.

"That's quite right if they were still interned in Palestine in April 1948. The British deported all remaining Germans to Cyprus when it became inevitable that the mandated territory would be partitioned and they could not guarantee the safety of the internees beyond the end of the mandate."

They arrived at the parkland surrounding the old mill site and strolled through the park to the Yarkon River as Miriam explained, "This was the site of a water mill; the Sarona residents used to come here on bike rides or on donkey and horse rides. Young people would swim in the river and the mill pond. Sometimes, on their way home from the beach, the young Saronians would stop here wash off any salt and freshen their appearance. As you can imagine, the paths under the tall eucalyptus trees along the river bank provided a pleasant place for strolling, especially for young couples who needed time together away from the prying eyes and gossip of the settlement. Unfortunately though, nothing is left of the mill building."

"What a charming place! And romantic – I can understand why the young couples used it. The mill pond with its quiet waters is an idyllic setting with the water birds and the tall shady trees. Oh! The water race is still in place and I can see an old stone grinding wheel lying in the grass over there."

"Heinz, it really is time for a bite of lunch as we still have a full afternoon ahead of us. Can I suggest a lovely little eating place in town and then to spend the rest of the day in Sarona?"

It was just a short drive to town and because it was not yet midday, they easily found a table for two. "This is Gold's Patisserie and Café which specialises in German and Austrian cakes but also serves light meals. The Gold family started a cake shop here in the 1920s when many Jewish immigrants came to Palestine after World War 1. The little shop soon became well known for its delicious cakes, baked by Mrs Gold herself. Of course, since then the business has changed hands several times but it still has a good name for quality some eighty years after its establishment. Because it was established when the Sarona settlement had become quite prosperous, some of the more adventurous Sarona Germans patronised it - who knows, members of your own family may have enjoyed a cake and coffee here."

"Do you think that they would have come here to a Jewish coffee shop? I would have thought that they would have gone to their own businesses. I read that they were fairly enclosed."

"Yes, they were a group that kept very much to itself and they almost certainly preferred to support other German businesses, but I understand that in the late twenties and into the thirties the German settlers did go out to eat at Jewish restaurants in Tel Aviv and bought many items, especially clothing and shoes, in Jewish-owned shops. Quite possibly, the mobility offered by the automobile was a factor. Likewise, many Jews, especially German, Hungarian and Czech, visited Sarona to enjoy German cooking and baking, or to experience again the cafe culture they knew from Europe. It was only in the late thirties, when Nazism excluded the Jews from German society, that this mingling between the communities became strained."

"I am quite astounded that you know so much about the German communities that once flourished here in Israel. From where did you learn it? I'm sure you didn't learn it in school."

"You're quite right, it isn't in the school history syllabus, but before the war my family lived nearby the Sarona settlement and my family knew a few of the settlers. I grew up in the area and although I was very young I can still remember the high barbed wire fence around the Sarona Camp during and just after the war. My mother sometimes took me for walks around the outside of the camp and I can recall seeing people and buildings on the other side of the fence.

"In my teen years my curiosity grew about this place in central Tel Aviv, which was out of bounds to the general public: the government and defence forces had their offices and administration centres there. The Israeli Broadcasting Corporation's broadcasting and transmission facilities were established and still transmit from here. Later, I began researching some of the district's history by talking to family members and friends – in fact, anyone I could find who had any connection with Sarona.

My interest was really aroused in the 1990s by the protests that arose when the Tel Aviv City Council wanted to clear for redevelopment the entire area that the military were vacating. Some academics, historians and the Society for the Preservation of Historical Sites vigorously opposed the total destruction of the site because of its historical value. Like most members

205

of the public, and probably many within the government administration, I knew very little of the history of Hakirya - it was just a dilapidated area with huge potential for development given the high land values in central Tel Aviv. The City Council also wanted to widen Kaplan Street, a very busy thoroughfare which was a chronic traffic bottleneck where it ran past the old Sarona settlement. The protests were well-organized: deputations were made to government and the City Council; brochures were published and widely distributed; and articles were published in the daily papers and influential journals. The struggle continued unabated for more than ten years before a compromise was reached and the preservation and restoration of a number of buildings was secured. During those years I learnt a great deal about Sarona and the people and who had lived there. I will explain more when we are on the site."

After their snack the pair set off for Sarona Garden. As they left the cafe Heinz-Erich commented that the piece of cake he had was as good as any he had enjoyed in Germany.

"I told you Heinz, the quality is first-class. The Gold tradition continues!"

SARONA GARDEN MAY 2009

As Miriam drove east along the busy wide Kaplan Street she remarked, "It is hard to believe that this major artery was originally just a sandy track leading from Sarona to the main north beach – the area where you are staying. The Templers of Sarona called it *Meer Strasse* (Sea Road)." Miriam turned right into Ha'arba Street where she parked on the southern boundary of Sarona Garden, near the old winery and wine cellar. They entered the site on foot and Miriam gave Heinz a map of Sarona Garden before she began her commentary.

"Sarona was designed by the surveyor, Theodor Sandel, who established two intersecting axes, a north-south road and an east-west road. Lesser roads were laid out symmetrically and parallel to these axes. Sandel also laid out one of the very early Jewish agricultural settlements, Mikveh Israel, the Hope of Israel, not far from here - it has also been preserved and now serves as an agricultural college. There are many similarities between these two old pioneering settlements.

"You can see that much of the area has been cleared and landscaped to create this beautiful park. Of course, the lawns and paths are new, as are the flower beds that line the narrow roads; many of the smaller trees and shrubs are recent plantings, but the large trees and shrubs were planted by the settlers more than one hundred years ago. These significant plantings have also been placed under heritage protection because we now recognize the botanical heritage - many of the species, such as the eucalypts, were the first of their type to be planted in the Holy Land. The Templer settlers were certainly the first to plant eucalypts in large numbers in the Holy Land; they started in the 1870s.

"The huge winery building in front of us is one of the most important buildings here. It was built in the very early days of Sarona and was still in use when the Templers were removed from Sarona. The wines produced here became well-known for their quality and much of the production was exported to Europe. The underground cellars are enormous, indicating just how important the wine industry was to the settlers. Under the spot where we are standing, a tunnel runs from the cellars to the distillery, that building opposite, which produced a range of spirits. Part of that building was converted to a printing works in the 1920s.

"When the State of Israel was declared, Sarona became a government and military complex - the first Israeli fighter planes were assembled in the wine cellar and some of Israel's early banknotes were also printed there. The solid and secure walls of the winery house a great deal of history so it is one of the most significant buildings on the site – of course, it is marked for preservation and restoration."

"I can't get over its size and its solid construction, Miriam. Even by today's standards it is an imposing structure - it must have been a landmark in its day - I'd love to see it inside and to explore the tunnel."

"Unfortunately, Heinz, I am not authorised to take you inside. Open days are held here from time to time; I don't want to make you jealous, but I have been inside and it certainly is a grand building. I have also walked the entire length of the tunnel - do you know that it was cut straight through the sandstone so it has no lining.

"We will now head towards the intersection of Kaplan and David Elazar Streets, which was the crossroad at the centre of Sarona. David Elazar Street, the main north-south axis of the settlement, was originally called *Christoph Strasse*; as we walk you will see a number of historic houses and functional buildings constructed of the local sandstone, Kurkar stone. There were several phases of construction in Sarona, each with its distinct architectural style. The first homes built by the settlers were of course based on the solid and enduring model they brought from Europe. The southern end of Christoph Strasse was the main entry point to Sarona from Jaffa; it joined what the Templers called the Nablus Road, today known as the Petah Tikva Way"

Miriam allowed Heinz-Erich some time to take photographs of the winery and distillery before moving on, but they had only gone a short distance when Miriam stopped to point out a pair of tall Washingtonian palm trees. "This is where the Mamlock Pharmacy once stood. Mamlock was a Jewish pharmacist who although a devoted Zionist, was both respected and trusted by the Sarona community. The pharmacy was the only Jewish business inside Sarona; the shop was built by the settlers in 1924 to entice him to locate his business in their midst. When he opened, he planted one palm on each side of his little shop. They still stand today eighty-five years later as testimony to his work and as a physical link to the past when the Jewish and German communities lived in harmony here for several generations. For that reason there were many protests and deputations to save the shop from demolition, but to no avail."

"It is such a pity when landmarks and symbolic buildings disappear because they can never be replaced. I suppose I can also understand the authority's point of view because not everything can be preserved." Heinz-Erich said, surveying the small empty site.

"Just across the road is the building which housed the first mechanized mill in Palestine. The Pflugfelder mill produced oil and has now been restored to working order."

After strolling further, Miriam stopped. "That house," she said, pointing at a two-storey dwelling, "was the Bergerle house: the house you came to see; your grandparents' family home; the place where your father grew up." Heinz-Erich was silent as he gazed at the house in awe. Its external walls covered with cement render which had cracked and flaked in parts revealing the sandstone; the old window shutters closed over the windows; unprotected windows boarded up; the wooden door frames still supporting solid wooden doors; the barred cellar windows just above ground level; the red-tiled roof; and the tall trees surrounding the house together formed a deep impression in Heinz-Erich.

"I am staggered at the size of the house - I really didn't know what to expect, but certainly not a house of this size. It is enormous and must have been glorious in its heyday. I know so little of my father's family- my mother knew him only for a short time. I am speechless!

"Are we allowed to go inside? I would dearly love to see it," Heinz-Erich asked.

"No, as you can see all the houses are all locked and, where the shutters are missing, the windows are boarded up to prevent access. Not only is it too risky and dangerous to allow public access, but the interiors could be damaged or vandalized making the restoration work even more difficult. Some of the interiors were altered by the military during their occupancy. However, I believe that access will be allowed when the restoration is completed. I am able to take you inside another house that has been fully, painstakingly, restored to show the original colours and interior decorations. That house is open to the public on special occasions."

"Who will eventually live in these houses, Miriam?"

"No, Heinz, they are not being restored as dwellings; they will become public buildings such as libraries, art galleries, coffee shops and the like. One will definitely become a museum. The City Council has invited individuals, companies and community groups to submit tenders."

For a while, Heinz-Erich walked around the house, taking photos and trying to peer into the interior through narrow gaps here and there; Miriam stood aside to allow him to take in the atmosphere of his ancestral home and its garden. "If only these walls could speak," he thought. "This house and the other buildings here must have really stood out in this barren area." He walked up the few concrete steps onto the rear verandah and faced the sturdy wooden door in its stout timber frame set in the thick stone wall. He tried the door handle only to find that it was indeed locked as Miriam had said. How he wanted to go inside – his father must have passed through this very door countless times, perhaps his first steps outside the walls of the house were through this door and down into the garden.

Heinz-Erich wandered into the back yard where a few tall trees still stood like silent sentinels; each had a small metal plate affixed to designate it as subject to heritage protection. One of the trees was a gnarled fig tree, clearly old judging by the thickness of its trunk, and he wondered by whom it had been planted and when and whether his father had eaten its fruit.

Suddenly, he turned to Miriam, "What became of their possessions?"

"All the furniture and other items were removed from the vacant houses and stored in the wine cellar. After the war, when it was finally decided that the Saronians would not be allowed to return, much of the furniture and personal possessions were stolen and the remainder was distributed to needy refugees."

"We know that some of the settlers concealed valuables before they were deported; a few years ago, an old Saronian in Australia recalled precisely where he had hidden some gold coins in a wall cavity before his deportation. They were found and returned to him, much to his joy, after being hidden for seventy years. Unfortunately, almost all of the people who would have hidden valuables have died and taken their secrets with them – it would be a fruitless task to search for them now."

"I wonder if my grandparents hid anything – I guess I'll never know," Heinz wondered aloud.

"Yes," Miriam responded, "they may have. But we'll never know unless something is found during the renovations."

After a period in deep thought, Heinz-Erich turned again to Miriam and asked, "Do you know where the orange groves and market gardens were?"

"The agricultural enterprises were all on the outskirts of Sarona, not in the residential zone. The orange groves and fields disappeared quickly when Tel Aviv grew rapidly with the arrival of thousands of displaced Jews after the war.

"As you can see, the entire residential zone has been landscaped; all the sheds and outbuildings, wire mesh and picket fences were demolished as they had no heritage value," Miriam explained.

When they reached Kaplan Street, Miriam explained, "This was the crossroad at the centre of old Sarona. On the other side of this busy road was the northern sector of Sarona. As you can see by the high security fence and guarded entrance, it is not accessible as it is still occupied by the Israeli Defence Forces. The large tower building with the heliport building is the Matcal Tower. I've never been into that area but have been told there are still some very beautiful homes - in fact, the former stately Aberle house was chosen by our first Prime Minister, David Ben-Gurion, to be the Prime Minister's residence in 1948. Other Israeli Government departments and authorities also chose buildings there as headquarters and that is why so many of the buildings have remained intact.

"In the northern sector was a large school, built by the settlers in the 1930s. It is no longer standing but it served as a hospital for many years after the war. Near the school was a large sports ground where the Sarona Sports Club had its headquarters. Sport was a key activity in the settlement and an annual Sportsfest, mainly an athletic and field sports' event, was held there. It was also the location of football matches against the other German settlements and also against British and Jewish teams.

"This part of Kaplan Street is very modern; a few years ago the Tel Aviv City Council arranged to physically move several of the homes and buildings to allow the widening of Kaplan Street and provide access to the underground parking of the new buildings. It was a huge and costly engineering feat involving both local and overseas engineers, but some of the houses were original buildings of the settlement and of too great a historical value to demolish. The buildings were only moved twenty to thirty meters but there was not a single mishap."

"I've never heard of whole buildings being moved. It must have been an extremely delicate task." Heinz-Erich gazed in amazement at the relocated buildings.

"Yes, but not one building collapsed. They were placed on a concrete slab on new foundations built to replicate the cellar walls of the original building. It was a painstakingly slow process that attracted many spectators, me amongst them – it was even shown on television.

"The building on our right is the old community building built in 1871; the newer, and larger, community hall, over there, was built in 1910 - nearly 100 years ago."

"I must say, I am surprised at the size of this place. I visualized a much smaller settlement – just a few old buildings."

"I will show you even more. In 1939, Sarona was a substantial village with more than one hundred houses and a population of approximately four hundred and fifty.

"Can you see that long building on an angle? It looks a little like a military barracks but it was a bowling alley, a skittle alley, or *Kegelbahn* in German - another first in Palestine. It was originally built as an open air alley, but was enclosed and roofed after the First World War. It was privately owned by the publican and was a popular meeting place in Sarona. Naturally, it was used mainly by the local settlers but several Jewish groups also regularly played skittles there until the mid-1930s. Kuebler's Bar, where drinks and meals were served, was right next to the alley. Kueblers had a courtyard, shaded by trees, which was also a popular place to meet and socialize.

"Directly opposite is the restored house I mentioned to you earlier. It looks splendid with its outside repainted, the window shutters fitting neatly and the balcony being a real feature. Inside the rooms have been repainted in their original colours and the decorative wall borders painstakingly repainted by hand. The walls, windows and doors have all been restored to their original state."

Miriam and Heinz-Erich proceeded down the narrow street which was lined with newly established colourful flower beds. "This was another important place," Miriam said as she stopped and pointed to a fine building. "This was Günthner's Patisserie and Coffee Shop - its reputation for fine cakes spread far and wide and it was not only popular with the locals but especially with the British administration and military personnel and their wives and girl-friends. In the evenings the young people often came here to dance."

They walked past the old joinery workshop before taking a break on a seat under a shady tree in a large lawn.

"This part of Sarona was developed just before the First World War - the houses are of a different style. That one on the corner is a marvellous example of a building constructed of textured Wieland cement bricks with a stone façade - even the spouting is made of stone. In the late nineteenth century the Wieland brothers started a large cement products factory near Jaffa. They also made ceramic floor tiles with absolutely brilliant colourful designs and patterns which can be seen in many of the houses here. When the floors were cleaned, the colours were as bright as ever. The Germans were industrially advanced and very innovative.

"On the far side of the road stand three beautiful stately houses built in the 1930s in the Bauhaus style. To my mind they reflect the wellbeing of many of the Sarona residents and the overall wealth of the settlement at that time. The house with the arched windows is of an unusual design - in the shape of a cube.

"That large building over there was the Home for the Aged, another Sarona community social initiative. I could just go on and on about the rich social life of the settlement. This lawn is where the Sarona tennis court once was. It was built in the late 1920s. And over there, behind the fence was the swimming pool - it was really a large concrete water storage for irrigation, but used as a swimming pool in the warmer months. I am sure that is where your father learned to swim.

"The first motorized water pump installation in Palestine was recently discovered near the swimming pool. It was installed by the Wagner Brothers Engineering Works in the late nineteenth century and was a key factor in the huge expansion of orange groves and other agricultural ventures. Later another underground motorized installation pumped water from the artesian aquifers into a a large water tower, since demolished, from which water flowed in pipes to the houses in the settlement. The supply was sufficient for a water flush sanitation system to be implemented. These initiatives were the first such domestic water systems in Palestine. Your forefathers reaped great benefits from having a good clean water supply at home and irrigated fields and orange groves.

"The fenced area is a secure area for the main transmission station of Israeli radio and television in the Tel Aviv area. Sarona was founded on a small rise in the Sharon Plain so transmission can reach far from here."

"From what you have told me, Miriam, the early settlers really changed things – not only with their building and planning but with agriculture and industry as well. I imagine that they must have done rather well and been quite well off. What happened to all their land when they were moved away from Sarona?"

"In the end, especially after Wagner's assassination, the remaining interned citizens, who had already been moved from Sarona, reluctantly agreed to sell the agricultural land to the Municipality of Tel Aviv. They negotiated a contract for the sale of certain plots but the British authorities rejected the proposal and compulsorily acquired all of the agricultural properties and paid the landowners only a token compensation. Then, in the post war years the whole area around Sarona became urbanized.

"It was not until the City Council wanted to clear the whole area for development that the significance of Sarona became generally known. The prolonged protests forced the Council to commission a detailed study of the former settlement and this resulted in a revised planning proposal for development which stipulated that many of the old buildings had to be preserved and restored.

"After the recent opening of the widened Kaplan Street, the area was renamed Sarona Garden as an acknowledgement of the past and a logo designed showing the old winery building encircled by new high rise buildings - linking the past, present and future. I have a copy here."

"It is a striking emblem," Heinz commented. "I must say that the experience of visiting my father's former village has been extraordinary. Words are hard to find, but to see these somewhat humble and plain but nevertheless marvellous solid buildings standing in this parkland oasis, surrounded by modern high-rise buildings in the heart of Tel Aviv makes me wonder what my father would think if he could see it. I am so glad I came and I'm most grateful to you, Miriam, for showing it to me and explaining its history in such detail. You seem to have a real passion for this place and you have helped to fill a void in my life."

"It has been such a pleasure for me. Of course, it is my job as a tourist guide to show people around and I do enjoy my job. But it is particularly rewarding for me when I can guide someone with a real and personal interest as distinct from general tourism.

"Now, it is getting late so I think I will take you back to your hotel to freshen up and have a small break. I still want to show you the southern side of Jaffa where the settlers relaxed at the south beach, and I also want to you to meet someone who had a close association with Sarona before the war. If you have any old photographs, please bring them along.

"That sounds good to me. We should make the most of the day whilst I am here. I haven't any photographs of Sarona, I only have a few photographs of my father."

Heinz-Erich was silent during the short drive back to the hotel, but emerged from his reverie when the car stopped at the front entrance.

"I will see you in an hour, at about five-thirty in the lobby," Miriam called as he alighted from the car.

SOUTH BEACH 2009

Miriam called for Heinz-Erich as arranged. After driving through the busy peak hour traffic of Tel Aviv and then the narrower streets of Jaffa they came to a raised area overlooking the Mediterranean and parked. The area was landscaped with lawns and palm trees. Stone steps lead down to the golden sands of the wide beach. Where sandy overgrown dunes once rose from the beach, strong bricked terraces now held back the sand, plantings had been established to stop erosion and concrete paths meandered along the top of the dune ridge. Bench seats had been installed on the terraces to allow people to rest or just sit and meditate as they gazed out across the sparkling sea.

Heinz-Erich could not help but notice the large blue and white Israeli flag with the Star of David fluttering from the top of a large black rock just a short distance from the shore. "That's a prominent place to fly a flag," he commented.

"Yes, it certainly is! You really can't miss it! Before the war that rock was called Adam's Rock by the Germans who regularly came here. It was always a challenge for the young to be able to swim out to the rock and clamber onto it. Your father probably stood on that rock many times.

"This whole area is abuzz in summer. It is one of the best beaches in Israel and today with cars and modern transport it is easily accessible and very popular. Many family groups come and the children can play on the wide sandy beach or go swimming.

"Similarly, before the war many German settlers, especially those from the inland settlements such as Jerusalem, would spend their summer holidays here.

"The Sarona people came here for day excursions. They would erect semi permanent shelters on the beach with palm fronds on the roof to provide some shade. They even employed an Arab lifeguard with a boat to make sure no-one drowned. Arab merchants would stroll along the beach hoping to sell food and other items to people."

Miriam led Heinz-Erich down some stone steps onto the beach.

"It is marvellous down here the sand is so clean and fine. No wonder the people love this beach," Heinz-Erich said picking up a handful of sand and letting it run through his fingers.

"Well, it wasn't always like this - during the war the British authorities established a rubbish dump for Jaffa's waste just on that headland," Miriam explained pointing north towards old Jaffa. "Even after the war, rubbish was still being dumped there and it polluted the whole area. The northerly wind carried the terrible smell and sometimes rubbish would blow right along the beach. Thank goodness that was stopped, the dump site cleared, and the beach restored as part of the restoration and redevelopment of Jaffa and the beach front."

They had walked only a few hundred metres along the beach when Miriam turned up one of the numerous access paths up the terraces. When they reached the top Heinz-Erich noticed a rather frail looking elderly lady seated on a bench. She was wrapped in a light shawl. Miriam approached and greeted her, "Hello, Imma, I am sorry we're a few minutes late. Heinz, I would like you to meet my mother, Ruth. Imma, this is Heinz the gentleman from Germany that I have been guiding today. As I mentioned to you he has a very special interest in Sarona."

"I am pleased to meet you, Ruth," Heinz-Erich said, somewhat nonplussed. "Please, no need to get up." He extended his hand and shook Ruth's hand; her grip was firm and she held his hand for quite some time before letting go. Despite her age, her dark penetrating eyes looked him straight in the face. Her hair was silver grey, she was of slight stature and had a few wrinkles on her face, but her skin was clear and her voice firm.

"I am also very pleased to meet you. Please do sit - it is much easier to talk."

Erich and Miriam sat on the either side of her.

"Now I know that Miriam showed you around Sarona Garden, but what else have you seen today, Heinz?"

"I have had a once in a lifetime day. Since we set out at eight this morning right through it has just been a wonderful, wonderful experience. I have learnt so much. Even our lunchtime snack was a learning experience at Gold's Patisserie."

Ruth smiled. "You know, Heinz, I worked at Gold's before the war – it was my first job. Mrs Gold baked many of the cakes they sold - she and her husband worked hard to establish the business and its good reputation."

"I was not disappointed. But, of course, the highlight was my visit to Sarona Garden. My father lived there until he left for Germany and I even saw my grandparents' family home, although only from the outside."

"You said that your father lived in Sarona. Did he tell you much about the settlement and its people?"

"No, nothing at all – you see, I never knew him because he was killed during the war before I was born. I knew a few sketchy details about Sarona from my mother and I made a few inquiries. I learned so much more today from Miriam about the settlement and its people. There were so many things I had no idea about."

"What about your mother, was she also from Sarona?" Ruth asked.

"No, she was born and raised in the city of Würzburg. My parents only knew each other for a short time. Mother had only a few recollections of what father had told her, that is why my visit here today was so significant."

"Is your mother still alive?" Ruth asked.

"No she died in 1970. I was only twenty-seven and not yet interested in my family's background. She often spoke about the war and her tough life but as a youngster I was not really interested. It is only in later years that I became more curious about my family's history."

"Do you have any brothers or sisters?"

"No, I am an only child - my mother never remarried after father was killed. She really had a very sad life - her first husband was killed in action in the first few weeks of the war in 1939. She was a nurse working in a rehabilitation centre for wounded soldiers when she met my father after he was wounded in the Ukraine in 1941. She often said that fate had brought them together – a young war widow and a lonely wounded soldier, far from his home in Palestine. He was a member of the elite Brandenburger Division and was often sent on dangerous special missions behind enemy lines. After his discharge from rehabilitation, my grandparents invited him to their home in Würzburg for Christmas in 1941. He was again assigned to the Russian front during 1942 and was actually serving on the front near Stalingrad when he married my mother who was in Würzburg on their wedding day. It was one of those distance field weddings which the German Army conducted during the war. My mother used to say that they had their honeymoon before their wedding!

"Early in 1943, just before I was born, my mother was notified that my father was missing. Despite numerous inquiries by my mother she never found out what happened to him. His comrades said he just vanished – nothing was ever seen or heard of him again. We assume that he was sent on a secret mission and never returned. It was during that dreadful winter of 1942/43 when the battle of Stalingrad took place and thousands of German soldiers were either killed or captured by the Red Army. Many more thousands of other soldiers were listed as missing like my father and their final resting places are unknown – they just vanished in the vastness of Russia.

"My mother never really recovered from the trauma of the war. She was twice widowed during the war and then in March 1945 she lost both parents in the devastating bombing raid on Würzburg. Today, with hindsight, it can be seen as a senseless attack on an historic city with no military importance; more than ninety per cent of the city was destroyed in the attack and more than five thousand people perished. Luckily, like nearly all young children in German cities, I had been evacuated to a rural location and was living with relatives in the country.

On the day of the air raid, my mother was visiting me. She always carried her personal papers and a few photographs with her whenever she left the house – she told me that in war you never know what will happen next, so I always carry my precious documents with me when I leave home. After the war she was one of the *Trümmerfrauen*, I do not know how you say that in English, maybe rubble women, who helped to rebuild the city. Times were very tough in Germany and she had me, a four-year old to care for as well. Somehow she managed and raised me and provided for me during those difficult times. Anyway that is all history now - just like the Sarona settlement."

"Miriam said that you can remember Sarona as it was before the war. Did you know my father's family, the Bergerles?"

A wry smile appeared on Ruth's face. "Yes, I did, but not very well. Was your father's name Erich and did he have a sister Helga?"

"Yes, Erich was my father, and he did have a sister Helga."

"Is Helga still living? From memory I recall that she was older than Erich."

"No, Helga was killed in a car accident many years ago in Australia. Also both my grandparents on my father's side died in Australia; my grandfather in 1959 and my grandmother in 1968. I never met them nor had any contact with them. They probably never knew that they had a grandson living in Germany.

"From what I can gather, my grandfather was deported from Sarona to Australia in 1941. He was interned there in a camp in southern Australia. When released from internment he lived in Melbourne where he found work. He was not allowed to return to Palestine. My grandmother and aunty were interned for years in Sarona until they were expelled from Palestine in 1948, when they migrated to Australia to be reunited with my grandfather – they had been separated for seven years."

Ruth sighed deeply and paused. "Before the war Sarona was a beautifully well kept settlement. It was always spick and span, colourful gardens surrounded the large homes, the tree-lined roads were well maintained and there was a sense of orderliness throughout. It had a wonderful village like atmosphere about it. On Sundays everyone was well groomed and dressed. Many people visited the settlement on weekends for walks or a coffee. Until the mid-1930s many Jews also went to Sarona to enjoy the hospitality and atmosphere.

"At the outbreak of the war, Sarona became an internment camp and the German Saronians lost all contact with the outside population. As you said, in 1941 many of the internees were deported. I can remember watching the buses departing. The sad faces, the tears as they waved good bye - they probably did not know that they would never return. My brother was one of the guards that accompanied them as they left.

"Those remaining were kept behind the high barbed wire fence that had been erected around the Sarona settlement. Only a few authorised people, such as doctors, the pharmacist, veterinarians and government officials, were allowed into the camp which had only one main gate and was under guard around the clock. We often watched as the internees came to the gate to give instructions to the Arab workers who were still employed by them to tend the orange groves, vineyards and vegetable gardens outside the fenced area. If we walked around the perimeter of the camp we could see the internees going about their daily business. It must have been very frustrating for them to be cooped up in the camp.

"Several other groups of internees left the camp for Germany during the war. By 1945 the camp was deserted as the handful of internees that were left were transferred by the British to another nearby camp at the former German settlement of Wilhelma, now known as B'nei Atarot. Nearly all the houses there are still standing and many have been very tastefully restored. It is certainly worth a trip there to see the rural village setting. It is not far from the airport.

"Anyway, getting back to the Sarona internees. Occasionally after the war we would see small groups or individuals come back to the camp, which had become a British base for police and military personnel, to collect some of their possessions. They were always escorted by guards. I think it was for their own safety as attitudes towards the Germans after the war were extremely hostile. Finally in 1948, all remaining Germans in Palestine were deported to Cyprus. Your grandmother and sister were probably in that group.

"You have to realize that the situation here in 1948 had become extremely volatile. The State of Israel was about to be proclaimed; the British were preparing to leave and an all out war was starting between the Jews and the Arabs. We were fighting for our very existence as a nation."

"I suppose you never heard anything further from the German internees or had any contact with them," Heinz-Erich asked.

"No. I know of no-one who had any contact. After they were gone that was it," Ruth replied. "We never saw nor heard anything from the Saronians. It seemed as if they had just disappeared!

"In recent years some of the younger descendants like you have come to see where their forefathers lived. Some of the descendants now living in Australia have been very helpful in providing information and photographs for the restoration of the houses and buildings in Sarona. Also when in 2005 a major exhibition on the Templers in Palestine was held at the Eretz Israel Museum here in Tel Aviv some of the exhibits were of Sarona. I remembered the old community clock which had been restored was put on display. Some Templers also came to Israel to view the exhibition. There is now a greater awareness of and interest in the history and achievements of the Sarona settlers especially after the Israeli Television Corporation produced a documentary a few years ago. It has been shown several times on television here.

"With the passing of time and the rise of new generations, the bitterness between the Jews and the former German settlers here will wane to be replaced by a growing understanding and appreciation of each other's contribution. Time heals many wounds. I am a very old lady and have noticed a higher level of tolerance than forty or fifty years ago.

"You know even in the late nineteenth century and right up to the mid-1930s the local Jews and German settlers lived in harmony here. Sure, we each had our own religion and beliefs; we lived in our own confined settlements and communities but we respected one another; conducted business and worked alongside each other – there was no open hatred and intolerance."

"I can understand the feelings and emotions from both sides. The Jewish people's anger and anguish after the Holocaust and the anger and despair of the German deportees. They and their forefathers, like my father and his family, had lived here for generations and suddenly had to leave everything behind. It must have been extremely difficult for the older ones who were born here and had worked the land or established flourishing businesses to be told they cannot return to their homes and properties where they had grown up. Their plight probably became even more difficult as they had to start and rebuild their lives again in a foreign country. No wonder there was little dialogue between the two groups."

"Yes war always creates so much bad feeling between people, but although none of us can forget there comes a time when we should move on," Ruth said philosophically.

"Did you bring the photographs we spoke about earlier?" Miriam asked.

"Yes - there are only four of them," Heinz-Erich replied as he undid his day carry pack to take out a small folder. He opened the folder and took out three photographs. "This photograph is one of my mother and father. It was taken in Würzburg at Christmas 1941," Heinz-Erich explained as he passed the photograph to Ruth.

She looked at it silently for quite some time before finally saying softly, "Yes that is Erich Bergerle."

"This next one is of my parents and my maternal grandparents; it was also taken around Christmas time in 1941 when my father was visiting my mother's family in Würzburg."

"They appear to be a very happy family group. Your mother looks very charming and your father is very clean cut and good looking. I can see much of him in you," Miriam said whilst Ruth looked intently at the photographs.

"How interesting that you say that, because my mother often said the same thing. This last photograph is one of my father. It is the only one I have of him as a portrait shot. It is an enlarged copy of the original which was a very small photograph. My mother had it framed and kept on her bedside table for as long as I can remember. It was something very special to her. At times I would see her gazing at it as if looking for inspiration and no doubt wishing my father was there to help and support her in her time of need."

When Ruth held Erich's image she began to sob and tears ran down her cheeks. She opened her handbag and took out a handkerchief to dab the tears. Miriam put her arms around her to console her as Heinz-Erich looked on in astonishment.

"Everything will be alright," Miriam whispered. "My mother just became a little emotional when she saw the photographs. She will be fine."

A few minutes passed before Ruth was able to compose herself again.

"I am sorry for that, Heinz, but the photograph of your father brought back so many memories," she whispered.

"Please don't apologise - I certainly didn't mean to upset you." he answered, puzzled by all the emotion. Even Miriam's eyes seemed to have gone watery.

"Heinz, thank you for coming to see me. I am so glad that you talked to me about your family and showed me these photographs. You will never understand how much this has meant for me and how many questions you have answered."

"You have also answered one big unknown for me," Heinz exclaimed as he took out the last photo which he had kept separately in a small plastic sleeve. He passed it to Ruth. "Do you know this person?"

Ruth and Miriam stared at the photograph dumbstruck.

"Yes, that is me," Ruth finally said. "Where did you get it?"

"It was with my father's personal possessions at the base near Stalingrad. One of Erich's comrades sent his personal belongings back to Mother. She of course did not know who was on the photo. She thought it may have been Erich's sister or possibly a former German girlfriend from Palestine. Anyway she kept the photograph with the others ones she had of father. When I met you and saw your face I immediately thought it could be you."

"Oh my God, I gave that photograph to Erich in 1939 and you are telling me he still had it with him in 1942 – three years after we said good-bye. I cannot believe it!" She wept quietly, the tears flowed freely down her cheeks as Miriam consoled her mother.

"What you are saying is that he kept this photograph of me to his very end," Ruth said between sobs. "My Erich did as he promised."

Heinz looked on in utter amazement as Miriam held her mother. When Ruth had composed herself, she continued in a strong and steady voice, "I would like to talk to you about a few other matters; I have brought a few items to show you." She took a small leather-bound folder and a little jewellery box from her handbag. With care she opened the folder and delicately removed a small, old black and white photograph which she passed to Heinz-Erich who looked at it intently.

"Do you recognize that person?" Miriam was the first to break the silence.

"It looks very much like my father," Heinz-Erich said hesitantly. "In fact I am ninety-nine per cent sure it is my father in this youth."

"You are correct," Ruth said. "It is a photograph of Erich Bergerle taken in Sarona before the war. It was probably taken in the mid-1930s: he gave it to me when I was a teenager and he left for military service in 1936. Just turn it over."

Heinz-Erich turned the photo over and read the faded writing *"Dein Erich"*.

"He gave me the photo enclosed in this envelope and card." She said as she handed Heinz-Erich a small card embossed with blue forget-me-nots. Heinz simply stared at the card and photograph – unable to find words.

"You see, I have not forgotten him but there is something else which he gave to me." Her arthritic hands trembled as she tried to open the little box.

"Let me open it for you, Imma," Miriam said reassuringly, "Here it is open now."

Ruth folded the lid back to reveal a sparkling gold bracelet. "Heinz, this is my most precious possession. I have had it for nearly seventy years now. Here, take a look at it and read the engraving on the inside," she said as she handed him the bracelet.

He handled it very gently as he looked at the bracelet before turning it on its side so that he could read the engraving *Liebste Ruth, Mit aller Liebe, Erich. August 1939.*

"So, you knew my father very closely. More than knowing him, in fact. From what you have said and shown me you were deeply in love with one another."

"Yes, I knew your father very well and we were deeply in love with one another but because of the political situation prevailing at the time and the feelings that had developed between the Germans and the Jews we had to keep our love secret. The war tore us apart and I never knew exactly what happened to your father until you told me just a few moments ago.

"You can now understand why I became so emotional. For many years I hoped against hope that one day we might meet again but it was not to be. I am neither angry nor jealous that your father married, quite the contrary I am happy for him that he found some one else even if it was only for a very brief time. Under the circumstances he and I could never have married. Your mother was so fortunate to meet and marry such a fine man.

"I asked Miriam to bring you here because the beach here was a special place for your father and me. We often walked along here." Ruth pointed to the steeper rise at the end of the beach. "See way over there, that is the old Greek cemetery. Near there we had our own secret hideaway. There we knew we would not be seen and spied upon. It was our place where we could sit and talk freely and openly. We could look out across the blue sea and contemplate what lay ahead of us as the dark war clouds gathered over Europe. Our lives were caught in the political storm of that time and as individuals we knew there was nothing we could do to change our destiny. Before the war there were shrubs and bushes and prickly pear plants right along the dunes, with only a few sandy tracks here and there leading down to the beach.

"I am just speechless! Not in my wildest dreams could I have expected this dramatic revelation! What an extraordinary day this has become! Please, Ruth, tell me more about my father. Tell me as you lived through all the drama and hardships and what happened."

"It will be a long story, but I am more than happy to share Erich and my story with you - as his son, you deserve to know."

"Yes, please go ahead" Heinz-Erich replied. "I have plenty of time to listen."

"I first met your father in Gold's Patisserie where I worked as a waitress when he called in to have a cup of coffee and a piece of cake. He was in such a happy mood because he had just passed his motorbike licence test. I had never seen him before but you could say we were both smitten with each other the first time we met. It really was love at first sight," Ruth's voice was firm and calm and she clasped her hands as she spoke. Her eyes were fixed straight ahead across the sea as if looking for inspiration.

Heinz-Erich and Miriam sat quietly listening as Ruth spoke from the heart about her love for Erich during the tumultuous times in Palestine just before the war, her life with Miriam during the war and later when she volunteered to work for the Haganah before enlisting with the Israeli Defence Forces. How she worked with the communications units during the Arab-Israeli War 1948 to 1950 and other conflicts. She concluded with the statement, "Erich never knew about Miriam."

When she finished the three sat silently together.

Miriam broke the silence "So, today after so many years, I know that I have a half-brother." She got up and kissed Heinz-Erich.

"I am quite stunned. It all seems like a dream. I also never had any inkling that I had a half-sister."

Heinz-Erich and Miriam put their arms around Ruth and the three sat silently looking out to sea as the sun sank, its fading golden rays illuminated the gold bracelet on Ruth's lap and picked out the engraving, *Mit aller Liebe, Erich.*